PRAISE FOR POLLY DUGAN'S

The Sweetheart Deal

"*The Sweetheart Deal* hits all of my favorite topics: loss, pain, friendship, betrayal—but ultimately love. It's the most romantic story I've read in years."

—Elin Hilderbrand, author of *The Rumor* and *Winter Stroll*

"A charming, poignant novel of dealing with grief and finding love again, this is the perfect lighthearted page-turner for the shore."

—Marisa Spyker, *Coastal Living*

"Heartfelt and wise, Polly Dugan's *The Sweetheart Deal* reminds us that every difficult ending can lead to a beautiful new beginning."

—Sarah Jio, author of *The Violets of March* and *Goodnight June*

"A sensitive portrayal of friendship, family, and loss."

—Mary Ellen Quinn, *Booklist*

"*The Sweetheart Deal,* a beautifully written debut, proves that the best love stories are the unconventional ones. Fans of *Good Grief* and *PS, I Love You* will adore this novel, which is brimming with heart and hope and perfectly balanced by the bittersweet."

—Sarah Pekkanen, author of *The Opposite of Me*

"A poignant exploration of a family not just recovering from loss, but growing stronger in its wake. Polly Dugan's debut novel moved me to tears and challenged my assumptions as it explored what any of us would do when offered a second chance at love."

—Miranda Beverly-Whittemore, author of *Bittersweet*

"*The Sweetheart Deal* intimately explores how grief can affect a family."   —Joy Gunn, *Library Journal*

"There is tender romance here, but it's more richly a story of an old family falling away and a new one beginning."   —*Kirkus Reviews*

The Sweetheart Deal

A Novel

Polly Dugan

BACK BAY BOOKS
LITTLE, BROWN AND COMPANY

New York Boston London

ALSO BY POLLY DUGAN

So Much a Part of You

Copyright © 2015 by Polly Dugan
Questions and Topics for Discussion © 2016 by Polly Dugan and Little, Brown and Company

Hachette Book Group supports the right to free expression and the value of copyright. The purpose of copyright is to encourage writers and artists to produce the creative works that enrich our culture.

The scanning, uploading, and distribution of this book without permission is a theft of the author's intellectual property. If you would like permission to use material from the book (other than for review purposes), please contact permissions@hbgusa.com. Thank you for your support of the author's rights.

Back Bay Books / Little, Brown and Company
Hachette Book Group
1290 Avenue of the Americas
New York, NY 10104
littlebrown.com

Originally published in hardcover by Little, Brown and Company, May 2015
First Back Bay paperback edition, May 2016

Back Bay Books is an imprint of Little, Brown and Company, a division of Hachette Book Group, Inc. The Back Bay Books name and logo are trademarks of Hachette Book Group, Inc.

The publisher is not responsible for websites (or their content) that are not owned by the publisher.

The Hachette Speakers Bureau provides a wide range of authors for speaking events. To find out more, go to hachettespeakersbureau.com or call (866) 376-6591.

ISBN 978-0-316-32035-1 (hc) / 978-0-316-32034-4 (pb)
LCCN 2014958394

10 9 8 7 6 5 4 3 2 1

RRD-C

Printed in the United States of America

For Patrick

Who's gonna take the place of me?
—U2, "Who's Gonna Ride Your Wild
Horses"

The less we say about it the better
Make it up as we go along
—Talking Heads, "This Must Be the Place
(Naïve Melody)"

And, by the way, I'm gonna love you anyway
—National Flower, "Riot"

The
Sweetheart
Deal

Leo

I know Garrett never thought I was serious when I told him, If I die, I need you to marry Audrey. Make my wife your bride—she's meant to be a bride, not my widow. And I know she didn't think I was either, but I'd never been more serious about a thing in my life. I was a firefighter; I risked my life every day. Surely I couldn't be the only guy in the department who thought about such a thing. And then, after 9/11, I knew asking him had been the right decision, and I felt even better about it. Of course I did. Garrett is my best friend. We met in 1983, when we were fourteen, and it's as true now as it was then. I had other friends, good friends. I had Gallagher at the firehouse—easily worth ten men—but Garrett is like a brother to me. It's as simple as that.

The three of us had joked about it for years. How many times did Audrey shout to me, when Garrett called, "Leo, it's my second husband! You going to pick up?" Then she'd say to him, "Bye, sweetie, here he is," and he and I would talk. My love, my everything, the mother of my sons—of course I wanted a plan in place. Of course she didn't expect me to die. It was all in good fun.

I didn't think about them being intimate. I couldn't. I only thought that if Audrey and the boys were left on their own, if I had anything to say about it, Garrett was the one person I'd choose to take care of them. I wouldn't be around to know about any of the rest, which they would figure out.

You have these precious, priceless responsibilities in life, the sources of pride you've created, earned, acquired: your children, money and property and assets, pets, even—treasures that demand you nurture and protect them properly—and in the event that you no longer can, you leave them in the hands of someone who can't possibly replace you. Assigning the job of the best care and love only you can give to someone who isn't you—that's the stuff of madness. When Audrey and I finally bit the bullet and wrote up our wills, everyone we considered seemed newly and certainly too flawed, crazy and unworthy to care for the boys. The list of family and friends we had to choose from got very short very quickly, but we conceded to name her conservative brother and sister-in-law, then my sister and brother-in-law as backup, all of them on the other side of the country. When Christopher was still a baby, we wrote up specific instructions and extracted promises, requiring attendance to Catholic school and exposure to open (progressive) political minds. Of course they'd agreed. If they'd ever be forced into the roles of guardians, we would never know if they honored our wishes or not.

Audrey and I had been married for six years when Garrett spent Y2K with us in Portland. It was the first time we'd seen him since our wedding. He'd been my best man.

"I bought my ticket and I'm flying out," he told me in November. He was in graduate school again, his second stint. "It's about time I come to Portland, and if it's all over with the millennium, I'm going out with you two."

On New Year's Eve, we got a sitter and had an early dinner downtown in time to be home and drink with the New York countdown. All was relief when the world didn't end. Audrey was pregnant with

Andrew and begged off to bed at ten-thirty, kissing us both, and Garrett and I stayed up. Christopher and Brian were still so little and would be awake early.

So as 1999 shed its skin and became 2000, we sat in the backyard smoking cigars by the fire pit, and I got drunk and sentimental. It was a dry, clear, cold night, a rare thing during Portland's December. I was overcome the way people are. On such a night, with such a friend.

Garrett and his women. That's what we'd been talking about. You could set your calendar by them. Anywhere from eighteen to twenty months—or less, but never for two years—he'd be with someone, and then he would end it. After a period of solitude, like a cleansing fast, he'd be on the market again. I could tell the ages of some of his lovers from their names alone. He'd been with an Acacia, two Zoës, a Piper. During that visit he was with a Nichole.

"And she's a student?" I said.

"She's a graduate student," Garrett said. "She's not *my* graduate student. She's a big girl. Jesus, Leo, I'm not going to let my dick get me arrested, or cost me my job."

"Why don't you find a nice Mavis, or an Edith?" I said. "What about an Opal?"

"What's going on here?" His voice got flat. "What's with the shitty judgment? I'm telling you about this woman, Nichole, who I'm very happy with, and you're being kind of a prick."

I had to tread lighter. The year and a half of what Garrett considered happiness, replaced by another of the same length, but with a different woman, wasn't what he would call a problem.

So while we argued about his future with Nichole, I pushed.

"You know they want to marry you, right?" I said. "After a few months in, they imagine themselves years down the road with you, living in the brownstone, with a library full of books from floor to ceiling, maybe a basset hound—no, a terrier. You, smoking a pipe, wearing your glasses and sweater vest."

"What the fuck?" he said. "I would never wear a sweater vest or smoke a pipe."

"Not now." I giggled. "Later. In the happily-ever-after. Maybe even the occasional cardigan."

"Fuck you," he said. "You're tittering. You titterer."

I sprayed my drink from my mouth and folded into a hysterical pile until I managed to speak again. "Titterer!" I said. "You're the titterer!" We often reduced ourselves to juvenile behavior when we were together, even then, when we were successful adult men. There's no denying that.

"I'll be right back," I said, and stumbled inside for paper, a pen, and a flashlight. At the kitchen counter, I scribbled on the sheet of paper. When I got outside, I shoved the paper and pen at him. "I need a favor. Sign this."

"Sign what? I can't sign something in the dark," he said. "Man, you're wasted."

I flashed the light on the page. "This," I said. "It says, 'I, Garrett Reese, in the event of the death of Leo McGeary, promise to marry Audrey McGeary.' All you have to do is sign it."

"What are you talking about? You're off your rocker," he laughed. "You're loaded."

"Just sign it." I shoved the paper at him again. I poked his arm with the pen. "I love that woman, and if I die on her, I need you to take care of her, to take care of my family. You're the only person I'd trust to do that."

Garrett took a puff off his cigar. "You stupid fuck." He was still laughing. "*I* have a life. And you're not going to die, but if you do, what if *I'm* married? I love your wife, but not *like that*. I'm not your plan B man, I'm my own plan A — Jesus. You call this a *favor*?"

"I don't sit on my ass for a living," I said. "I need some insurance and I'm not going to hold my breath waiting for your wedding. You want to keep discussing that probability? And you would figure out how to love her *like that*. Pretty easily, I'd expect. Let's not talk about it.

"If you're married when I'm dead, I can't hold you to a promise that you can't keep. There'll only be so much I can do at that point."

He took the paper and rested it on his leg in the dark.

"Move the goddamn light so I can see." He scanned the words I'd scrawled. "You're smashed," he said. "I'm with Nichole, *remember?* You're going to have to find someone else to give this to."

"Oh, for Christ's sake," I said. "I'm not going to die tomorrow. Nichole's got nothing to worry about. Will you sign it already and I'll bring us more drinks."

"I'm only doing this to get you off my fucking back. It's the new millennium for God's sake, and you're being morbid as hell. Refill me." He signed the paper and handed it back. "It's your word against mine, dead man. That doesn't even look like my signature."

"Thank you," I said. I took the paper. "I really mean it. That's a load off. Hand me your glass. Stand up. Give me a hug."

He did, and our embrace manifested all the years of our friendship.

"I love you, brother," I said. "I'll be right back."

"Love you too, man," he said.

Leo Thomas McGeary 1969–2012

Audrey

The day Leo died on Mount Hood, as the night skiers arrived my concern started to nag. When the weather changed and the sky darkened while I waited, for a short time I thought a joke was coming. Leo's jokes were a fixture in our marriage, but he still always got me. I was never onto him because he was discriminating and patient with his timing. No more than two good ones a year, and his best schemes were grand and I never expected them.

It started with him moving my wedding ring from where I'd left it. The first time, during the first year of our marriage, I took it off to do the dishes or clean the bathroom. It was so precious, I couldn't bear to wear it during those menial parts of my day. When I went to put it on again, I panicked when it wasn't in the porcelain dish on the kitchen windowsill. I was certain it had fallen down the drain and was gone forever.

"You don't lose things, Audrey." He was cavalier. "It will turn up, I'm sure."

"Well, can you at least take the sink apart, please?" I begged. "Find it before it goes down any farther."

It pissed me off that he didn't care more. My wedding ring. The one he had given me. "I don't think it's down there," he said. "But if you need me to, I will. Let me grab some tools."

Then he called from the living room, "Babe, it's in here. It's on the mantel."

He brought it to me, smiling. "Did you leave it there and forget?"

"I absolutely did not," I said. "That's not where I put it. And I don't lose things."

"I know you don't. Strange." He could pull off his pranks, wearing a poker face for weeks while I was ignorant, but once I was onto him, he caved. He tried, but he couldn't curb his grin, like a boy who hadn't yet had years of practice. "Maybe we have an elf or a gnome in the house. Cheeky little bastard."

"Bastard is right," I said, and he surrendered and laughed, found out. I never ever lost my wedding ring but he moved it at least once a month. One weekday, just a month ago, he was working on the addition, and the boys were back in school after the break. I was cleaning what remained in the fridge from Christmas and had taken it off. I still kept the routine.

He came into the kitchen, dressed to work, tool belt and kneepads. "Hey, have you seen your ring?" he said. He spread his arms. "Here's a hint. It's somewhere on me. Find it." That was a lovely afternoon we spent alone.

Then there was the much-needed and overdue girls' night out years ago that I'd planned with Erin and some other friends. I knew Leo's schedule, I'd double-checked, we'd arranged it weeks earlier. He was at the station, at the end of his shift, and I was getting dinner ready for the boys, ready for the handoff when he came home and I'd leave. When the phone rang, it was Leo, full of apology and regret, saying he had to cover at the station because a bunch of the guys had called in sick. They'd all eaten the same bad brisket at work.

"I'm so sorry, babe," he said. "I know it's your night out. Thank God I'm not sick too."

"Goddamn it, Leo," I said. "Sometimes this is too hard." The doorbell rang. "Jesus, now someone's at the door. Will you be home early at least?"

As he was saying, "No, I'll be here all night, I'm afraid," I opened the door to him standing on the porch with a bag from Tumbleweed, a shop on Alberta I loved.

I took the phone away from my ear, and he smiled then, handing me the bag with flourish, like a proud cat bringing home the prize prey. I shook my head. He walked in and kissed me. "Open it," he said.

It was a beautiful little dress. Something I could wear over skinny jeans, or by itself in the summer. A sweet print of blue and red, with ruching at the bust, and an empire waist. Exactly my style. That's the sort of thing he would do. The man could shop for me better than I could shop for myself. My friends, begrudging me nothing, hated their own husbands a little for it.

On my thirty-ninth birthday, I was getting my hair done. I was in the chair, and Suzanne was finishing up. Leo and I had reservations for dinner at Blue Hour at six. The sitter was coming—all I had to do was go home and change. Leo had been working all day on our bathroom remodel.

When my cell rang, Suzanne said, "Sure, go ahead."

When I picked up, it was Leo. "Don't panic, darling, I'm okay. I've called some of the guys and they're headed over. I think we'll be okay for dinner."

"What?" I said. "What happened?"

"Well, I was trying to level the tub, and the bitch fell on me and I'm stuck. Goddamn thing weighs a ton. Nothing feels broken. I'm all right. They're on their way. Just hurry home."

I drove home in a fury, wondering why he hadn't had someone helping him. Why he'd thought he could move a claw-foot tub by himself. I knew we'd celebrate the dinner sometime, whether it was tonight or not. It wouldn't be the first time something like this had happened. When I opened the front door, panicked about what I'd find inside, a roomful of our friends shouted, "Surprise!" with Erin and Leo at the front of the crowd. There had been no trouble with a fallen tub, he had pulled off an impressive surprise, and it was a wonderful party, which I'd never suspected. Who celebrates thirty-nine?

The reason Leo's schemes always worked was because he wasn't greedy—he didn't overdo their frequency. And in a family with a firefighter husband and three sons, there were many times when a calamity or cancellation or interference with plans wasn't a ruse. Andrew fell at school and broke his arm when he was in first grade. Leo forgot to pick Brian up at preschool once because he'd thought I said I would, and the teacher had to call me when he was the only kid still left, sobbing and worried, forgotten by both parents. That's what made his pranks perfect. The reality and chaos of our lives made anything possible.

I never asked him why he did it. I didn't want to dissect the pranks' charms. When I was a teenager, I asked my father once why he loved my mother. I never thought of him as poetic, although he was a smart man and often loved the sound of his own voice, but his answer to my question was unexpected. "Audrey, if I thought about it, it would be like examining the unremarkable parts of a beautiful flower to see how together they make it exquisite. It would be disappointing." That's how I felt about Leo's stunts. I suspected they were an outlet, a panacea to offset the awful things he saw on the job. To create—and completely control—a fabricated crisis that he alone knew would have a happy ending.

I didn't know how they all coped. Beyond what I heard on the news, and from other wives, occasionally, I knew about only the calls Leo chose to share with me. At the Motel 6 on Southeast Powell, which had a reputation in the department as the destination for suicides—the man who'd set himself on fire being one of the worst. There was the three-month-old who'd drowned in six inches of water. And the bicyclist fatalities, at least one hit-and-run every year. The teenage boy who had killed himself with a shotgun in his parents' bed. And the congenial man with dementia—deprived of food and water himself—whose caretaker-wife had been dead in their house for days. Leo told me that when they entered his apartment, the man had wanted them to sit down and visit. "He said, 'Here you are. Maggie's run down to the store and should be back any minute,'" Leo said. "Christ, that poor, sweet man. Nothing but skin over bone." But he didn't always tell me. I knew after the shifts he finished when he didn't want to talk. When he brooded and his mood was dark. He'd tell me if he wanted to, when he wanted to, and the only thing I could do was give him the space he needed to transition back to us.

The night after the call with the man on fire, we were on the front porch with glasses of wine after the boys were in bed.

"Come here," he said. He patted the step between his legs.

I slid down and over from where I'd been sitting next to him, and put my glass on the step below me. He kneaded the base of my neck with his thumbs.

"I don't know how you get through a day like today," I said.

"You hope there's not another one like it for a while," he said. "But the very same thing could happen again tomorrow. Accountants get audited, right? Surgeons have patients die on the table, and executives get thrown in jail. It's what you sign up for."

How he could be so grounded that night I didn't know, but I loved him for it. I thought of my father and not dissecting the flower.

"Look at Gallagher," he said. Leo's closest friend at the station, Kevin Gallagher, had been a New York firefighter—a 9/11 survivor—before he'd moved his family to Portland. "Even after my worst shift, I'm lucky. That's not a cross I have to bear."

That's what I thought about, Leo's jokes and what he had to do to get through on the job every day, while the time on the mountain dragged and I waited. We had had a flawless day, nothing but blinding blue above and new powder beneath. Because of the exquisite conditions, Leo wasn't ready to call it a day. Minutes after he had said to me, *One more. This snow is too good. We never have powder like this—just one more run and I'll see you at the bottom, babe,* minutes after I tracked his orange helmet to the lift and watched it rise until I lost sight of it, the weather over the mountain shifted and the low clouds socked in, fast. I thought nothing of it. We had all skied in worse. One more run and he'd be done.

While I waited, I was glad to be warm and inside, my body having had its fun, and now having its rest. The boys changed out of their wet gear, got their games and books from the car, and ate. I kept checking my cell phone even though there was no coverage. The boys, by now used to their father often appearing when he did and not when he was expected, were busy and unfazed. But I kept looking and waiting for Leo to walk through the hallway in the lodge, back to me, maybe having done what he had as a teenager with Garrett: gotten lost skiing out of bounds to where they couldn't ski back. They'd had to find the road and walk to the lodge. Everyone was frantic, while the boys had had an adventure. They were fifteen. I tried to think of what else could have happened. Maybe his delay was because he was helping someone else. But I started to think I should call the ski patrol office. We had season passes, and with Leo's bracelet information, surely they could locate him. I had just told myself I would wait ten more minutes when I heard my name announced over the PA system with instructions to call a number.

"Mrs. McGeary, this is Richard Allen," said the voice on the other end. "I'm the physician here at the medical center today. Can you tell me where you are?"

"Please, it's Audrey," I said. "What is it?"

"Can you tell me where you are in the lodge so I can come to you?" he said. "Ski patrol was contacted for an incident involving your husband and they're bringing him down."

Him. They were bringing *him.*

I called the boys over and minutes later, three men in identical gear stood in front of us.

"I'm Richard Allen." He extended his hand. "And this is Nick, and Jeff." He indicated the other two. Then the three of them all reached for chairs, placed them in front of us, and sat down.

"A group of skiers observed your husband skiing downhill very fast before he collided with a tree," Richard said. "They contacted ski patrol and we responded."

"How badly is he hurt?" I said. "Can he walk?"

"When we got to your husband," he said, "he had no vital signs, and despite trying to revive him, we were unable to." He leaned closer to me. "I'm very, very sorry, Audrey. I know this is a terrible shock."

The boys and I sat there. I was waiting for more. I was waiting for Richard Allen to say *but. But in a few months he'll be fine. But he'll be able to tell you about it himself in a few minutes. But I recommend he be more careful in the future.* He was a very kind man, but he said none of these things.

Andrew started to wail and Christopher and Brian clutched him and the three of them attached themselves to me, no space between us. All I could do was kiss them and feel my body, heavy in the chair. My sons surrounded me like a small herd, which I tried to comfort and contain. They were all crying now, but Christopher and Brian still tried to soothe Andrew. I didn't cry. Not then. *My sons have lost their father.*

"But you said you're bringing him down," I said.

"They're bringing his body down," said Richard. "We'll call the medical examiner to transport him to the funeral home of your choice, or to the one in Hood River until you decide. Is there anyone else you'd like us to call? When you're ready, we'll go so you can identify him."

"But he was wearing a helmet," I said. "How could this happen if he was wearing a helmet?"

"He was," Richard said. "We have his helmet. He was going so fast, there's no way to know if he suffered a head trauma or another internal injury from the force of impact."

Every day that Leo had gone to work, the possibility of his death hovered. That, I'd learned to live with, but not this.

"Is there anyone you'd like us to call?" Richard asked.

Who should they call? I would have to call my parents, Leo's parents and sister, my brother. So many people. Which was worse, making the call or getting it? It was a call no one wanted to get and I didn't want to make.

"Yes, please," I said. I gave them Kevin's number, and Erin's. "They're close friends. Kevin and Leo work together." Nick and Jeff stepped away and dialed.

And Garrett. It felt like the middle of the night here, though it wasn't, but it would be late in Boston. When did I last talk to him? Leo had told me he'd called Garrett on Christmas Eve, from work, but I couldn't remember the last time I'd spoken to him. That was a call I had to make. And our families. Erin could do the rest.

Nick and Jeff returned to their chairs.

"I reached Kevin," Nick or Jeff said. "He's coming with the medical examiner and will drive your car home. I'll give him your keys."

"Erin and her husband will be waiting at your house for you," the other one said.

"We'll have someone drive you all home," said Richard.

My hands were numb, as useful as two dead fish at the ends of my wrists. "He was a firefighter." I worked to move my lips. "He did what you do. He saved people. He had to do this too."

Jeff and Nick both nodded. "Yes, ma'am. We know he was."

Richard sat looking at his hands folded between his knees before he looked at me. "Take as much time as you need. When I hear from the team and you're ready, we can go see him. In the meantime, is there a funeral home I can contact? One less thing for you to handle."

"I don't know," I said. I kept kissing the boys. Andrew had wormed his way into my lap and curled up into a ball half his size. "I guess McKays? A lot of the Catholics use McKays, I think."

"I know Matt well," said Richard. "I'll call him."

They were like an envelope around us, Richard, Nick, Jeff, and the other Mount Hood Meadows staff that joined them as we moved from the lodge—*don't fall down, don't fall down*—to the private room in the medical center where they had Leo, to the car that took us home. I don't know if their job was to keep us away from other people—how our news would have ruined their time at the mountain—or to keep other people away from us. I suppose people around us wondered why we moved as a pack—my family surrounded by officials wearing matching jackets—intuiting it surely couldn't be good. I clung to the boys on the ride home, which was no longer the home any of us knew, shushing and comforting with words I mustered without thinking. On a very dark stretch of road on Highway 26, I hoped and waited for an instant head-on fatal collision. *Bury the five of us together*.

When we got to the house, the boys were asleep, and Erin and Mark came out to the car to meet us. Mark half woke the boys and got them all inside. Since we had taken my Subaru wagon to the mountain like we always did, Leo's Land Cruiser—his impenetrable four-door, more than twenty years old—loomed alone in front of the car that had driven us home. Its appearance looked exactly the way it had when we left that morning, suggesting that Leo was home and waiting inside for us, and I fell against Erin, unleashing the agony I'd harnessed for hours for the boys' sake—to not come undone in front of them—in waves of wild sounds I'd never heard before. We stood in the driveway, behind Leo's car, and I leaned on her and wailed until she shepherded me into the house and upstairs. Mark had put the boys in my bed, and they were all asleep again, and Erin helped me change, and tucked me in next to my sons. I lay there whimpering in the dark, with her sitting on the floor next to me, stroking my hair until I fell asleep.

Garrett

L eo and I had both grown up in Radnor, Pennsylvania, but we
didn't become friends until 1983, when we were fourteen, during our freshman year at the Shipley School. Leo had gone to
school there since kindergarten, and my parents, content enough with
the public education I'd gotten through eighth grade, had decided
Shipley, for countless compelling reasons, was where I would attend
high school.

Neither of us was big, but because we were both fast and accurate,
we played varsity basketball as sophomores. That first year, when I
was new to Shipley, Leo and I found each other through basketball,
and because of him, within weeks I had shaken the stink of being the
new kid. Once we were friends, it was like we always had been.

Leo, and three of his friends who'd all been at Shipley since kindergarten and who played ball too—though not nearly as well as the two
of us—took me in. We made five with Eric McGinnis, Ryan Wheeler,
and Keith Donahue. We each had our own quirks, but for the rest
of high school we were a unit. Eric refused to ever chip in for gas
when Ryan, the first one of us to get his license, starting driving us all
around, but as soon as Eric started driving, he started asking for gas
money and Ryan shut him down right away, reminding Eric he was

a cheap bastard and had been for months. Keith was the one we had to watch out for if we liked a girl. Once he got wind of it, she'd be the one he'd go for, with rare success, but he was on thin ice a lot of the time with us because he couldn't help himself. We put up with him anyway, and never let him forget when he'd gone for someone one of us liked and failed bitterly.

As tight as we were in general, in spite of our squabbles, when Lisa Ponti died right after our junior year ended, it changed us and cemented us together in a way that wouldn't have happened otherwise. Lisa was in our class, one of the four Ponti girls, and was a superb golfer, a prodigy. All her sisters were too, but Lisa was on track for a golf scholarship, colleges and universities already fighting over her, and when she was killed instantly by a drunk driver, coming home from the course the Friday afternoon a week after school let out, in the car her parents had bought her for her birthday in January, her death froze everything in town and cast a pall over what should have been a carefree summer.

Without any discussion, like a flock of birds operating on instinct, the four of us packed sleeping bags, enough clothes, and our suits for the funeral, and lived together at Leo's house for five days, in the McGearys' basement rec room. It was an oppressively hot week, and Leo's mom, Libby, fed us around the clock while we got through the days together. The McGearys had a pool but none of us swam, as hot as it was. Before Lisa's funeral we waited, walked, watched a little TV, and played cards, and again for another two days after she was buried. Then we all went back home again.

Years later, I remembered few of the details, only the walks and card games and the waiting. There had been so much time to fill, I didn't know how we had passed it with so little to occupy us. Shock had its place, doing its unseen work to make surviving possible when death could come and pluck any one of us bright young things out of our shining life. We had all liked Lisa, a lot, but not like a girlfriend.

She was pretty and smart and cool—besides being the golf phenom-enon—and any one of us trying to date her would have tainted our friendship, which none of us wanted. Even Donahue knew it, and wasn't a dog for a change.

After high school, Leo and I drifted away from the other three, al-though our parents kept us updated. Last I knew, Eric had been living in Europe for years, and Keith had moved to Chicago and been di-vorced twice. Ryan still lived outside Philadelphia with his wife and four kids.

My family always spent every summer at our house in Surf City on Long Beach Island, and starting that summer after our junior year, through college, Leo came with us. His parents had a house in the Po-conos, where he'd learned to ski as a little kid and where I learned as a teenager, after I started going there with his family. The summer be-tween sophomore and junior years, my dad got me a job with Costello, a construction company, light stuff at first, and Leo and I both worked there the next summer, starting weeks after Lisa died. During the day we learned everything from framing to finishing these crazy geomet-ric houses right on the beach that people dripping money could afford for us to build. On our breaks, we'd run and jump in the ocean to cool off, and got in this flirty back-and-forth thing all summer with a few of the badge checkers who always gave us shit because we were on the beach swimming without a badge—*Not really,* we'd say, *we're work-ing, same as you*—before we'd run back and change into dry clothes and return to the hot, sweaty work. On our days off, we went to the beach wearing our badges and showed them off to the checkers who'd harassed us.

One of them, Amy, on the days she didn't work would walk the beach looking for sea glass, wearing her Walkman, and we'd flag her over and she'd sit with us, and sometimes we'd all swim before she re-sumed her walk. We'd always beg her to stay longer, playing desperate for her company. "You'll see me soon enough," she'd joke. "I'm going to nail you guys if it's the last thing I do this summer." That reduced us to raunchy laughter. She knew what she'd said, she was in on her own joke, but nothing ever happened with either of us and Amy. She was like Lisa, cool like that. Instead, we met other girls on the beach, and at night we went to where they were babysitting and hung out, or met up with them somewhere on the island—miniature golf or the arcade or the ice cream or pizza places—and drank and smoked and sometimes made out. A couple of times more than one girl seemed like she could be a summer girlfriend, but neither Leo nor I wanted that kind of ball and chain. It was summer and the island was full of so many girls, there was no way that was going to happen.

That first summer he spent with us, Leo had bought a unicycle and taught himself to ride it, so if we didn't borrow my mom's car, he'd cycle and I'd skateboard on our rounds. No helmets in those days. One night we went to Twenty-Third and the Boulevard, where a girl I liked from the beach was babysitting. While we were there, Leo rode his unicycle down the brick front steps of the house. I never forgot the place, which years later became a law office. Leo's stunt was impressive, no question, but as soon as he did it, that girl stopped knowing I was alive. Without me saying anything, Leo knew it too, and that was the last time we ever spent any time with her.

After Lisa died, we never drank and drove on the nights we borrowed my mom's station wagon and went to The Ketch, a bar in Beach Haven where there was always action. One night, when Leo was driving, I threw up all over the passenger door of the car. The next morning he pretended to be all wrecked and hungover, and, on his own, he finished the half-assed cleanup job we'd started the previous night, before he'd pushed and hauled me to bed. He told my mom I was still in bed because I was fuming and wanted to kill him.

After college graduation, I went to Europe for a year with a fraternity brother, Curtis, which was easy to do back then. He and I traveled together, until I took up with a girl named Katya for a few sweet months, before I left her for another girl named Estelle and a time that was far less sweet. Leo had gone back to working for Costello full-time, and lived in a cheap apartment over a pizza parlor in Ship Bottom.

That fall he met Audrey in Wilton, Connecticut, at the September wedding of Charlotte, Audrey's best friend from high school, and George, a college pal of Leo's. Charlotte and George had met in Scotland, at St. Andrews, during their junior year abroad. Audrey was a year older than Leo and she had a fat job in Portland at an ad agency. They danced together, to the exclusion of all the other guests, and stayed up for hours talking after the reception ended. After he got home, Leo found a note in his pocket that Audrey had put there: *If you have good long distance, you should call me.*

So he called her. And he went to Portland a month later and drove up to Wilton to see her at Christmas, and flew to Portland again in February, and in March he left the East Coast for good and moved in with her. Leo was a hoarder with his money—he always had been—and so he had a cushion until he found a job.

We'd talked on the phone twice while I was abroad, and when he told me he was living in Portland, I gave him shit for following a woman.

"Fuck yeah, I followed her," Leo said. "Before another man can. I'm not going to let it be anyone else but me."

The next summer, after I'd returned from Europe and was at my parents', he called me. *Welcome home, let's go out tonight,* he said. *I want you to meet Audrey.* They had flown east to visit both sets of parents when he knew I'd be back. I hadn't seen him in a year. When I got to the pub that was our old haunt, they were playing darts. After I hugged Leo, the way he introduced me to Audrey—with the combined giddiness of a boy and the confidence of a man—told me he was going to marry her.

She hugged me like it was a reunion instead of an introduction, and kissed me on the cheek. "Leo," she said, "get Garrett a drink, and we're going to sit while you play. Come on." She linked her arm through mine and pulled me over to a booth, herding me onto the bench before sliding in across from me. She had moved, and moved me so quickly, since I'd walked in, it wasn't until I was sitting that I had the chance to really look at her. She put her elbows on the table and rested her chin in her hands. She wore a red sundress, and a broad spill of freckles flecked her chest and trailed down under the neckline. She was blond, which I didn't expect, because Leo had always gone for dark-haired women. I'd pictured her a brunette before that night, and in seconds I'd had to adjust my expectations to the woman in front of me.

Leo brought us our drinks, and they shared a look before he left us alone. "Come on," she said. She drank from her beer and laid her palms flat on the table. There was nothing coy about her curiosity. I could tell that she had been waiting for this. "Tell me everything. So I can fill in the blanks."

We talked while some other guys joined Leo at the dartboard, and for every detail, large or small, that I shared, she had at least one question. Even then, I'd always thought I was good with women, charming, cagey if I wanted to be, and was naturally, not withholding exactly, but careful about what I'd share in conversation. Though it was far from uncomfortable, by the time we were finished talking and joined Leo to play darts and then pool, I felt like a criminal suspect who'd been grilled, then released. From that night on, it was as though I'd known her as long as I'd known Leo. When they got married in Wilton the next summer, I was the best man.

After their wedding, I didn't see them for six years, but we called and wrote—that's how you kept up a friendship back then—until the rare visit we could coordinate, living as far from each other as we did. I went back to school for one graduate degree, then taught high school, then got a second graduate degree, became a college adjunct, then went back for my PhD. I didn't stick with most things for very long, and made the switch easily to something new when I was tired of what I was doing, but I did like being in school, on both sides of the desk.

I still had that fucking piece of paper he made me sign all those years ago. Leo had dated it *December 31, 1999/January 1, 2000,* and mailed it to me a few weeks after my trip. He had enclosed it in a thank-you card—as our mothers had taught us to send for far lesser things, or at least tangible things we could unwrap and hold, a gift or a check. *So you'll have it if you need it,* he'd written in the card. I wondered if Audrey knew. Sobriety was evident in his straight, clean handwriting, so for reasons I couldn't understand, he was serious. I wasn't a worrier by nature, but for the next several months, I was anxious and afraid that he was going to die, like he eerily knew something was coming that no one else knew about, the way you heard people say they did. Maybe it was the millennium that had done it—both before and after, until people settled down—it had made the world skittish. After enough time passed waiting for the tragic news about Leo that didn't come, I stopped worrying. Except during our time that New Year's Eve, and Leo's card, we never mentioned it again. Even the "second husband" banter between the three of us, fueled by Leo and fed, tongue in cheek, by Audrey, had run its course and died a natural death.

But I had saved the paper anyway, not like the years of tax returns I was paranoid to part with, but as an unlikely souvenir, like the photograph that's a bad picture of everyone in it but the only tangible proof of the good time had by all when it was taken. I had the note in a manila folder in a hanging file in my desk, in with cards and letters from both Audrey and Leo. A joke that had become something much graver, although it was far from a binding document of any kind.

I couldn't wrap my head around it. That Leo was dead. I thought I should have known, that I should have felt something happen the moment he died, but maybe Audrey had. Of course, if there had been any kind of an alert, she should have been the one to get it. And not being a believer, or with murky beliefs at best, maybe I wasn't a fertile recipient primed for the goodbye one soul says to another.

When we'd lost my mother to pancreatic cancer three years earlier, we were all there at the house in Radnor, sitting vigil while she was dying. Sometimes we were together, but mostly we took shifts. My father, my sister, Kate, and me. We had been ready for days because of what the hospice people said, the signs they recognized. I loved those people, doing the hardest work I could imagine with their unwavering and infinite kindness and compassion.

When my mother finally did die, on a Tuesday, all three of us were there holding her hands. Her death was peaceful and dignified, like her, and afterward we stayed with her, adjusting to those first minutes of her being gone. When we finally left the room and my mother's body alone, I called the funeral home. They were expecting our call. After I hung up the phone, I saw something happen to Kate, who was sitting in a dining room chair.

Like responding to a reflex, Kate began talking aloud to no one in particular. "Oh my God. Oh my God. I keep having this feeling. I can't stop having this feeling." Her face was flushed and lovely. Her hands clung to the arms of the chair. "I can't stop having this feeling." Five minutes earlier she'd been sobbing. The purest word I could think of to describe what happened to her was *epiphany*—a genuine spiritual ecstasy—that lasted less than thirty powerful seconds. We'd discussed it many times, my father, Kate, and I, and the only thing she could ever articulate was during that short, intense spell, Kate *felt*—didn't think, she felt—that for the rest of her life she would never feel sadness that our mother was dead. Although she had the memory of what happened to her, she'd returned to her grief after the sensation passed, and had told me more than once since how she wished she could call that feeling back up whenever she wanted.

I don't know why it was my sister and not my father who experienced what she did. My mother and Kate, they'd been as thick as thieves, with their tennis and their Junior League, and were both good Catholics. And when my mother was terminal, in those last months, Kate had suffered insomnia and a pervasive anxiety about my mother's death, about her leaving our lives, our physical world. I concluded later, in spite of my skepticism—I had witnessed it, after all—that Kate's euphoria was my mother's last message to her, letting her know she'd arrived safely in heaven, or the afterlife, or that her energy had traveled onward into the universe and its new destination. My family, whatever else you could say about us, we were consistent about one thing we asked of each other: *Call me when you get there. I want to know you arrived safely.* Our parents demanded it of us our whole lives, and when we got old enough, Kate and I demanded the same of them, and each other.

Leo flew east for the funeral, alone. My mother had loved him and had loved that we had stayed friends. He read the Twenty-Third Psalm at her funeral mass. We got drunk after the burial, and both wept over my mother, and he left the next day. That was the last time I'd seen him.

When the phone rang, late here, and I saw it was Audrey, maybe I should have known something was wrong. The late-night call. But it wasn't late on the West Coast, and Leo had called me on her phone before. Maybe he was having a beer and feeling chatty, too lazy to find his own phone. So I'd answered, "Hey." But instead of Leo a little buzzed on the other end, it was Audrey, crying. "Oh, Garrett." That was the first thing she said.

Although we'd been already asleep—it was after midnight in Boston—I told Celia to go home, I was sorry, I didn't know what to do, but I wanted to be alone. I knew she wanted to stay but I asked her to please, please just do this. She didn't know Leo, although I had told her about him. The last time I'd talked to him was less than two months before, on Christmas Eve when he'd called me from work. He'd told me the addition was going well, when he had the time to spend. He was doing most of the work, and Kevin from his firehouse was pitching in quite a bit. *Once it's finished, if it doesn't kill me, you have to come visit again,* he said. *I'm sure it will be as good and solid as if you'd built it with me.* When he had started the project in October, he had emailed me after he'd poured the foundation. *Audrey and I decided, we can't move out of the house, so we're moving the house out,* he'd written. They had drawn the plans together with Mark, Audrey's best friend's husband, who was an architect. Everyone was in on the project. I wondered how far he had gotten, if there was a gaping hole left in the house.

After Celia left—I knew she was pissed—I poured whiskey into a tall glass and sat on the couch and drank. "Fuck you." I railed at a dead man in my empty apartment. "Goddamn you, McGeary."

I knew, in terms of what lay ahead, Audrey thought she could handle it by herself. She cried on the phone while she told me the news, but I heard her resolve underneath, her commitment to meeting it head-on, like potty training a stubborn toddler or running a race in a good time. Even though she hated help, she couldn't do this by herself, no one could. But that was her default. A few weeks after my New Year's visit, when she was pregnant with Andrew, Leo called and told me that while he was at work that morning she'd had a scare—she couldn't feel the baby moving, so she went in, and everything had turned out fine. The baby had only moved behind the placenta, where it was harder for her to feel him.

"Can you believe her?" Leo said to me. "'Why didn't you call me?' I asked her. 'If something had been wrong I should have been there.' Do you know what she said? 'If something had been wrong, you would have been, because I would have called you and then you would have been there.' What am I supposed to say to that?"

"I don't know, man," I said. "You seem surprised that your wife is the woman you married."

That's how she was, but this was without precedent. The longer I sat there drinking, it came to me: *I'll go and finish the house.* We'd worked so many jobs together all those years ago that after I caught up, I'd know exactly where he'd left off and where to pick up again. And there were plans. There was nothing in Boston that wouldn't still be here, or somewhere else, later. If he could have, he would have done the same for me, I thought, as I filled my glass again. That stupid old promise had nothing to do with it. It really didn't. If there hadn't been what he'd left behind, unfinished, I wouldn't have had any reason to up and leave, but there was one thing out there I could fix. I took my glass, sat down at my desk, rifled through the drawer of files and found the paper, soft from folding and time, and forgotten for so long. Staring at it through my whiskey blur, I wanted to shred it, burn it, break a window with it clutched in my fist, but instead I tucked it deep into a pair of rolled-up socks, left the socks on top of my dresser, and went to bed. Initially—and for so long—the paper had been insignificant and juvenile, but with one phone call, it had turned into a sobering artifact from a careless night: *What you think will never happen, might.*

Audrey

In the hours, then days and then months after the recovery of Leo's body, when I keened when I saw him, with Richard Allen's firm hand on my shoulder, and the helmet that did no good—*don't fall down*—I was grateful that he hadn't died on Brian's birthday.

We had planned to go up to the mountain the previous Saturday, February 4, the day Brian turned fourteen, but the fridge, which had been on its last legs for weeks, tanked overnight. I opened the door early that morning, planning to pack lunches when it was still dark and everyone was waking up, and a sour warmth poured out. Everything was spoiled, and the food in the freezer was tepid to the touch. I was furious. I had seen this coming. The fridge wasn't old—it was a high-end model we'd gotten on clearance because it seemed like too good a bargain to pass up, but in hindsight, there'd been a catch. The icemaker hadn't worked for months, and for weeks the element inside the freezer had been caking with ice so that every other day Leo defrosted it with my hair dryer, insisting he could keep the whole thing working. When I badgered him enough to repair it properly, he finally made some calls and told me the model had been discontinued and parts were no longer available.

"Well, goddamn it, Leo," I said. "We need a fridge that works, for Christ's sake. For as much food as we go through in this house."

"Audrey, it's fine," he said. "It's not old enough to die on us. I'll figure something out. There have to be parts I can find somewhere, or an old-timer who can extend the life of this thing."

So that morning of Brian's birthday, when I took coffee up to Leo, I broke the news.

"The fucking fridge is done," I said. "We can't go up today. I knew this would happen. We need a new fridge. I'm going back downstairs to toss out all our rotten food. All our balmy, rancid food. So Brian's not going to have the birthday we said he would."

Leo sat up in the dark. "What are you talking about?"

"The fridge, Leo. It's done, dead. It's almost *hot* inside there. I told you this would happen. I'm going back downstairs. See you down there. Take your time."

"Well, shit," he said.

So we went the following weekend, and since the skiing was better than it had been the previous week, it felt like serendipity.

During that ride back from the mountain, and for months afterward, I sought comfort in one never-ending thought that flowed like water smoothing a stone: *Brian, my sensitive, sage soul. He would never have gotten over it.* But then, when I was awake at two in the morning, pacing the house, I'd think, *What if we had said fuck it. All the food was past salvaging. We should have gone anyway. Even if conditions did get lousy, we would have had a good morning. The fridge could have waited until Sunday.* We hadn't had to stay home, but I had insisted on dealing with the fridge, which wasn't a matter of life and death, so I blamed myself. Since I couldn't undo what had happened and couldn't let myself off the hook, I worked to accept the relief that for the rest of his life, Brian didn't have to share the day of his arrival in the world with the one on which his father left it. Three days later, on Valentine's Day, I accepted that I was a widow. Nobody's sweetheart.

But other days, I was enraged that he had insisted on making that last run, alone. And then, I raged at myself for the very last thing I had said to him before he skied down to the lift: *Don't be long.* I hadn't said, *Hurry up* or *Make it quick,* but I'd tacked on that last statement after *Be careful.* Why hadn't I stopped there? Because the care was really what mattered, always—the time was nothing at all, it just came out. And if one of the boys had gone with him, surely he wouldn't have skied so fast. Leo had learned to ski when he was four years old—when he was finally ready to but wouldn't go on his own—and his mother had pushed him down the bunny hill in the Poconos. She skied behind him the whole way, although he didn't know it until they both reached the flat. He had sobbed and fretted the whole way down, but by the time he got to the bottom, he couldn't wait to go up and do it again. And yet. After surviving whiteouts and stupid stunts as a kid in the Northeast, the mountain that Leo had mastered and dominated for more than twenty years had taken him.

After all the years of shifts he'd been on. My worry every time he went to work, *Maybe he won't come home tonight.*

"It's a wonder you're alive," I told him more than once.

Every time, he laughed and said the same thing. "It's nothing short of a miracle, I'll admit."

He wasn't afraid of death, he'd often said, not back when he was young and careless and felt immortal and not later as a grown man, putting himself at risk in a different way. "How can I be if I want to do my job well? What's the cause of death, anyway? Being alive, right? Being afraid doesn't change that, and it doesn't help."

After he was gone I kept waiting for him to send me some kind of message, some comfort that it wasn't something I should be afraid of either.

Garrett

I called Audrey early the next morning. I had a headache and was
dehydrated, but my thoughts were clear. Shaky as I was, I was
full of tenacity and ambition.

"When's the funeral? I'll fly out tomorrow or Tuesday, after I talk
to people at school," I said. "Then I'm staying. You can't say no. I'm
not asking. I'm going to finish the house."

"The funeral is in a week, on Saturday," she said. "No, Garrett, I
can't let you do that. Aren't you living with someone? Aren't you trying to get tenure? Come and then get back to your life."

"I told you, I'm not asking," I said.

She exhaled a quiet laugh. It was a small, unexpected sound. "It
will get finished someday, and I don't even give a fuck about the house
right now." She wasn't saying anything I hadn't expected. Then she
started to cry. "I'll have money," she said. "Leo increased his life insurance two years ago and didn't tell me till after he did it. You know
what he said when he told me? 'It's a guarantee that you'll never need
it.'" I could hear her trying to compose herself. "You have a life. Come
and then go back to it."

"I told you, I'm not asking." We were deadlocked. "And no, I'm
not living with someone. That was last year. Don't spend your money

on that, Audrey. You'll use it for what you really need. I'll text you with details."

"Okay." Her voice was hoarse. "I'm so glad you're coming, Garrett. I'm really glad you're going to be here. For however long."

I started packing and called Celia. I got her voicemail and left a message.

We had been together for three months, doing what we were doing, and I liked her, I did, or rather, I liked things about her. We had met at a birthday party of a mutual friend. Celia taught English and drama at a private school in the city, and she was funny and beautiful, and thirty. When I emailed Leo about her, he emailed back, *Good for you, no Amber or Trixie. How old is she, anyway?*

In bed, I couldn't complain, but out of bed, she did things that made me feel worked over. She hadn't seemed impressed with me at the party—she talked to a lot of men that night, but she and I sang a karaoke duet when I grabbed her hand and pulled her up to join me at the mikes. I got her number, and when we went out two weeks later, she acted, a tiny bit, like she was doing me a favor. After all the women I'd known, if nothing else, I was hard to fool. From the beginning, she acted independent—for independence's sake, not because she really was. Whenever I asked her out, she was always busy and suggested a day or two later—every time. I started counting and after the fifth time figured out the pattern. Because I was feeling played, I asked if she was seeing other people, which was fine, I said, but I wanted to know. She fell all over herself telling me she wasn't, and asked me if I was, and I told her I wasn't either, not currently. So I thought that was good to get out in the open, but her games continued. Once I offered to pick her up at the airport and she said she'd take a cab. And some nights when I thought we'd spend the night together she'd get up and leave, saying she really wanted to sleep in her own bed, even if it was late.

None of those things alone was a deal breaker, and neither were all of them together, but nothing was ever *easy*, and her other, conflicting traits were more revealing. Every time she cooked dinner for me, it was a new, elaborate recipe that she slaved over in the kitchen, like a surgeon fighting to save the patient; her concentration and desire were so fierce. And within the first two weeks, although it was too early to be leaving personal items at each other's places, she had a new, full bottle of my favorite Scotch at hers. The way she clung to me, curled against my body, the mornings after we did spend the night together made me think she was trying very hard to seem one way but was really another. I would have preferred that she was genuine, no matter how she thought I might interpret her investment in our relationship, or her falling for me, or her ambivalence. I couldn't stand a phony, and I could stand Celia easily and well enough, but early on I'd recognized that her approach to our relationship was contrived. Not trying too hard, not being too needy—it was like a romance recipe she'd researched and was following to the letter. The thing was, I had been with women who had been genuinely independent or transparently attached, and it never made a difference. I only wanted each of them as long as I'd wanted them. So, when the time came, the way it did, Celia was an easy one to leave.

When I called her, I checked the time, set the stopwatch on my phone, and after twenty-three minutes, Celia called me back.

"Hi," she said. "I'm sorry I missed you, I was in the shower. How are you doing? I'm so sorry."

"I'm okay," I said. "Can we talk? Can you come over?"

"Well, I'm meeting a friend for breakfast, how about later? Or tomorrow?" she said.

"I'm leaving town," I said.

"Oh," she said. "For your friend's funeral? I'll see you when you come back."

"I'm not coming back," I said. "If you want to see me before I go, it has to be this morning."

"Okay," she said. "I'll come over. Is now good?"

"Now is good," I said. And I hung up.

She was at my place fifteen minutes later. Dressed and made up, not beautiful and barefaced with her hair still damp, like I'd expected, her coming over on the fly.

I let her in and we sat on the couch.

"I'm doing something you may not want to hear, but it's what's happening," I said.

"You said you're not coming back," she said. "I thought you'd just be gone for the funeral."

"Hang on," I said. I went to the fridge and got two beers, came back, and sat down. "You want one?"

She shook her head. I opened one and set them both on the table.

"Celia, Leo's family needs help," I said. "What happened changes a lot of things for me, so I'm going to stay out there and help. It's the one thing I can do."

"I'm really sorry about your friend—"

"Leo," I said. "His name is Leo."

"I'm really sorry about Leo, I am. It's terrible this happened, but what about your life?" she said. "I'm not talking about me. Garrett, you have a job." She hadn't planned for this. This wasn't something she'd had time to research, or ask her friends about.

"I uproot pretty easily," I said. "Like a weed."

"A weed." She crossed her arms.

"I hope this never happens to you," I said, "but if it ever does, then you'll understand." I reached out to touch her hand—a gesture seemed called for, since what I was saying wasn't doing any good—but she pulled it away. "Maybe I'll see you when I'm back."

"Do or don't," Celia said. "It makes no difference to me." And she stood up and walked out of my apartment.

When things are messy, that's when you learn what a person is made of. I knew everything about Celia I needed to that morning, and I guessed she learned what I was made of too. If I had loved her, or felt an affection on my way to loving her, I might have asked her to come with me, told her I needed her, bought her a plane ticket. And if she had had a shred of empathy—an unrehearsed selflessness and accommodation for me—things might have been different. As it was, Leo's death shined the spotlight on the facade we were playing at, which, once illuminated, couldn't return to the shadows. Leo, even dead, saved me a lot of wasted time with Celia.

I finished the beer, opened the second one, and kept packing. I put the socks with the note inside at the bottom of the suitcase. I left a message for my landlord and then called Mitchell Britton, the academic dean at Boston College.

"Good morning, Mitchell," I said. "It's Garrett Reese. I apologize for calling on the weekend. Can we meet sometime today?"

"Garrett, I'm sorry," he said. "I'm in Philadelphia for my granddaughter's baptism. The mass is at eleven. Is everything all right?"

"No, Mitch, no it's not," I said. "I hate to do this over the phone. I have a personal emergency. There was an accident. My friend, my best friend, Leo, his wife called last night from Portland—he died yesterday. I'm flying out as soon as I can."

"Oh my God," Mitch said. "Garrett, I'm so sorry. Of course, go. I'll take care of it."

"The thing is, Mitch," I said. "I'm going to stay out there for a while. I don't know how long, maybe a few months."

There was silence on the other end. I waited.

"Garrett, this is unprecedented," he said.

I was on track for tenure along with the rest. We were like puppies scrambling to get to the tit first, the status, the *title*. The dangling security seized after years of scrutiny. "Mitchell, I know," I said. "Of course it's unprecedented. No one plans for something like this."

"You'll pardon me for saying so," Mitchell said, "but this isn't your family, correct?"

When I was quiet, Mitchell hurried to fill the silence. "Again, forgive me," he said, "but we're not talking about your wife, child, or parents. This isn't your family."

"They may as well be," I said. "Mitchell, I'm sorry, I didn't call for advice, and I understand you don't understand. I'm only sharing my terrible personal news and how I'm handling it."

"This is suicide, Garrett," he said.

"Well, I won't have this job," I said. "But not having it isn't going to kill me."

"I'm sorry," he said. "You know what I'm talking about. You won't have a position to return to. And you'll be damned for a position elsewhere. You've painted a very different picture of who we've come to know and the expectations we had."

We weren't getting anywhere. I already knew everything he was saying.

"Mitch," I said. "You've got talented people who want what I have. I have a syllabus, and you've got resources to tap. I'll send an email and take full responsibility. Thank you sincerely for everything these past three years. I'm truly grateful. But, really, I'm doing the only thing I can."

He softened. "I'll look for the email. I'll get some things together—come by my office tomorrow. And, Garrett, I'm very sorry about your friend. I do wish you were making a different decision, but I wish you the very best of luck."

I moved some money around, paid some bills, forwarded my mail. I drove to campus and packed my office. I cleared off my computer, saving what I needed onto a thumb drive. I made a folder for Leo's emails. Some of them were years old, but I couldn't delete a single one. A student had given me a jade plant that had survived its time with me despite my lack of doting. When I got home, I knocked on my neighbors' door. Rob and Morgan had moved into the apartment across from me the previous summer, before the school year. They both taught at the college too, in different departments, and were pregnant and due in two months. I went into as much detail as I had with Mitch and told them I'd be gone for a while, and gave them the plant. I thanked them and declined their offers to do anything else.

I made coffee and wrote the email for Mitch and everyone else who needed to know. A choice was easy to make, no matter how small or great, when you only had one, and sometimes the hardest one was the right one.

I booked a flight for six o'clock Tuesday morning, Valentine's Day, and texted Audrey. *I'm flying out early Tuesday. I'll see you in the afternoon.*

Garrett

I didn't sleep on the plane—I never could. Sleeping is such a private, vulnerable state, I was always fascinated when adults packed in a plane among strangers surrendered to it. *Sleeping together*. So I felt ragged and useless when I got to the house. Audrey was sitting on the porch. She stood up and waited, and cried against me after I dropped my bag, and I wept too. There was nothing to say.

The boys were all so big. At fifteen, Christopher looked so much like Leo, with the same dark good looks, only a year older than his dad was when we met. Brian and Andrew were handsome too, with Audrey's eyes and mouth, and both seemed more mature than middle-schoolers, having aged overnight, I thought. They all hugged me without hesitation. I hadn't seen Audrey and the boys in six years, when Leo had brought them all east for a visit with both sets of parents. I'd rented a place on Martha's Vineyard and they'd spent a week with me.

The house was much as I remembered it, but it had matured with the boys. What had been the guest room was now Christopher's room, and what had been the playroom was the guest room, around the corner from the kitchen. The baby gates and the other children's accessories that had littered every room the last time I'd been here were long gone. Because the family had filled as much room as the house had to offer, Leo had started the addition. Their bungalow in the northeast quadrant of the city had four bedrooms and was larger inside than it looked from the street, but with three boys, Leo had written in one email, there was no such thing as too much room. I thought the rooms downstairs were painted different colors than when I'd been here before. The dining room was red now, striking, and I didn't remember it that way. Audrey and Leo might have re-painted, but I didn't ask. Maybe the paint was the same and I was different. I might not have noticed such things twelve years ago. Photographs lined the mantel. School portraits of the boys that I'd never seen. Several of all five of them. Leo and Audrey with Christopher as a baby. A portrait of Audrey and Leo on their wedding day, and one of the two of them from a day they'd gone skiing, their goggles pushed up, Leo's bulky glove wrapped around Audrey's shoulder. She had to know it was there. I'd only been in the house five minutes, but I felt like taking it down and putting it away. No one needed to see that. There were at least eight flower arrangements, a few sitting in each room, that looked like they had been set down haphazardly and with-out much thought.

"I made coffee," she said, and poured me a cup. "How was the flight?"

"It was fine," I said. "It got me here."

"Did you sleep?" she said.

"Nah, I couldn't."

"Do you need to take a nap?" she said.

I sipped the coffee and shook my head. "It will just mess me up for tonight. I'm fine."

"Okay," she said. She hadn't stopped moving since we'd walked into the house. "Listen. My parents and Leo's parents are here, Mau-reen and my brother are too. Everyone's at the same hotel."

I knew Leo's family—his parents Glenn and Libby, and his sister,

Maureen—as well as I knew my own. I'd met Audrey's parents, Marty and Claudia Lanigan, and her brother, Gabe, at their wedding.

She rested her hands on the counter and looked out the window above the sink. "Glenn keeps saying to me, 'Whatever you need, Audrey, whatever you need.' What I need he can't give me, no one can. They've lost their son."

"I know," I said. I had traveled this terrain when my mother died, but hers had been a very different death. "People don't think they know what to do, but they're always capable of more than they imagined. If you can, just give them some direction. Or I will if you want me to. My father will be here on Friday."

She turned away from the window and looked at me and nodded. "That's so nice of him." She got a tissue and blotted her face. "So I need your help," she said. "Maybe you want to shower first, but I need you to help me buy a suit this afternoon. A suit for Leo."

"Okay." I wasn't sure what she meant.

She wiped the counter and loaded the dishwasher. She was back to moving again, confused but committed. "I have to take his clothes to Matt MacKay, to the funeral home, and I need a suit," she said. "I'm sure everyone expects me to bury him in his dress blues, but I won't. I'm not putting anything in the ground with him that he's ever touched or worn. So I'm buying a suit for him to wear for one thing only. And with a closed casket, it doesn't matter anyway. Let everyone think they know what he's wearing inside."

"Okay," I said. Now I knew what she meant.

"You have to try it on," she said. "I know if it fits you, it will fit him." I felt like I was scheming with the wife of someone who was still alive, a wife who wanted to surprise her husband with a gift.

"Okay," I said for the third time in a row. Maybe that's all I was going to do while I was here. Agree with everything Audrey said.

We drove out of Portland, to a vast mall, and when we walked into

Jos. A. Bank, four salesmen descended upon us, and one woman. She was the one Audrey spoke to.

"We could use a little help," she said. "Can you give us some time to ourselves after we find what we're looking for?"

"Absolutely," said the woman. "I'm Deirdre. I'm here to help as much or as little as you want. Please let me know what you need."

"Thank you," Audrey said. "Can we look at some of your nicest suits? We're looking for navy." She put her hand on my shoulder. "For him."

We followed Deirdre and we weren't there fifteen minutes before I was wearing the suit—Leo's suit—Signature Platinum Wool, Navy Thin Stripe. It was five dollars shy of $2,200.

"If you don't mind my saying," said Deirdre, "this is beautiful on you, and the right size, but taking it in a bit"—she pulled at the back of the jacket and looked at Audrey—"don't you think, will make it exquisite."

"Thank you," said Audrey again. "It's actually a surprise for my husband and I think it will be a perfect fit." I felt lightheaded. I realized I'd been holding my breath. I exhaled. "If he tries it on and we need to adjust it, we'll be back." I needed to sit down. I wanted to take the suit off.

"Oh, I'm very sorry," said Deirdre. "I thought you were together."

Audrey smiled. "Thanks again for your help. I think we have what we need, but we'll let you know if we want to see something else." I knew she was doing what she needed to, to get through this purchase she insisted on making, but I was about to come undone.

Thank God Deirdre got the hint, since those people don't always, and she left us alone.

"Thank you, Garrett," Audrey said. Her eyes filled. She put her arm through mine and we looked at our reflections in the mirror staring back. "This is what I wanted. It's close enough to his uniform. Leo always looked so good in blue. So do you."

"It's a good suit," I said to the mirror. "It's a beautiful suit." I couldn't wait to rip the fucking thing off.

Audrey wiped her face. She seemed at once the most fragile of creatures and a peerless force to be dealt with. "I'm going to pick out a shirt and tie," she said. "I'll take this with me." She slipped the jacket off my shoulders. She patted my back, draped the jacket over her arm, and walked away.

I went into the dressing room, sat on the bench with my face in my hands, and took deep breaths until I was ready to meet Audrey and hand over the pants. The fatigue from the flight and the weight of buying Leo's suit combined and refused to waver. I couldn't look in the mirror and acknowledge the image of my living self, so I turned my back while I changed. I don't know how many men had tried on that suit, but I was going to be the last person who did before Leo wore it till the end of time.

Audrey

The day after I bought Leo's suit, I went to Ann Taylor alone. Erin offered to come with me. "You need help," she said.

"No, I can do it by myself," I said. "But if you could, would you take the boys shopping and I'll meet you downtown? Christopher is the only one with a suit."

"Done," she said.

I didn't think about it until I was shopping alone. How Garrett had tried on that beautiful suit while I lied to that nice woman who helped us. He looked sick by the time I paid, and I wondered if I had asked too much of him. How would I have felt if someone had asked me to be the model for a dead woman who would be the next and last person to wear what I'd tried on? Garrett hadn't said anything, of course he hadn't, and by the next day it felt too late for me to bring it up. After we'd left Washington Square, I'd dropped him off at the house and had taken the suit, shirt and tie, socks, and boxers I'd bought to the funeral home. *This is what he's wearing,* I told Matt MacKay.

I knew what I wanted at Ann Taylor and declined all the offers for help. A dark gray suit—I refused to wear black, and I refused to wear a skirt or a dress—and one was easy to find. I was in and out of Pioneer Place in fifteen minutes. It had taken me longer to park.

Erin had picked up Brian and Andrew when I'd left the house. I texted her as I walked the few blocks to Nordstrom. *We're here, in the Boys Department,* she wrote back.

By the time I saw them, Erin had already found each of the boys a dress shirt and suit; navy for Brian and gray for Andrew. No black for them either, and I was so relieved and grateful for Erin's having made exactly those choices, even though I hadn't said anything the way I'd meant to but forgot. The boys were both quiet and stoic, Andrew looking angrier than Brian, and Brian looking like he couldn't leave the place soon enough.

"They look terrific," said Erin. "Both of them."

"Thank you." I hugged her and whispered into her hair. "Thank you so much."

She clutched me back. "Of course. We're going to go grab a snack — do you want anything?"

I shook my head. "I'm going to buy them each a tie and I'll meet you outside."

There was a customer in front of me so I had to wait. After she finished, I piled everything on the counter and the cashier folded it all and filled the shopping bag. She was very kind, but more reserved than I was used to the Nordstrom staff being, always so predictably outgoing, with their *How's your day going?* and high level of genuine professional interest in you for however long you spent with them. I was waiting for her gentle inquiry: *Special occasion?* But she only said how handsome the boys looked in the suits and what nice sons I had. I was prepared for her to be more solicitous, and I was glad that for whatever reason she wasn't.

"Thank you for your help," I said when we were finished.

She came around to my side of the counter and handed me the bag. "You're so very welcome," she said. "Please, take good care."

Erin and the boys were waiting on the corner across the street, outside Starbucks, and the four of us walked in the direction both of us had parked.

"Did that tall woman working help you guys at all?" I said. "At Nordstrom. Or did someone else?"

"No, she did," Erin said. "She was great. That's why we were practically done when you got there."

"Oh, that's good," I said. "I was just curious. She didn't have that usual bubbly chatter they always have, you know? I didn't want for you to have had any trouble. It was such a huge help."

"No, no." Erin shook her head. "Here. Let me take that." As soon as she took the Nordstrom bag from me, she clutched my empty right hand in her left. "Sweetie, she was wonderful. I told her why we were there and asked her to not say anything to you. But she told me how very sorry she was. She'd seen the paper."

After the funeral, I had my suit cleaned and I donated it to Dress for Success, hoping it would be just the thing for a woman on the cusp of taking her life in a new direction. I thought of a single mom. Maybe she would be only twenty-two or twenty-three. Maybe she'd recently finished school or a class where she'd developed new skills she was proud of. Maybe she'd gotten an interview she was really excited about, for a job she hoped to get. Like Leo's suit, I wore mine for only one occasion, despite the expense. I couldn't bear to hang it in my closet, where it would wait futilely to be worn on a happier day for an occasion that would never come. I knew when I bought it that I wouldn't wear it again. But the suit could mean all the difference for this woman I imagined. She'd be so excited about finding it, she'd call a friend. Maybe the suit would be part of what got her the job she wanted. And whomever it ended up with, I hoped at the very least the woman would feel lucky. She'd have no idea of the sadness it was part of before it came to her.

Brian

I didn't know about Christopher and Andrew, but I was glad Garrett was here. Our grandparents and Aunt Maureen and Uncle Gabe had been here for a few days already, and everyone was a wreck but trying not to be for us kids—it was obvious. As soon as he got here, it seemed like Garrett decided his job was to try to keep everyone from going completely crazy and off the rails, I could tell, even though no one asked him to. Even though he was a wreck too, he'd known my dad's family forever so he knew how to deal with them the way no one else could have, even though I'm sure he was doing something he never wanted to have to do.

Both sets of grandparents had come out to visit us right after Christmas like they did every year. They always came in the summer, and then again right after Christmas, so it was messed up to see them not even two months after the last time we did, when we had exchanged presents and both grandfathers had worn Santa hats. I sat with the adults sometimes and listened when they talked about my dad, crying, trying not to cry, my grandmothers hugging each other, laughing about him and how he was, then crying again. It seemed like everyone was always drinking, and Granddad Marty and Grandpa Glenn were usually quiet, and drinking made them both quieter or cry more often, depending on the day. We ate the food that people brought and it was mostly good even if it was weird eating a dinner every night that someone we didn't know had made for us.

My best friend, Michael, and sometimes his younger sister, came over with his mom, pretty much every day, and I was always glad even though he seemed as sad as I was and all we did was watch TV with Andrew. Joe Assante came over a few times and he and Chris would leave the house for a while, even though it seemed like nobody else left the house that week, and sometimes Chris looked better after they came back and sometimes he looked worse, although every day he pretty much looked ruined, like he never slept at all.

Because of Michael and Joe, I felt bad for Andrew that he didn't have a friend come over like we did. Andrew had a lot of friends he liked the same, not just one super good one. So if he was around when Michael and I were watching TV, I'd ask Andrew to pick the show he wanted, and that's the one we'd watch.

Garrett

The night before the funeral, Matt MacKay opened Leo's casket for the only people who would see him for the last time: Audrey, the boys, Leo's parents and sister, Audrey's parents and brother, Kevin Gallagher, my father, and me.

When I saw the suit again, I floundered for composure following the shock I hadn't anticipated. *You can still make the suit.* While helping Audrey buy it was something I couldn't forget, in the days since, I must have suspended the memory the way people do during such times. My only thought was that Leo's body dominated the clothes with far more authority than I had, and I had to remind myself they were the same ones. The suit did look good—it fucking better have—and although I couldn't say Leo looked good, I had expected him to look far worse. The work the funeral home had done to restore him as completely as possible was evident. And yet despite all the mortician's care and cosmetic mastery, it was only the final rendition of Leo—not him at all anymore—and I could look at it for only so long.

It was my father who made me think of doing it. After my mother's viewing, with Kate and me beside him, my father had taken off his wedding band and slid it onto my mother's left ring finger—Kate had inherited our mother's rings—and with that gesture he transitioned to no longer being married, by surrendering the symbol that he had been for forty-one years to accompany his dead beloved into the ground.

So before we'd left the house, I had taken the signed promise out of my rolled socks and tucked it in the inside pocket of my jacket, and if I'd had the discreet opportunity—which I didn't, as we were all there together the whole time sharing our last looks—I would have put the note in Leo's jacket pocket, returning it, to rid myself of the physical thing in the hope that doing so would enable me to forget about it. But since I didn't have the chance to accomplish something so furtive, all I could do was periodically finger it throughout the night, making sure it was still there. And because I never had a chance to do what I'd wanted to, which would have involved at least a minimum of physical contact, I didn't know how to otherwise touch Leo for the last time, or where, so I didn't touch him at all, not even to graze his hand with mine, and after the chance to do something had passed, I berated myself for the inability to muster what his family had. The boys had each touched their father one last time, and Audrey, shaking from inaudible sobs, had leaned into the casket and pressed her cheek against Leo's. For the rest of the night I had no one to share my insignificant private shortcoming with and no way to lessen its hold.

The honor guard who'd been assigned stood vigil for the calling hours, which had been scheduled for two but almost exceeded four, the line of people waiting spilling out the front door and curling around the block, appearing to never shorten. In lieu of an open casket, all there was to see of Leo were the three framed photographs on display: a group photo of the Station Twenty-Five men, one of him and Audrey and the boys that wasn't recent, and Leo's professional department portrait.

The next morning dawned with clouds, and their smudge clung, blocking the sun even as the hours of the day pressed on. We were all up early, taking the quiet, heavy steps to prepare for mass at eleven.

Leo and Audrey's parents, Maureen and Gabe, and my father all arrived, dressed and ready, sitting or standing until they were given a job to do. When I handed them a list and directions, Marty, Glenn, and my father drove to New Seasons for bagels and came back with too much food—pastries, muffins, cinnamon rolls, and the bagels that no one touched. Libby and Claudia tied their grandsons' ties, and made the boys sit with them. The boys were subdued and exercised restraint with each other, and let their grandmothers fawn over them. Everyone distracted one another with whatever means available.

I hadn't shaved since I'd arrived, and my hands shook that morning as I did for the first time. *I can't do this. I just won't shave. Fuck, I have to shave.* I tried to slow down and take my time but gave myself three bleeders anyway.

We got to the church at ten. Kevin and Alyssa Gallagher and their three girls met us there, and starting at ten-fifteen, the firefighters arrived—the other seven pallbearers among them—and occupied the pews at the back with respect and quiet valor, waiting to be invited closer to the front, the off-duties all in Class A, a hat in every lap, the on-shifts, ready for a call should one come, badge shrouds to a man. Leo's captain, Dave Bradley, and his wife, Violet, came early too, and after talking with Audrey, showed the same deference, waiting to be told what to do.

In the half hour before mass, the clouds that had threatened rain surrendered to bleak sun that never brightened but maintained its weak, consistent light for the rest of the day, and by eleven o'clock, when the procession started, the church looked filled to capacity. Kevin read the first reading, from The Book of Wisdom, and the first words, *The just, though they die early, shall be at rest,* waylaid my attempts to control my emotions, so I was already weeping when I began the second reading, the Twenty-Third Psalm, which I managed to get through, my grief and perseverance each warring to get the upper hand the whole time I read.

After the committal, at the reception at the Pittock Mansion, I stood or sat with my father when I wasn't with Audrey, and when I wasn't, her parents, Leo's parents, or Alyssa and Kevin Gallagher were. Erin and I made sure the boys ate something, and when it was time to leave two hours later, she didn't know where any of them were. I finally found the three of them out on the grounds of the mansion sitting on one of the benches that looked east out over the city and toward the mountains. There was nothing good about the day, but I was grateful that while the boys sat, because of the overcast, they didn't have to see the mountain where their father had died.

Although the parking lot was at capacity and the guests who'd arrived late had a long walk back to their cars, when the reception was over, everyone behind the wheel seemed patient and kind, making generous spaces to wave in other drivers, no one bullying anyone else to be the first to get home. Before we got to Burnside, Audrey asked the limo driver to wait, so we did, until behind the very last car, the men from Station Twenty-Five drove their truck, followed by the engine, down the hill.

Audrey

I thought the calling hours would never end, and that we might stand there all night until the last, patient mourners, after waiting so long, were able to share their condolences just in time for us to leave and go directly to the funeral. There were so many people, strangers I'd never seen before among the hundreds of faces I recognized—police officers, paramedics, firefighters and their families, and families from the school, the church, the street and neighborhood, the boys' preschool, the sports teams—they all waited for as long as it took for their own turn to talk to us.

I didn't think I'd sleep the night before the funeral, but the few hours I did took the edge off enough that I didn't feel so raw and like I couldn't cope—but barely. I didn't know how I could have gotten through it without Erin. I couldn't have. That morning she asked me if I wanted a Xanax—she was a terrible flier—and I'd told her no, and sobbed in the bathroom alone despite the whiskey I nursed while I showered and dressed and dried my hair. There wasn't anything that could dull my sorrow, or enough of anything to blunt the ordeal of burying my husband.

Erin wouldn't let me do a thing that day, acting as the hostess in her own house refusing offers from helpful guests. She scrambled eggs while the coffee brewed, one pot after the other, as the mugs were drained and refilled. She cooked and fed everyone who would eat. Her son, Michael, had been Brian's best friend since kindergarten, bringing us together in the process, and over those eight years she had earned the right to take over and to take care of me. Since Leo died, she had been there at least once a day, bringing Michael with her, and sometimes her nine-year-old daughter, Rory, taking charge after people started to drop off meals. She had marked all the containers' lids with the dates and stacked them in the basement chest freezer, with the oldest ones on top. There were too many flowers to manage—they overwhelmed me—and after covering every possible surface in the living and dining rooms, Erin ferried the ones that came later to the addition, a room I avoided. She put the arrangements on boards laid over the floor joists around the room's stark, skeletal perimeter; then when they passed their prime, as soon as they started dropping leaves, she got them out of the house and into the compost bin.

After we had all gotten through the morning and it was time to leave for the church, everyone filed out of the house and piled into the limos the funeral home had sent along with the hearse, but Andrew wasn't with them. I found him in bed, fully clothed, his shoes still on, bunkered in his comforter, which I peeled away as I coaxed him out as best I could. "Andrew, I would give almost anything right now to crawl in there with you," I said. "But I can't do this without you. Please, sweetie, you have to come."

With so much grace and kindness it humbled me, Kevin Gallagher had helped Father John and me plan the funeral. Kevin presented the decisions and desires the department offered on its behalf, provided they were acceptable to me. Together we chose the most reverent and ceremonial options. The men had put up the bunting at the station. The protocols reminded me of the rigorous rules for coronating European royalty: they seemed as relevant to my life, and to Leo's life, and who Leo had been, as a monarch's taking the throne in another country.

"It's everything we wanted to do for him," Kevin said. "I know it's a lot of pomp and splendor. Thank you for being okay with it. He deserves the best we have to give him."

And without spending more time than I could bear, I picked the plot for both of us in the cemetery Matt MacKay had helped me select. Years or hours from this time—I didn't know which to hope for—I would be in my own casket next to Leo. I ordered a dark granite headstone with a Celtic cross atop a base, under which Leo's name, birth and death dates, and five words would be engraved:

Son

Brother

Husband

Father

Friend

By eleven o'clock, when the procession started, the church was as full as on Christmas and Easter—even the balcony was packed. Kevin read the first reading, from The Book of Wisdom, and I sobbed, tucked in to myself, from the first words, *The just, though they die early, shall be at rest,* my parents and the boys close to me on either side. Garrett read the Twenty-Third Psalm, his voice breaking up as soon as he started. In the church and school parking lots, the fire department's trucks were queued side by side. The engine and truck from Station Twenty-Five, Leo's house, were parked in front of the others.

Leo's death was a loss not just for our family but also for the community he'd served, and the procession to the cemetery—where his captain, Dave Bradley, spoke at the graveside—clogged traffic. As the hearse, and fire engines and trucks, and cars with headlights on all passed the perpendicular streets, drivers whose routes had been disrupted stood outside their cars and saluted, or placed their hand over their heart, and remained that way until the motorcade passed and they could resume driving. Of everything that day, I didn't know if seeing those respectful strangers had been the most harrowing, or if it had been the eight pallbearers—strong but compromised men, Garrett the only civilian among them—who carried Leo between them with both the tenderness of holding a newborn and the determination of moving a mountain, all while the bagpipes played.

Dave and Violet Bradley, who had no children of their own, had insisted on having the reception following the committal at the Pittock Mansion. Because they were longtime donors—part of the elite Pittock Patron membership specifically—not only would they not take no for an answer, but because of how much money they had donated to the estate and since she was a distant Pittock descendant, Violet appealed to both the Pittock Mansion Society and to Portland Parks and Recreation and got them to close the mansion to the public that afternoon—an unprecedented allowance. Violet orchestrated all the catering, and while capacity had been daunting at the church, it was another in the Pittock's oval social hall. I thought the fire code was clearly breached, but no one seemed to give it a second thought on account of the organization that would have issued the violation being the one committing the infraction.

The winding road from Burnside up Barnes to Pittock was wide enough for one truck not passing another vehicle coming down from the top until it reached the fire road. So only the engine and truck from Station Twenty-Five drove up, and the other on-duties headed back to their stations. Once the upper lot was full, the overflow of cars was sent to the lower areas until they were full too, and some people had to walk up almost all the way from Burnside, from the closest spots they could find. The bar was ample, and the on-shifts who were still dressed at the ready nursed their tonic waters and club sodas, and the off-duties remained stoic, even as they got sloppy.

At the top of the marble staircase, before we descended the flight down to the social room, Violet Bradley, Garrett, the boys, and I stopped at the grand leaded windows, and Violet pointed east.

"When it's clear, you can see all the mountains," she said. I knew her attempt at conversation was benign and her carelessness was unintentional. "The Pittocks had exquisite views as far as the eye could see."

Even with the sun, the visibility was still not clear enough to see the peak of Mount Hood. *From how many wakes can you see the place where the person died?* I knew the mountain was there, but I was glad it was shrouded that day.

"How nice for the Pittocks," I said. And we continued down the stairs.

All I had to do was talk and hug and cry for, or let cry for me, everyone who came. For that whole time one of my parents or Leo's sat or stood with me, and then Garrett, or Kevin or Alyssa Gallagher. As generous as the Bradleys and all the people who had come had been—generosity that I'd been forced to accept—I couldn't wait to get out of the Pittock Mansion with its mocking view of the mountains and go home. When it was time to leave and I couldn't find the boys, I asked Garrett to look for them, and after he brought them inside we all got back into the limo for the ride home.

Although we were the first to leave, I asked the driver to wait when we got to the bottom, before turning onto Burnside. I wanted to see everyone drive away until the very last car left, and the truck from Twenty-Five, followed by the engine, finally came down the hill. Then we drove away from the estate too, close to three o'clock, and I thought, *Did you see how many people came to your party?*

Erin got to the house ahead of me and waited for everyone, even though it was only us, and it was like a replay of the morning, only with different food and now with booze. She had brewed coffee again and opened bottles of wine and put mixers next to liquor on the sideboard in the dining room and filled the ice bucket. When I walked in she offered me two glasses—a glass of red and a tumbler of whiskey—and I took the wine and she kissed me on the cheek and went back to heating casseroles and slicing meat and cheese and opening boxes of crackers.

Erin and Garrett took care of everything, and close to seven—it was coming up on a twelve-hour day—after everyone left, my house and kitchen showed no evidence of what had happened. My parents, Leo's parents, Maureen, Gabe, and Garrett's father, Julian, went back to the hotel.

Garrett's father left the next day, and Leo's and my family the day after that. It wasn't until they did that I could finally let go.

Dealing with Leo's parents, I suspended my own loss. I loved Glenn and Libby, and Maureen and I were as close as sisters-in-law who live far apart and differently can be. While they were with me, their grief supplanted my own. Glenn and Libby had lost their older child and only son, and Maureen had never known the world without Leo.

My parents and Gabe had been their steadiest, best versions of themselves. They did everything that needed doing or tending, and took care of the boys, and the McGearys, until they'd done all they could. They had loved Leo, but they respected that the loss was the McGearys', and mine. My father made many runs to the market, and Gabe handled the phone calls. My mother kept us fed, and although we talked, she mostly touched me—stroked my hair, rested her hand on the middle of my back, squeezed my forearm—any time she was close to me.

Garrett

I drove my father to the airport the day after the funeral. I parked and walked with him as far as I could. He knew I'd left my job, and Boston, for an indeterminate period of time. *I see* was all he'd said. *Well, you know what you're doing.*

"How long are you planning to stay?" he asked. He knew how lean I lived, and he knew I had money; it was from him, from both my parents. After my mother died, he sold the house I grew up in and moved into a condo, and later the same year, after much deliberation, he sold our house in Surf City. He had always been very smart with his money, both my parents had, and he had given Kate and me each a generous share of his assets after planning what he needed for himself in the short and long terms in his new life as a widower. *I want you to use it and be happy while I'm still alive,* he'd said. *No point in waiting till I'm dead to enjoy it.* He had also, within six months of my mother's death, begun a companionship with a widow named Judy, whom both my parents had known, with whom my father had reconnected, and who, I knew, despite his unnecessary discretion, made him very happy. They each lived alone but traveled together frequently, and there were several nice framed photos of them at his place, mixed among the ones of my parents, my mother, Kate and her family, and me. I had met Judy and had dinners with them more than once when I'd visited Radnor. I didn't know why he was so bashful about the two of them; Kate and I were both happy they'd found each other.

We stood near the security lines forming for his concourse. It wasn't the place I would have chosen for our conversation.

"I don't know, Dad," I said. "I haven't thought that far ahead. I guess until the house is finished. Whenever that is."

"I know how fond you are of Audrey," he said. He looked at his shoes and then at the line of people he'd have to join. He didn't have all the time in the world. "People need each other—we're not built to be alone. I don't know how you've done it."

"Done what, Dad?" I said. "I haven't been alone." I laughed, but I couldn't bullshit my own father.

"You know, Judy is a very good friend to me," he said. He always called her that, and Kate and I let him. "Our spending time together, our friendship, it in no way dishonors your mother." My sister and I called them the Js, even to my father—*What are the Js up to?* I'd ask him when I called, and he would chuckle quietly, *Oh, we're just fine,* like the cat wasn't entirely out of the bag. He never tired of defending his relationship with Judy, or thinking that he needed to.

I put my hand on his shoulder. "Dad, I know," I said. "Please tell her hello from me. You've got a plane to catch. I can't tell you how much it means to me that you came."

It was like we were doing two different things—I kept lobbing a ball, unreturned, and he was gathering leaves, which the wind kept scattering—even though we were standing in the airport looking at each other.

With my hand still on his shoulder, he let go of the handle of his suitcase and moved his coat from where he'd draped it over his arm and rested it on top of the suitcase. He reached out with both his hands and cradled my jaw, staring at me. It was a stance we hadn't shared in decades.

"Garrett, I know your business is your own. But when people are lost, and they need each other, it's not something to ignore. It's a gift. I know how fond of Audrey you are," he said again. "Down the road she may need you in ways you aren't aware of right now."

"Jesus Christ, Dad." I took my hand off his shoulder, but he left his hands where they were on my face. "I'm happy for you and Judy— after three years already, you have my blessing. What the hell are you even talking about? We just put Leo in the ground."

"I know, son," he said. "I know we did."

He pulled me against him and grasped me hard and held me before he stepped back and kissed me. He picked up the coat, put it back over his arm, and grasped the handle of his bag. "I love you, Garrett," he said. "I'll talk to you soon." He walked away, straight and true, with his long easy strides, neither slow nor fast, to the end of the line. He stood behind the last person, and when he put his bag down again and turned and lifted his hand, I waved back.

Andrew

I t was because of me that my mom asked us all to go to the Dougy
Center, to talk with other kids who had a mom or dad who died
too. *At least once, please,* she'd said. *This has happened to other families and sharing can help. I have to know you're all right.* Even if they
went just once, I was ready for Chris and Brian to complain about it,
and I was ready to fight back and remind everyone that Chris had
turned into a creep who always had the door of any room he was in
closed, and that I couldn't believe no one else noticed, and that Brian
was freaking out in his sleep, but my brothers didn't say anything. And
neither of them was punching or biting people. But I had had it with
things.

It really bugged me that Christopher took up all the hot water in
the shower every morning, like the rest of us didn't have to use it and
he could shower forever. And that he was always shutting the bathroom door. None of us ever shut the bathroom door, even my parents,
and if I had to go, I had to go. I didn't care if a door was open or shut.

"I have to pee!" I announced when I walked in the bathroom.

"Get out, Andrew!" Christopher shouted.

"Hurry up!" I said. "Other people are waiting!"

"Go downstairs!" said Christopher.

"Why should I!" I said.

But what bugged me more was what an asshole Gannon Keegan had turned into after my dad died and how because of him I started getting in trouble at school. The basketball season had ended the first week in February and my dad had been our coach. He had coached since I started playing in third grade, and he was great at it, not like the other lame coaches who didn't teach their guys any real skills, so our team had ended the season with a winning record. My dad had been a basketball player, a really good one, so he knew what he was doing. He had us run suicides, and he did them with us, slow at first so we'd pace our breathing, and then he'd step it up, but they weren't bad—they didn't make us drop dead or anything. We practiced layups with guys crowding the net, and passing and guarding separately and then together, and shot free throws with our eyes closed sometimes, so we were pretty scrappy. That's what my dad had called us, *scrappy*.

Gannon and I had gone to school together since kindergarten, and we'd been on the same team for three years. We weren't best friends or anything, and he was a good basketball player, but he wasn't the only good one on our team—he wasn't better than me. Gannon had always been a ball hog, like he was the only one who could take it down the court and score, which he'd try to do if he had the ball, rather than pass, and no one else did that. My dad never called him out, but when he emphasized teamwork and sportsmanship, I knew Gannon was the one he was talking to. I griped about Gannon to my dad, but he'd never bite. Like I said, he was a good coach, and he'd always say Gannon was competing with himself on the court as well as against the other team, and it was everyone's job to rely on the skills of our other teammates. That we succeeded or fell together, not alone.

But Gannon had *always* bugged me a little. After my dad had come to our class in second grade to talk about being a firefighter, like a bunch of other parents did during Career Week, Gannon got all obsessed with firefighters. That year he had his birthday party, which I went to even though I didn't really want to, at the Belmont Firehouse, and you would have thought he owned the place or that he lived there. The rest of the kids just wanted to play games after we'd had the tour, and Gannon kept wanting to drag people back into the museum to show them one thing or another again. Then after that, he never stopped asking me if I went to my dad's firehouse, and could he go with me sometime. I told him I never went, I wasn't allowed to, which was a lie, but I was embarrassed he wanted to go so bad, and because he wasn't my best friend or anything, I never would have taken him. I couldn't figure out what was wrong with him. He had his own dad. I didn't like him being so crazy about mine.

Gannon had always been bigger than me, which never meant anything before, but after he became an asshole, it did. When we played basketball at school during recess—right after the season ended and my dad died—even though we'd play the same side, he'd try to get the ball from me to make his own play, doing that thing again like he was the only guy on the team, and when I didn't let him, when I hung on to the ball, he acted like I hurt him, clutching his stomach, like I'd fouled my *own* player, which made the teachers monitoring the playground come over and break up the game and send me inside to the principal's office.

He didn't do it every time we played—he spaced them out—but after the second time I got busted because of him, not long after I was back in school again, I told him to cut it out.

"What are you talking about?" he said, like he had no idea.

We were sitting at the same table during lunch. "That"—I wanted to say *crap*—"stuff you say I do when we're playing basketball. Don't be so greedy for the ball; if you're smart and you move, maybe I'll pass it. That's garbage that you say I hurt you just because I won't let you steal the ball from me when we're on the *same* side."

"You're not me," Gannon said. "You can't say whether I'm hurt or not. If you hurt me, you hurt me."

"Oh, brother," I said. "Whatever. I'm not hurting you, Gannon, and you know it. And you don't do that to anybody else. So cut it out."

So the third time he did it, when Gannon acted like a little girl after the teachers broke up the game, and pretended to cry even though as usual I hadn't done anything to him and he wasn't hurt at all, as I walked off the court past him, I whispered, "Asshole. You're just an asshole."

That made him yell for the teacher, "Swearing! Now Andrew's cursing at me!"

Maybe Gannon had only liked me, or pretended to, because of my dad, and now that he was dead, Gannon didn't have a reason to anymore. He didn't have to like me—I didn't care—but he didn't have to be an asshole. I hated sitting on the bench outside the office and bringing home conduct referrals. The third one got me detention after school. But I hoped it made people a little afraid of me. I could be dangerous. If people pushed me, they'd find out what I would do.

My mom was really mad.

"Andrew, you've never been in trouble at school," she said. We were standing in the kitchen after the third time, and I told her I had detention the next week. I knew she was saying the things she could think of that would be helpful. "We're all going through this terrible time, I know. I'm angry a lot of days too. But you can't fight like that, you just can't—not during recess, at school, not anywhere. Can't you come home and punch a pillow when you're mad? Would that help?"

"Punching a pillow, really? Mom, are you serious?" I shouted. I started to cry. "Gannon Keegan is who I need to punch. I hate him. I want to kill him. I'm not doing anything and he's getting me in trouble."

She stared at me. She looked miserable. "I know," she said. "I heard it. The pillow, that was dumb. Maybe it's something you can talk about at Dougy?" She sat down in the middle of the kitchen with her legs crossed. "Come here," she said, but I kept standing. "I know, Andrew, just come here." I walked over and let her pull me into her lap and curl me up against her the best she could, even though I'm pretty tall, but not as tall as Gannon. "Oh, my baby," she said. "Sweet boy, just sit with your mom for a minute. What are we going to do?" We sat like that for a long time on the kitchen floor even after I stopped crying, and I didn't get up until she did.

Christopher

We didn't go back to school until after the funeral, so that week Joe Assante texted and asked if he could come over. When he showed up I told my mom we were going for a walk, and we walked without talking until I started to cry, and without saying anything Joe put his hand on my shoulder and the weight of his hand helped me keep walking, and then I did both things. I kept walking and crying. Joe didn't say anything and I didn't know how long we walked that way, but it was long enough that I could go back to my house and be in it with everyone who was a mess.

Joe came over again twice and brought homework for me, and when he asked me if I wanted to know about what was going on at school, I said sure and he filled me in with some funny things that might not have even been true, or could have, it didn't matter, but I could tell he was trying to get my mind on something else, even for a few minutes, and that meant a lot.

But I still woke up crying the morning of my dad's funeral like I did most other mornings that week—crying overcame me as soon as I wasn't sleeping anymore. When I was awake, I couldn't ignore the reality that my dad was dead, and even though I felt like I had to do whatever I could to help my mom and my brothers, as soon as

I was awake, the fact that my dad was gone made me want to sleep for years.

And now, because he was dead, my mom had asked us to go to the Dougy Center, and we'd agreed to try it but I didn't think I'd go more than once, or Brian either. I wasn't much of a joiner, and Brian was so private, I knew it wasn't his thing. They arranged the groups by age, and Brian and I were together but Andrew was in a different one. We went around the room and said our names and who had died and how. Some of the kids had been coming for a long time and talked about how much better they were than when they started. I wondered how long Brian would have to come before he'd stop screaming in his sleep.

The only thing I knew or thought about the Dougy Center before we went was that three years earlier, on Father's Day, they'd had a bad fire that my dad had fought. Station Twenty-Five was the first one at the scene because my dad's firehouse was literally one minute away. Since he had to work, we celebrated on Saturday instead, and served him breakfast in bed. I scrambled the eggs with my mom hovering while I cooked. We planted Andrew up in bed with him so my dad would stay put, and Andrew took credit for the success of the whole thing because my dad kept trying to pretend to get out of bed and come downstairs to see what we were doing, and Andrew had held him off—which my dad of course had let him do.

After the fire they had to rebuild, and the new building was really nice, not at all like a place where you'd expect a bunch of kids with dead parents to go to try to feel better. It was more like the nicest house that one of your friends had, a place you'd rather hang out at than at home because it was bigger and fancier and the kitchen had all kinds of gadgets yours didn't. I wished my dad could have seen the place, it was so nice. I wondered if he had; he'd never said anything about it, but he didn't talk about work much.

The one thing that I liked was that nobody was weird talking about their dead parent, not like how everyone was at school. No one was afraid to say the word "dead" and nobody put on some kind of fake face or attitude. One girl's mom died in a car accident when she ran out to the grocery store for milk. Another boy who was super quiet and struggling to keep it together had lost his dad, who had been sick with cancer for a really long time. One kid was there because his dad had drowned during a triathlon. Anywhere else, hearing about the deaths that had gotten us there together would have horrified and appalled people, turned them stupid or at least useless with no idea what to do or say. But here, all of us heard each other and didn't even flinch. Our dead parents brought us together in a way that nothing else could have.

I *was* grieving, like they said in group—we all were, it was no secret—but Garrett was here now and my mom had enough to worry about. Brian was all fucked up, screaming in the middle of the night like a crazy person, then my mom was up, running in there every time he did. And Andrew had turned into a royal little shit. He'd always been the peacemaker, the happy, kind one. When he was a little kid and he stopped liking a toy, he'd give it to a friend, or start collecting them in a bag for my mom to donate. He was bighearted like that, but not lately. He was getting in trouble at school, and he bit me one night when we both reached for the ketchup and I got it first. I wanted to smack him but I didn't. Someone had to keep it together.

My dad was a firefighter, and a really good one, but although I never thought he'd die, *really die,* I knew he had a dangerous job, and sometimes when he left for work he said goodbye to us like he was never going to see us again. Not creepy or sad, just super emo. *I really love you. I'm proud of you. I'm lucky to be your dad. Be good to your mom.* But it was cool. He wasn't like that all the time and I never worried about him when he went to work.

I still couldn't understand how it happened. He was wearing a helmet, which he'd always made us all do, and he ran into a tree and died anyway. It was enough to make you say, *Fuck the helmet—if I'm going to die if I crash anyway,* right? But we'd always had to wear them, on our bikes, scooters, and skateboards too. He taught us all to ski and we were all pretty good, although Brian was the best.

He made us do fire drills too, as soon as Andrew was good at walking. *The smoke detector goes off and what do you do?* Dad said. *You get low and you stay low and you get out of the house. But if the bedroom door is closed, feel it, and if it's hot, or you can see that the stairs are blocked and you can't get out, close your door, get low, shelter in place and wait until the firefighters or mom and I come get you. We'll get you out.*

He tried to make the drills not like a game exactly—he wanted us to take them seriously—but he expected us to do the best we could, like when we learned anything new. Because of his work schedule, he'd told us he might not be home if a fire happened, or he might not be able to get to us, so we had to know what to do and be able to do it ourselves without panicking. Our neighbor's porch was our meeting place. My dad would time us, and we did the drills until he was happy that our time was fast enough. I was six and Andrew was only two when we first did them, and Andrew would laugh through the whole thing, like it was the best game ever, which maybe it was to him, running as fast as he could on his short little legs to the Thompsons' porch, but Brian, who was four, cried every time. I knew just talking about the drills worried Brian, even before we did the first one. The idea of a fire was terrifying. None of us wanted to think about it happening, but Brian was the most nervous of all of us. That's just how he was.

So after we went to Dougy for our one time and after everyone at school stopped acting so weird around me, all I could think about was Mrs. Maguire—Colleen Maguire—my friend Ben's mom. But I couldn't talk to anyone about that. Ben and I had always been okay friends, but when I'd started hanging out with him more, it wasn't because of him. Colleen didn't seem like a mom type at all—she was beautiful, and sexier than stupid singers who grind against stuff in their music videos. I thought she was prettier than Meredith McCann, who I'd kissed a couple times, who said I was a good kisser. Meredith was always texting me about tests and teachers and what her friends and her were doing on the weekends—*LOL, Theresa is craving Jamba Juice so we're at the mall*—but I knew there was more to it.

I didn't want to hang out at the mall. I hated the mall, but I knew, for reasons I didn't understand and didn't want to, the girls liked going there, especially in the winter. Instead, I biked to Grant Park and played ball and hung out with the guys, especially on the nice days during the winter. That's where Meredith and I kissed the two times, on the bleachers at Grant, when we were hanging out. We'd taken a walk over there and sat down and kissed for a while, before we walked back to everyone else like nothing had happened. That was in January, before my dad, during a really warm week without any rain, and I thought that was cool. I thought Meredith was cool. Till she started to bug me.

I texted her back sometimes but not nearly as much as she texted me. I could be her boyfriend, but I didn't want her like that. Nothing was going to happen with Colleen, but I thought maybe someday it could. It would be worth the wait.

In fifth grade, our class had the sex talk, and it was disgusting, and it was even worse when I asked my dad that night if he and my mom did it.

"We do, Chris," he said. "That's how the three of you got here, buddy. Sorry, I know it's weird to think about your parents like that. I don't like to think of mine either." He laughed.

"It's not weird," I said. "It's disgusting. It's not something I'm ever going to do."

"I know you feel that way now." He sighed. "But one day you're going to change your mind. And, Chris, that will be weird for me."

I felt like I should say something back but I didn't know what.

"Listen," he said. "We don't have to talk about this anymore right now if you don't want to, but if you can, I want you to promise me that anytime you want to talk about it again, anytime you have any questions, you'll let me know. Can you?"

I nodded and let him hug me, then got out of the room as fast as I could. I wanted to forget that sex talk in school and the talk with my dad ever happened.

But now, if I could, maybe I'd make good on the promise. I didn't think sex was disgusting anymore, not when I thought about Colleen Maguire, which was mostly in the shower. I thought about her washing her own body. Everybody showers. I liked to take my time, but I had to be quiet and hoped no one walked in on me, especially Andrew, who would walk in because he didn't care what anyone else was doing or if a door was closed because someone wanted a little privacy. That kid. It wasn't like when my friends and I elbowed each other when we saw women wearing tight jeans tucked into their boots and pushing their kids in strollers. When I thought about Colleen it wasn't like that at all.

Even though nothing could come of it now, it wouldn't be that long till it could, only three years. Till then I'd practice. Maybe next year Meredith would still want to be my girlfriend and I'd let her and maybe we'd have sex and maybe I'd have another girlfriend or two after her, and get good enough at sex so I'd know what I was doing, and Colleen would be impressed that I was experienced. Of course she wasn't the kind of person who would have an affair, so I didn't know what to do about Mr. Maguire. His name was Paul. I didn't know him at all, but I'd seen him at church and they were a nice family. But what if he died? I didn't want anything bad to happen to him, not really, but I figured if my dad died, it could happen to anyone. I didn't want Mr. Maguire to have a disease or suffer and be in pain, but what if he had an aneurysm or was traveling alone and was in a plane crash? I felt bad thinking about that but not as bad as I would have felt if Colleen cheated on her husband with me. Or maybe they'd get divorced before

I was eighteen. Maybe Mr. Maguire *would* be the type of person to have an affair—although I didn't want that to happen to Colleen and I couldn't imagine a man cheating on her—and by the time I was old enough, she'd be ready to date again. Maybe by then Ben and I wouldn't be friends anymore—not enemies, just would have drifted apart—so it wouldn't seem so weird his mom liked me. We'd both be men by then, almost.

It wouldn't be long until I was in college and I'd get an apartment off campus. Colleen could come and spend weekends with me and I'd see her when I came home for breaks. It worked for Demi Moore and Ashton Kutcher, until he turned out to be a total dog. Their whole age thing was a big deal to everyone at first and then it wasn't, and Demi and Ashton never cared. Since I didn't even like girls my age now, if Colleen and I were together, there's no way I'd leave her for someone younger. I'm not that kind of guy.

It was really too much, all these things I didn't want to think about but I couldn't help some days. Colleen in the shower, getting Mr. Maguire out of the picture and being Ben's mom's boyfriend. Even if my dad hadn't died, I wasn't so sure I'd be able to tell him about any of it. When he asked me for that promise in fifth grade, I bet he'd had no idea I'd ever be thinking about stuff like this.

Brian

Every morning after it happened again, my mom was in my
room, leaning over me first thing.

"Sweetie, how are you? Brian, are you all right?"

I mostly wanted to be left alone for a few more minutes before I
had to get up. "I'm fine, Mom," I said. "God. I'm not even awake yet.
Can you leave me alone?"

"Of course," she said. "I know. I just need to make sure you're
okay."

Andrew, the little shit, had started calling me "screaming meemie,"
but I mostly felt bad about waking up everyone else in the middle of
the night.

The dream was always the same. It scared me so much, I wanted to
die. In it, we're all at home, and it's my birthday, and there's cake and
presents and everyone's happy but my dad is missing. Not like *missing,*
he's not dead, he just isn't there, and no one thinks anything of it. My
mom and my brothers are singing to me. Everyone's having a great
time but I can tell I'm the only one who knows something bad is about
to happen. And when the bad thing happens, everything changes, just
like that. Something dangerous is loose in the house, wanting to hurt
us, and the party is over, and my mom and brothers are afraid and ev-

eryone has run from the table to find somewhere safe to hide. That's what I want to do too, run and hide. But what makes the dream so bad is that I can't find any of my family—even though I look everywhere, fast, in closets and under beds—and when I can't find them I realize I'm the one who is supposed to save us from the bad thing happening, the loose thing in the house, which is after me now, since everyone else is hiding and safe. And I can't find anywhere to hide—no place I can think of is good. It doesn't even look like a person, or look like anything really, the dangerous thing, it's just a terrible force I can feel, but it's after me, and I think if I can just get far enough ahead of it, I *can* find a place to hide, and lose it, and protect my family at the same time since it's chased me, and if it doesn't get any of us it will just go away, but it's always right behind me, gaining, and I can't get any distance from it, so I start to scream as loud and hard as I can, and wake up. Every time I woke up, my mom was there trying to hold me and keep me still. It was hard because I'd push her away and try to run from my own room. Sometimes I crawled on the floor, sweating, scrambling away from my bed when she came in, and I would keep crawling, even after she was there, trying to grab me and convince me I'd had a dream. Now that Garrett was here, he came in with her once or twice too, when it was really bad, and I'd managed to get away from my mom, when I was still freaked out beyond reason.

Like Chris, I'd told my mom I'd go to the Dougy Center one time and if I changed my mind about going more, I'd tell her. It was such a weird thing that the building where we went had replaced the one where my dad had fought a fire. I didn't say anything to anybody, but it was almost like he was there, kind of. We were in the same place where my dad had done his job the best he could. All those firefighters hadn't been able to save the building after all.

What I hadn't expected were the murals, which decorated the rooms on the first floor. It was such great work that I couldn't believe I'd never heard of the artist, and that she wasn't an artist for her job.

When I asked the people there they told me her career was something else, in real estate or something financial. I would have gone there every day if I could have just stared at all those scenes on the walls instead of sitting around waiting for my turn to talk.

One of the things we talked about the time I went was if we thought we could have done something to prevent the death. Even if it was a totally unrealistic thing, we could say anything we wanted to—like for the one girl, never running out of milk, like not ever. Or the other guy, what was he supposed to do, tell his dad he shouldn't compete in a triathlon when everyone else his dad knew was so excited about it? But I bet that kid wouldn't ever compete in a triathlon himself, and maybe if he heard about someone else training for one, he'd tell them to do a marathon instead, and why.

It hadn't been a big deal to me. I knew we couldn't go skiing on my birthday, that we needed a new fridge, even though my mom was always saying, *The way you boys eat, food doesn't have a chance to go bad in this house*. But she liked things taken care of, and the fridge did suck. And that morning after it broke, all the food stank, then it stank up the whole kitchen while my mom divvied it between the compost and the garbage until my dad came downstairs and said he'd take care of it. I hadn't thought about it until they asked us in our group, and even after that, I didn't think there was anything I could have done. If I were a totally different person and I'd thrown a huge fit about my life being ruined because we weren't going to ski on my birthday, it's not like my family would have done things differently. *Oh, Brian's having a fit, forget the fridge, we better go skiing*. I wasn't like that and my family wasn't like that. Nobody caved about something important because someone was having a fit or not getting their way. The fridge was important. We needed it, and so we went the next week. That's just what happened.

And even after he died, when I thought about the fridge drama, I still thought it had been funny. My dad blow-drying the freezer trying to make the thing last, those weeks before it tanked, that had cracked me up. So I sketched him doing it—I had a lot of chances—which annoyed him the first few times he was working, lying there on his side waiting for the ice to thaw, pointing my mom's blow-dryer at it like a gun, but when he finally saw what I was working on, it cracked him up too and it became this big joke between us, like he was a superhero whose power was The Blow-Dryer. So all the times he tackled the defroster after he saw my drawing, he'd geek out, hamming it up, all stealth and unstoppable, which was totally corny and he knew it, but because he was so aggravated, I thought he had to do something so he wouldn't blow a gasket. My mom didn't think it was funny at all when he strutted around with his sunglasses on, creeping up on the fridge. She would shake her head and exhale really loudly, she was so pissed, and leave the kitchen so she wouldn't have to see it. Then my dad would swagger away after he was finished, with his sunglasses pushed up on his head and blowing the tip of my mom's dryer the way sharpshooters always do with their pistols after they've saved the town or killed the villain.

Anyway, my drawing was pretty good, and what I'd liked about it the best was that what I'd drawn had turned not a terrible situation, but a frustrating one, into something that made my dad laugh, something he'd made into a kind of game. We had egged each other on. My mom was annoyed and Chris and Andrew didn't care. When I finished the drawing, I gave it to him and he took it to work and I hadn't seen it since. I wanted it back, but I didn't want to remind my mom of anything about the old fridge and my dad's goofiness and my birthday and the day my dad died, and I didn't know who else to ask about the drawing. Maybe I'd ask Garrett to help me get it back. But what I was afraid of was that all my dad's stuff was already cleaned out from the fire station and some firefighter who had no idea what it was had thrown it away instead of giving it back to my mom with all his other stuff.

It was only later, after the one time I went to Dougy, after we'd talked in group about what we thought we could have done to prevent the death, when I hadn't said anything and neither had Chris, that the idea crept into my head that maybe if I hadn't made the drawing in the first place, if it hadn't temporarily made my dad goof off and delay the solution, if instead, without my drawing, he'd dealt with it the way he should have, like the guy he was who took care of things, maybe we would have gotten a new fridge earlier, or at least the freezer might have been repaired by someone who knew what they were doing, long before it broke down completely, preventing what happened later. Without my drawing and all the goofiness it had started, maybe the fridge problem would have been solved and my dad would still be alive.

Garrett

They were all so damaged, and I had no idea what I could do except finish what Leo had started. Now that I was alone with them, I realized I didn't know any of them as well as I had assumed I did, even Audrey, and that sense of estrangement made me regret the distance Leo and I had lived from each other for so long. Without him as the bridge between his family and me, I felt like an interloper, my usefulness limited to helping Audrey buy his suit and what I'd done the day of the funeral. Refusing Audrey's initial wishes that I not stay made me feel like a bully, and now that I was here to do what I'd said I would, I knew I wasn't being entirely altruistic—I was also staying for me. I would never again be able to spend an hour or a day with Leo, and I couldn't make up for lost time with his family, but I could create new time. It was later than I wished, and under circumstances that I would have changed if I could.

Scabbed onto the back of house was a fresh wood box, bright and uniform in color, with holes cut out for windows. Edges of Tyvek that had come loose flapped in the weather, like the corners of a wrapped but battered gift. The yard was dotted with piles of scraps: stacks of Hardiplank siding, rolls of Tyvek, two-bys, and berms of dirt dug from the trench that Leo hadn't backfilled. The windows he'd ordered were stacked against the back, the glass smeared with grime. Tarpaper covered the top and plastic was laid over it. Inside, the floor joists had sheets of plywood piled on them. On one plank laid across two sawhorses, bags from Home Depot and Lowe's with the receipts still in them, blueprints and sheets of paper with notes and lists in Leo's handwriting, a coffee cup with cold, shallow remains in the bottom and a plate sprinkled with careless crumbs.

As much as it pained me to fasten Leo's kneepads around my own legs, and to drape the straps of his tool belt over my shoulders and buckle it around my waist, when the weather cooperated, the roof was where I started, slowly, laying the tarpaper Leo had already bought. The days the weather made it hard to work up there, I did what else I could. I got organized and oriented myself with the plans and the progress Leo had made. One afternoon I backfilled the trench in the rain. But first, after the funeral, after everyone had left, I asked Audrey if she would take me to rent a car.

"Sure," she said. "But what do you need a car for? You're welcome to use mine. I guess if you think you should have one, okay, but—No, no, you can't do that, it's too expensive."

"I'm driving up to the mountain," I said. "I want to be there. I want to see it. I want to get a good look at Mount Hood."

Because she insisted, I took her car. "I won't need it till you get back," she said. "And if you need chains, you'll have them."

It wasn't a short drive. For people who go up to ski every weekend, no doubt it becomes routine and the ride seems shorter, but for me there was a lot of ground to cover between Portland and Government Camp alone, at the base of Mount Hood. Off Route 84 into and through Gresham on 26, then through the town of Sandy, "The Gateway to Mount Hood," and the other hamlets and mountain villages—Welches, Zigzag, Rhododendron—that peppered the national forest banking the road on both sides. I alternated between listening to NPR—and Oregon Public Broadcasting—and local music stations until as the elevation increased I lost reception and the connections died away. With no CD in the player, in silence, with each mile I climbed, I retraced what had been, without his knowing it, Leo's last trip with his family.

There was more than one resort on the mountain, and after I got a coffee in Government Camp, I followed the signs to Meadows and found an empty place to park in the crowded lot. I walked around and through the lodge, by the racks of skis and poles and snowboards, looking at the people I passed, none of whom noticed me, a guy with no gear, not dressed to spend the day. I got a drink and sat inside the lodge and watched the slopes and everyone gliding down; the awkward and the intrepid, the beginners and the experts, the little kids in ski school—fall and stand up, fall and stand up—the lines forming at the lifts, all from a chair by the window.

I didn't understand how he could die skiing, wearing a helmet. He'd been skiing since he was four. He made his kids do fire drills. It was a shameless taunt that of all those he'd saved, Leo didn't survive his own accident. He'd lived through so many mishaps with me on and off the slopes: icy conditions, the missed jump, whiteouts that only made us stop and wait, but not quit; the time we had to find the road and walk back to the lodge, his parents on the verge of cardiac arrest; the acid and mushrooms and drinking; one night during senior year, when he was sober but still drove too fast on Donahue's moped (no helmet) to 7-Eleven for snacks while the rest of us rolled joints. I couldn't wrap my mind around it. Surviving all that wild youth only to have this be his undoing.

The mountains out here were a far cry from what Leo had grown up skiing on and we'd skied together back east—Camelback, Elk Mountain, Killington—but he'd adapted and made this mountain his own for all the years he and Audrey and the boys had skied it, until the mountain had claimed him. Maybe mastery had been part of the problem. He was never reckless, neither of us was—though maybe his mother or Audrey might have disagreed—he knew his limits and was confident of his ability on the snow, in a variety of conditions, and I'd never seen him out of control. That's always what seems to be the fatal flaw in sports with any margin of risk: Once you think you know what you're doing—far from reckless but encroaching on invincible—that's when you're fucked. Once you become an expert at something you aren't exempt from making mistakes, you just make them less frequently. Still, all it takes is one. My sister had gone through a horse stage in her early teens, and my mother was never quite comfortable with any of it. So when Christopher Reeve had his tragic accident years later, well past Kate's own time riding, my mother said during one phone call, "Thank God she never got hurt. I'm so glad she didn't stay with it."

After I finished my beer I asked directions to the ski patrol office—*No, no emergency,* I told the woman, I was looking for someone I wanted to say hello to. When I got to the office, a guy, Tom, was waiting to meet me. I told him I was a close friend of Leo's and asked if anyone who had worked that day was here now. Tom was forthcoming with his condolences—he knew about it, of course, but said nobody who'd been there that day was in the office now, but if I wanted he could check who might be out on the hill. I thanked him and told him not to bother, but asked him to share my thanks with them.

"His wife told me how kind everyone was," I said. "I wanted to tell you how much that meant to her, and how much it means to me," I said.

"We did what we could," Tom said. "It's not a part of the job any of us ever wants to do."

I stayed less than two hours. I didn't need any longer than that, and after that much time, I had to leave. I drove back down the mountain the way I'd come, reversing my trip to Portland. Audrey had told me someone from the resort had driven her and the boys home that night, and as I drove west, all I could think about was how that journey must have pushed her to the brink of madness. What an agonizing trip it must have been for the four of them. A nightmare end to the day their family had begun that morning, the same as every other.

Audrey

I don't know how we—how I—got through that early time, the weeks before Daylight Saving and the first signs of spring. Like people always say, the goddamn sun still rose every morning. The weather followed its own erratic whims. The hummingbirds chased each other away when it was their turn at the feeder and the squirrels bickered and recovered what they'd buried, maintaining their fat and biding their time. The laundry piled, the mail came, the bills still needed to be paid, the food made, the dishes cleared and washed and used again. The boys had homework, and still argued, and each day Andrew simmered a little more with an anger that was unlike him, and Brian screamed in the night from his dreams, still needing his mother, still needing me. Christopher came right home every day after school instead of hanging out with his friends like he always had, though some days Joe Assante came home with him. And still, the sympathy cards kept coming, the phone kept ringing, and the voice-mail and my inbox kept filling.

After the boys returned to school, after I got them all out the door in the morning, I went back to bed. I told Garrett I was going to read, but I buried myself in bed and slept for hours, hiding from my grief and exhausted from the insomnia, or from getting up with Brian.

I never opened a single book. The fire bureau reached out with resources I wanted no part of.

I listened to Leo's voicemails I'd saved on the landline and on my cell. *On my way, babe. What a sight you'll be for sore eyes,* one said. And, *I wish I was home tonight, darling, but I'll see you when the tour's over.* At the time, saving them seemed unnecessary, and though I was grateful now that I had them, they gave me no comfort. I had the voice of a dead man talking to me, not me now, but to the me I was the day he'd left them, still alive. Since the voicemails could never be anything more, I went to bed, wearing the heaviest, warmest clothes I had, and every time, the last thing I put on over them all was Leo's fisherman's sweater.

Erin called and texted, but otherwise left me alone for three days after my family and the McGearys were gone. I never answered the phone, but I texted her back: *Thanks, got your vm, talk soon.* I didn't want her to worry about me, but I didn't want to talk to her either. All the energy I could muster I spent on the boys—after that, I had nothing left. Then, on the fourth day, she came over with groceries, did all the laundry and put it away. She came up to my room when she got there, and again before she left. Both times she lay down on the bed behind me. The second time, before she got up she said, "I'll see you again in three days. That's when I'll be back. I'll come sooner if you want me too. Let me know."

When she returned, when she said she would, after she dropped her own kids off at school, I was, as I imagine she expected, in bed. She lay down behind me again. "Sweetie, how about a shower?" she said. "Or do you want me to run you a tub? Tell me."

"Shower," I said.

She got me in the bathroom and set up, like I were an invalid. When I'd finished, she had changed the sheets and vacuumed and laid out clean clothes for me.

"Come eat something," she said. "I'll see you downstairs."

Garrett was already working, and Erin had eggs, toast, and coffee waiting.

"I can't eat all this," I said.

"Eat what you can. You can't disappear. I'm not going to let you disappear," she said. "After this we're going to take a walk, just a little one—it's not raining. And then if you want to, you can go back to bed and I'll come over again tomorrow. The kids have dentist appointments in the morning, but I'll be here right after."

I pushed around as much of the eggs as I ate and managed half the toast, but the coffee was good.

Her voice got thick and she started to cry. "Audrey, I'm so, so sorry. I wish there was something I could do."

"You're doing it," I said.

Then we walked without talking and when we came back, after she left, I didn't go back to bed, but I did lie on the couch under a blanket until the end of the school day.

The next morning, after the boys were gone, I tried, I really did. I took a shower and stood in front of my dresser in my bathrobe. I got tired of standing and sat down in front of it. I sat on the floor staring at the drawers for an hour, sucking in small but regular breaths, which were all I could manage. It was too much to decide. I didn't know how to do the next thing and the next and the next to get dressed. I couldn't manage it. Erin would be here soon and she would find me on the floor. I didn't care. But then I got angry, so angry—I put on the first thing I saw in the drawers I opened and the first thing I saw in the closet. I may have been broken, but I was a grown woman and I could dress myself.

Downstairs in the foyer, I put on one of Chris's ski hats—he would only wear Patagonia; Brian constantly called him a brand snob, but Chris claimed they were the only ones that didn't itch—and sat at the kitchen table with a cup of coffee. Garrett came in from the addition and refilled his cup.

"Good morning," I said.

"Good morning," he said. He looked at me with a curious expression and sat down across from me. "Did you sleep?"

"I guess I must have," I said. "I didn't for a long time, but then I wasn't awake when the alarm went off. How are you?"

"I'm okay," he said. "It's good to have something to focus on. He did a great job already."

I nodded. "Yes. He did."

Garrett stood up. "You want me to make you something to eat?" he said. "I can cook you an omelet, or scramble some eggs?"

I shook my head. "Not right now. I'll have something in a while."

"Okay," he said. "I'm going to make some toast. How about a piece of toast?"

"Thanks, no, that's okay."

The front door opened and Erin called, "Hello."

"In the kitchen," said Garrett.

I got up to refill my coffee as Erin came in the room. "Hi, Garrett," she said. He nodded his head and raised his eyebrows at her. He buttered his toast and left.

She hugged me and stepped back and looked at me from head to toe.

"Do you want a cup?" I said.

"I'll get it," she said. "So, what's happening here, sweetie?" She lifted and lowered one hand in front of her, then with both hands massaged the air between us. She smiled a smile I'd seen many times before, when I was being funny and on a roll and she was building up to laugh out loud.

"What?" I said. "What's happening with what?"

"You're up." Then the smile on her face vanished and her voice turned gentle. "And you got dressed. That's great. I hope you didn't rush because I was coming."

"No, I didn't rush," I said. "It actually took me a really long time."

I started to cry when I looked down and saw what Erin saw, and what Garrett had seen: a lace blouse with cap sleeves and a twirly green cotton skirt I'd worn most of the previous summer, the first things I'd seen and put on after I'd opened my closet. I stood in my favorite strappy wedges, shoes not meant to be worn for months.

"I got the boys off to school and then I dressed myself." I sat back down with my coffee. My tears blurred my vision. "I'm just getting started. It was really hard but I'm doing it."

"Oh, I know you are," said Erin. She pulled a chair next to mine and sat too. "I know that. I can see you are. But it's raining out and it's cold and I thought maybe if we went for a walk or got a sandwich later, you might be warmer in something else." She put her arm around me and pulled me toward her. She slipped off Chris's hat, put it on the table, and leaned in until our heads were touching. Resting against me, she started to hum, and I felt her vibrations as much as I heard her. Garrett came into the kitchen with his empty plate and put it in the sink. He leaned against the counter and looked at the two of us looking back at him.

Erin stopped humming. "We can do this," she said into the room. "We're going to be all right." She began to hum again, with her lips against my forehead, and the two of us rocked together, barely moving, and after a minute, Garrett left the kitchen and walked back into the addition.

Audrey

The next morning, because she came earlier, Erin found me in my bathrobe sitting on the floor staring at my dresser. The first thing she did was sit down next to me, and then we were both staring.

"It would be nice to stay like this, I think," she said. "I could sit here for a really long time."

"I know," I said. "So let's."

And we did, for I don't know how long, together, not saying anything. Then Erin got up.

"I brought you something—I'll be right back."

She went downstairs and came back up.

"I'd like to go back to sitting, but why don't you get dressed first?" She had a green pad of Post-its and a pen. When she reached her hand out, I took it and she pulled me up.

Together we rearranged my clothes so that similar things were together and I couldn't go wrong with what I grabbed. On the Post-its she wrote numbers one through six. And while I got dressed that morning, she stuck the Post-its on the drawers with my underwear (1), bras (2), and socks (3). She stuck Post-it four on one of my closets—I had two—the one Leo and I shared. On the other closet, where I hung my skirts and dresses and kept my summer clothes and shoes, she stuck the Post-it on which she'd written *Not Today*. Inside the number four closet—where every time I opened it I'd see Leo's things on his side—Erin stuck number five on the shelf holding my folded shirts and sweaters, and on another shelf she put the last Post-it, six, where I could pick any one of the pairs of pants stacked there.

Starting the next week, every Saturday, I drove to the cemetery alone. Every morning I went, it rained. I would bring the boys when I was ready. That first month, after I'd sat next to his grave and talked to him, my face was swollen and my body was spent.

Are you okay? I said. *I want to know you're okay. I'm sorry, we should have gone on Brian's birthday. I'm so sorry, Leo. I'm sorry you were alone. I'm sorry the weather changed. I don't know what to do.* It went like that every time, so I had to be by myself.

There had been so much to navigate. My family and Leo's family leaving had been as hard as it had been a relief. Fielding the firefighters and their wives, who all called and emailed after the funeral—some I knew well, some a little, and some not at all. The flowers, and cards, and the food Violet had people bring. When I read each card and note, more than once, it was disorienting that they were for me.

I had hung up Leo's skis in the basement, and packed his boots and ski clothes in a bin of their own. I didn't know what else to do with them. I couldn't throw them away. But I couldn't sell them or give them away either. It would have been a terrible thing to do to the equipment, and to an interested party. My husband died wearing them, skiing on them. Even free seemed too high a price for something a man died in. So I put them where they had always been stored, and didn't look at the skis when I was in the basement.

I refused to disturb Leo's things anywhere else around the house. Closets and drawers remained unchanged, since I saw no reason they shouldn't stay the same for the time being. His clothes, shoes, and coats waited as they had all the other days he hadn't worn them. But I had to do something about his boots on the porch. Our porch had always been the catchall, where everything landed. It was the place for basketballs, and baseball bats and gloves, cleats and skateboards, and the boys' helmets, muddy sneakers, flip-flops, and rain boots.

The boots Leo wore to work in the yard, or threw on to run out somewhere, were never anywhere but the porch. Their companion, what he called his "dear hat"—a black-and-green mesh John Deere cap that he'd brought to our marriage—always hung on the hook inside the front door. I couldn't leave them out among the other things. I didn't want to see them every time I left or entered the house, when I was able to. If I'd been told before he died how much the sight of Leo's boots and his ugly hat—*Hate the hat, not the man,* he always said when he put it on—would trouble me, I wouldn't have believed it. Before I could stop myself, I put the boots—with mud still caked on their soles—and the hat in a paper shopping bag, and before I put it in back of my closet—the *Not Today* closet—next to my boxed and preserved wedding dress, I took his wedding ring out of my jewelry box and dropped it in the right boot, and shook it down toward the toe. I still wore my wedding and engagement rings, but Leo's wedding band was the only other thing I couldn't bear to have in plain sight or within easy reach. Although I avoided sitting on the porch with my coffee in the morning or a glass of wine at night, at least I could come and go through the front door and walk past everything that was there.

We'd always been a two-car family, but I refused to drive Leo's Land Cruiser, and wouldn't let Garrett either, so we only used mine. But the truck was always there, in the driveway, with the last five CDs Leo had loaded in the player. Although I didn't drive it, I started it every Saturday before I went to the cemetery, part of my routine, to keep the battery charged. The first time I did it, I expected to hear the last music he'd listened to, but instead it was NPR talk radio that came through the speakers. After I let the engine run, I turned it off and left the station right where it was.

Garrett

For the next eight weeks, starting the Saturday after we buried Leo, which was the first weekend of Lent, I went to five o'clock mass, like a sheep, following Audrey and the boys, all our sufferings parallel with those of the liturgical season. Each time, we walked into the church, crossed ourselves at the font, and walked up the aisle until Audrey said, "Here," and we settled in a pew on the right, halfway between the front and the back. Of those eight masses, the intention for three of them was for Leo. Who had made the requests? I didn't know why masses were always said for the dead—I understood intentions for the sick or dying, but what about saying masses for those left behind, trying to live and survive? Those Saturday afternoons, when all of them were still and in one place, I observed these four people I barely knew.

I knew Audrey and Leo weren't the most devout Catholics, but they were involved in the parish and the parish's school, where Christopher had gone and Brian and Andrew still went. Leo had served hot lunch once a month, which Audrey called "hot dads' hot lunch." When I gave him shit about it, he'd told me, *No, it's fun. I get to see my boys in their day, in their place. And the other guys, they're all right.* Audrey had chaired the school auction one year, with much success, and volunteered serving meals at one of the homeless shelters in town. So I wasn't surprised that she seemed more relaxed, while still behind a shield of sorts, in this community of the church, than she did with the firefighters and their wives, all so hungry to reach out and help.

Each time we went to mass, she'd lift a hand to someone across the church, or sometimes hug someone on our way in, or was approached by someone when we were on our way out. But once mass started, she seemed to occupy a quiet place where she couldn't be reached. The way she held herself, her whole body announced, *I can't be disturbed.*

Since Leo's funeral, the church had been stripped down for the Lenten season and the crucifix was covered with a purple shroud. The altar society's decorations had disappeared as if the committee had quit the job and taken all their finery with them.

I had heard the Gospel readings my whole life. I wasn't a believer, but I strived to be open-minded, so for all those weeks I sat, waiting to be convinced, hoping for some comfort in *You don't have to see it to believe it.* And it was no surprise to me that it didn't come, that comfort, that confidence, that faith that I suspected so many of the people in the congregation had but I did not. That faith that my mother and Kate had had, and Kate even more so after the inexplicable sensation she'd experienced following my mother's death.

So Easter was a joyous but contrived celebration. As contrived as Christ's Passion had been. The resurrected undead didn't flow into the church, politely cramming into the crowded pews to join their families. How validating and horrifying that would have been, what a miracle, to have Leo waltz in, with my mother and everyone else who'd left behind people they loved, looking as unblemished as they had in life, thanking us for saving them a seat.

Audrey made a ham and although the boys were too old for it, had them hunt for hidden baskets with candy and something special nestled in the plastic strands of grass. I worked most of the day after we got home, but I took a walk before we sat down to eat, scanning the neighborhood. The day had turned sunny early after the clouds burned off, and I sought some proof that this day was different from any other. The first flowers shared their tentative scents, and the explosions of cherry and dogwood were stunning. But that had nothing to do with Easter. It was only because it was spring.

Audrey

After weeks of eating other people's food—I was so tired of their never-ending lasagnas—I had to cook for my family. I managed to get dressed—the Post-its were still up—and made a list and left the house. I was at the grocery store when Mary, the school secretary, called and told me I needed to come to the school and pick up Andrew. She said he'd been in a fight, but she wouldn't tell me any more on the phone. I left my cart, half full, in the aisle.

When I got to the school, Andrew was sitting on the bench outside the office with his backpack.

"Andrew, what happened?" I said. "What's going on?"

He didn't look at me. "Mrs. Donnelly wants to talk to you."

I went into the office.

"Hi, Audrey," Mary said. She leaned her head toward the door behind her. "She's waiting."

Barbara Donnelly, the principal, was sitting at her desk and stood when I walked in.

"Hi," she said. "Come in and have a seat." She closed her door.

I folded my hands in my lap and waited. The school had sent a magnificent bouquet and a card. Barbara had sent one personally. We were parishioners, and all three boys had gone to the school starting from kindergarten. She knew me and she knew what we were going through.

"I'm sorry," she said. "I know Andrew is having a hard time, but he punched Gannon Keegan in the face at recess today, and I need you to take him home. He'll have another detention next week. Can you tell me what's going on, Audrey? I don't know how to help."

I was so fucking tired of Gannon Keegan. Andrew was responsible, but since Leo died, Gannon had found an easy target in Andrew and pushed his buttons because he could. I had no idea why.

"Barbara, we're going through a terrible time. We're doing the best we can and the boys are coping in their own ways," I said. "And Andrew is so angry, which is so unlike him. We talk—I try to make him talk to me. Everyone else in the class has been such a good friend to Andrew, and so kind, or given him space. I get as much out of him as I can, and he's getting some help. But Gannon is provoking him and Andrew has a breaking point. Everyone does. I'm not saying it's okay, but Gannon has pushed him to his breaking point."

"No one else seems to be having a problem with Gannon," Barbara said. "And today I can't fault him for Andrew's actions."

"Andrew doesn't punch other kids," I said. "I have three sons, Barbara—I know what they're like inside and out. Did you ask him why he did it?"

She folded her hands on her desk. "I did. He wouldn't tell me. He just said he wanted his mom."

I refused to cry in front of her. "Well, I'll find out, he'll tell me, and then I'll get back to you." I left her office and walked back to Andrew in the hallway.

"Come on," I put my arm around him. "Are you okay?"

He nodded, still looking at the floor.

"Let's stop and get something at Starbucks on the way home," I said.

He nodded again.

When we got to the café, Andrew sat at an empty table and I ordered. I brought the snacks over and sat down across from him.

"Andrew, what happened?" I said. "I know Gannon is a problem for you, but we have to figure this out. This has to stop happening."

"I'm sorry, Mom," he said. He didn't touch his drink or the food. He still wouldn't look at me. "I know I'm in big trouble at school and I'm sorry."

"I know," I said. "Just tell me what happened."

"Well, we were playing basketball at recess," he said. "And he did that thing he always does, again, saying I fouled and hurt him, and I didn't, and then before the teacher came over and made us stop playing he called me a bad name and then he said he was waiting for me to cry."

"Were you playing with other kids?" I said. "What did they do?"

"Yeah, we were playing three on three, like normal," Andrew said. "But I think they didn't want to get in the middle of it. They never do. They don't want Gannon to get on them too."

Nice friends, I thought. What had I just said to Barbara about how great they all were?

"What did he call you?" I said.

Andrew shook his head. "I can't say it," he said. "It was p-u-s-s-y. He called me that and then said, 'Don't cry, p-u-s-s-y. You don't want to cry in front of everybody.'"

"Andrew, why didn't you tell Mrs. Donnelly that? Gannon was completely out of line. You can't punch him, you just can't, but he started the whole thing and was totally inappropriate."

"Mom," he said. "I couldn't tell her *that*. Gannon would have lied and denied it anyway, and I'm in enough trouble at school. Who's she going to believe?" He looked down again. I wanted my youngest son to stop feeling so crushed and burdened.

"Eat something, okay?" I said. "I'm going to talk to his parents and get this to stop, but I need your help. You can't punch him every time he tries to provoke you. You have to figure that out now, Andrew. I'm sorry, but you're going to meet plenty of assholes—sorry—like him and that's not the way to solve it. Can you play without including him?"

"Mom, please don't talk to his parents," Andrew begged. "That will make it so much worse. He'll take it out on me."

"We'll see about that," I said. "Eat. It's going to be okay. You have to trust me."

He nodded again and we took his drink and snack, untouched, home with us.

At four o'clock everyone was home, head down with homework in various rooms, Garrett working, when the doorbell rang.

Frank Keegan was standing on my porch looking like he'd raced to my house from the office.

"I need to talk to you about your son assaulting Gannon," he said when I opened the door. "I'm not happy."

Like that, all the boys were clustered around me.

Frank pointed at Andrew. "You're on thin ice, bud," he said.

"Don't speak to him, Frank. I'm standing right here," I said. "Boys, upstairs please. Finish homework." They scattered, but slowly, and I waited for them to go.

"You're welcome to sit down," I said.

"I'll stand," he said.

"Well, I'm going to sit," I said, and did. "I was planning on calling you tonight. I've talked with Andrew about what happened today. What he did isn't okay, but Gannon has been harassing Andrew. This has been going on for a while, Frank, and it's going to stop, one way or another."

"Your kid punched mine, Audrey, not the other way around. Gannon didn't get sent home from school."

"Gannon called Andrew a pussy, then baited him not to cry. Did he tell you that?" I said. "If I was Andrew, I would have punched him too. I've told Andrew he can't react that way, and he knows it, but I won't let this continue. If you don't deal with your son, we can start by meeting with the principal and the pastor and everyone else we need to until this stops. Andrew has enough to deal with, Frank—my whole family does."

"Gannon doesn't use words like that," he said.

"Well, he did today," I said. "There's a first time for everything."

Garrett walked into the room. He still had on the tool belt, and his safety glasses were pushed up on his head. I don't know if he heard us or if the boys told him what was happening.

He walked toward Frank and extended his hand. "I'm Garrett," he said. "What's going on?"

Frank took Garrett's hand and shook it and narrowed his eyes.

"Andrew punched Frank's son and was sent home from school today," I said. "Andrew knows he's in trouble, but Gannon has been provoking him. This isn't a new thing."

"Why would your son do that? After Andrew's father just died?" Garrett asked.

Frank crossed his arms and clenched his jaw and looked back at me, dismissing Garrett with his gaze. "I don't want you to take this the wrong way, Audrey—I am so, so sorry for your loss. For your family's loss. My whole family is. But if Andrew is acting out, if he's taking out his grief on other kids, physically, then maybe he needs to get some help."

"How dare you," I said. "If you're so sorry, then *you* can help by getting your deviant little prick of a son to leave Andrew alone. Gannon is taking advantage of a boy who is hurting, someone who is an easy target."

He crossed the room and stood over me, glaring. "Don't you talk about my son like that."

I laughed in his face. "Too late, Frank," I said.

In two steps, Garrett was next to him. "Frank, hey, Frank," he said. "Let's go, fella." He put his hand on Frank's shoulder and eased him to the door. Frank shook off Garrett's hand. "Outside, man." And they walked out.

Garrett

I walked that motherfucker out of the house, off the porch, and down to the sidewalk. "Who the fuck do you think you are?" I said. "What the fuck do you think you're doing coming into her house and talking to her like that?"

"This is none of your concern," he said.

"Yeah, it is my fucking *concern,*" I said. "This family is my concern. And I'll say whatever I want to you after you weren't a gentleman in there just now. You deal with your own kid and Audrey will deal with hers. And maybe dig a little deep for some compassion. Whatever it is the Catholics are recommending these days."

When I turned around I saw Audrey standing by the window watching us. She opened the door and let me in.

"I can handle him," she said. "I'm sorry I lost my cool. I shouldn't have said any of that. That was stupid. Talk about provoking."

"No," I said. "I'm not going to watch someone treat you like that in your own house."

The boys came into the living room. "Is he gone?" Andrew said.

"Yes," Audrey said. "Guys, homework, please."

They all groaned and left. "I'll talk to you later when you're all finished!" she called after them. "I need a drink."

We went into the kitchen and she opened a bottle of wine. "Thank you, though," she said. "Thanks for that. You want a glass?"

"Sure," I said. "He's a jackass. He didn't accomplish anything by coming over here."

She sighed. "I know—Christ. Neither of us did. I'll talk to the principal again, tell her what's going on and see if she'll at least be more vigilant. Maybe talk to the pastor. I'll tell Andrew to stay away from Gannon, not spoil for a fight. Even if it means he can't play basketball for a while."

"I know how boys are," I said. "You want me to talk to Andrew? Can I do something at school to help?"

"You want to start volunteering? You need a background check and have to take this class about pedophiles. Don't get me started."

"Maybe," I said. "My record's pretty clean."

"Talk to Andrew if you want to. It might be different coming from you." She put her head in her hands. "I don't know. I just want him to be okay. Why does he have to deal with this too?"

I put my arm around her. "Because people are assholes, sometimes at the worst possible times. What do you need to do right now?"

"Figure out dinner. Feed my family. So much for a home-cooked meal," she said. "Put one foot in front of the other."

"I can go get takeout," I said.

"I can go," she said. "I'll just go get a pizza."

"If you want. If you're sure," I said. "I'll see if Andrew wants to shoot some hoops."

She hugged me. "He'd like that," she said.

She walked to the stairs and called out, "Boys, pizza tonight—the usual?" They all whooped in response and thundered downstairs.

"I'll be back," she said. "Thanks again."

The boys were all there, their banishment over.

"You guys done homework?" I said.

"Almost," they all said.

"You guys finish," I said to Christopher and Brian. "Hey, Andrew, take a break and let's shoot for a minute."

He looked chastened. "Come on," I said. "Let's blow off some steam."

We walked out to the street and he threw me the ball. "Gannon's dad is mad at me," he said.

I threw the ball back to him. "You go," I said. "Don't worry about Gannon's dad. He's not worried about you."

He shot and missed. "Hey, let's sit down for a second," I said. I crossed the street and sat on the curb. He followed like a dog with its tail between his legs.

"Listen," I said. "People like Gannon are going to show up from time to time and make your life, or parts of your life, difficult. It's really fucking bad timing for you that you have to deal with a kid like that right now. Don't tell your mom I swore. And what sucks is his dad has blinders on about his own kid. He can't help it."

He shrugged.

"Andrew, you're going to have to stay out of your own way with this kid. It's not going to be easy, but you can't take his bait," I said. "And once you stop taking his bait, he's going to find someone else to bother, or he's going to get himself in trouble if he doesn't leave you alone."

"I know," he said. "I can't, though. I can't let him get away with it."

"That's what I mean about getting out of your own way," I said. "You've got to stop before you make that decision that's going to get you in a shitload of trouble, and walk away. Come home and throw stuff, you know, outside or whatever."

He frowned. "That's what my mom said. Punch a pillow. That's not the same thing."

"No, it's not," I said. "I know it's pretty lame. What about your friends—you have some good friends, right? Spend less time ready and waiting for Gannon and more time with them."

"I do, I guess," he said. "I did. They're still acting weird, though. Like I'm going to break or something. They're all being so nice. Not normal nice, too nice."

"It's a lot for you to deal with, right?" I said. "But your friends are taking their lead from you, you know? Is there someone you could have over and do something with? Like you used to? Try to pretend being normal even if nothing will be normal for a long time?"

"I don't know," he said. "Maybe I shouldn't be acting normal. My dad's gone. Maybe it's too soon to pretend to be normal. Did my mom ask you to say all this?"

"No," I said. "She didn't, but I told her I wanted to talk to you. I don't know how to be normal either. I'm working on your dad's house—that's not normal. I know that he wouldn't want you to be hurting more than you already are. He's gone and that hurts, but don't let Gannon or anyone else make that hurt worse. I think your dad would want you to do whatever you could so you're hurting less."

"Yeah," he said. "I guess."

"If I can do anything and help out with this Gannon thing," I said, "you let me know what and I will."

His little shoulders drooped and he put his face in his hands. "Maybe come get me at school some days. We could shoot hoops after. That would be cool."

I put my arm around him. *I had no idea I was in for this.*

"You're right, that would be cool," I said. "Is tomorrow good?"

His head bobbed.

"Okay, tomorrow then," I said. "Maybe we get some friends to play too, if you want?"

"Not Gannon," he mumbled.

"No, not Gannon," I said. "No way in hell."

Audrey

They screwed up my pizza order so I had to wait. I had no idea what to do about Frank and Gannon, and I wondered what Leo would do. Andrew's behavior and maybe Gannon's, too—I had no way of knowing—I was sure was because Leo was gone, but if Leo were still alive and our son was being bullied, what would he do? He wouldn't take any shit from another parent, I knew that. I wasn't either, but I couldn't help but despair that coming from a woman, it wasn't the same.

They redid my order and threw in extra breadsticks, and I arrived home a half hour later than I should have. When I got close to the house, from a block away I saw the boys and Garrett playing basketball, two on two, Garrett and Andrew against the older boys. I slowed down and pulled over to the side of the street and watched them. It had been a long time since Christopher and Brian had played with each other, or with Andrew, but looking at the four of them, it seemed like they played every day. Andrew was fierce guarding Christopher, funny because Chris was so much taller. He was taller than me now. Andrew, scrapping with everything he had, stole the ball from Chris, passed it to Garrett, who shot it in and high-fived Andrew. He looked so different from the boy sitting on the bench at school earlier today.

Chris and Brian had gone to the Dougy Center the one time without complaint, to appease me, but Andrew had been three times so far. His continuing to go had seemed like a favor to me, so I didn't touch it. All he'd said when I asked if he wanted to go back again was "Yeah. When I'm there I don't feel like I have to be ready for anything, the way I do all the time everywhere else." After that I drove us there each time without comment, wondering if it would be his last. I had gone too and joined other grieving spouses, most of them widows—some with four and five children, some whose husbands had left no life insurance—and their challenges, greater than my own, made me feel like I had no right to be there. But it was a serene and healing place, and everyone there was so tender and compassionate, that every time Andrew and I left, I was glad I'd gone. I remembered Leo working when they'd had the big fire there. When he finally came home, so depleted, the boys welcomed him, waving the newspaper, asking their questions, and he had been as gentle and patient as he could, but he refused to look at the paper or follow the news. He didn't need to.

The pizza was getting cold, but still I sat. I watched Brian and Chris pass the ball back and forth, Garrett and Andrew countering with an aggressive defense, but Brian made the shot and he and Chris did a goofy victory shimmy. Maybe they didn't even need me. Maybe they just needed to play basketball with Garrett until their mourning eased, and by then I would know what to do. Because every day, every morning I woke up, even when I thought I did, I still wasn't sure.

Garrett

The next afternoon I got to school before dismissal and shot some baskets by myself until the bell rang. I took the ball and waited by the front door. The eighth-graders came out and I saw Brian walking with a group of boys. When he looked up I raised my hand and pointed to the courts and he nodded. The sixth-graders flooded out and I looked for Andrew. He ran away from the swarm of kids and over to me.

"Hey, Garrett," he said. He didn't look happy exactly, but not unhappy either.

"You want to get some guys to play?"

He looked around. "Nah," he said. "Let's start shooting and see who comes over."

We walked past mothers pushing strollers and holding toddlers' hands, distributing Cheerios, fathers talking and texting on their phones, parents visiting with each other. It reminded me of Boston, and for the first time since I'd been here, I felt a pang, missing the swirling clusters of kids studying on the grass, rushing to and from class, couples holding hands, other professors on their way to office hours, meetings, their own classes.

"How was the day?" I said.

"Okay," he shrugged. "Yours?"

"Same," I said. "I had to save some energy for this. I'm old."

We got to the courts and passed the ball back and forth and took some shots. After a few minutes, Brian came over with Michael and joined us. We played two on two until two other sixth-graders joined us, Bobby and Marcus, with Marcus's dad, Luke, who seemed decent. When another one of Brian's friends, Kyle, asked if he could play, we were even again. When the ball got away from us and Brian went after it, Andrew came up to me.

"Garrett," he whispered. "There's Gannon—don't look, he's over there by the trash can."

Brian threw the ball back in, and after we started up again, I looked over. He was a big kid, with hair that hung down past his collar. He stood there alone, staring at our group. When I looked back ten minutes later, he was gone.

We kept playing until almost four, when nobody was left but us, the boys flushed and sweaty.

Luke shook my hand. "Nice meeting you, Garrett. Maybe see you back here again?"

"Yeah, maybe," I said. "I'll be around. Nice meeting you, too."

Brian, Andrew, and I got back to the house and shot some more in the street before dinner. Chris came out and joined us, and when Audrey called us in we all got to the table so fast, you'd think we hadn't eaten in weeks.

Brian

Chris and Andrew and I had all heard what happened between Mom and Gannon Keegan's dad and Garrett, and I was upset. Even though Andrew and I had lunch and recess at the same time, we both hung out with our own friends, and I had no idea Gannon was making trouble for Andrew, because if I had, I would have done something about it before it got to this point. I wasn't much of a fighter, so people had no idea, but when it came to my brothers, or my mom, you didn't fuck with me, because I'd kick your ass.

That night, after Gannon's dad left, I told my mom I would handle it at school, that Andrew had nothing to worry about, and Gannon would be sorry.

"Brian," she said. "I know you would, but please don't. I don't want you both in trouble because of a kid like Gannon. We're above that and he's not worth it."

I laughed. "Mom, I'm not going to get in trouble. I'm not going to touch him. I won't have to."

"No, Brian, please. Don't," she said. And the way she looked at me, I knew I'd be in a bad spot with her if I did anything.

It bothered me that even if I hadn't seen what was going on at school, Andrew never said anything to me. He had to know that if he had, I would've helped. He was always, really, the nicest one of all of us—Chris and I both agreed on that—but he'd gotten so mean since the accident, so nasty, and you could see his temper brewing all the time, about everything. Before Dad died, Andrew would have told me—although I probably wouldn't have had to handle it then—if Gannon, or anyone else, was giving him trouble. Before, he always told me everything that was going on with him. Sometimes I pretended I was listening because he'd talk on and on with no end in sight. And he always told me whatever I was drawing was good, even if what did he know?

I hardly ever liked my drawings, because it seemed like they never turned out the way I wanted them to. But people told me all the time, *I could never draw like that, you're so talented.* I tried to remember to say thanks every time, but because the drawings didn't look as good as I'd hoped, thanking people felt fake. I hadn't always said thanks—I used to shrug and say things like *It's not that good,* or, *It could be a lot better.* But last spring, when I was like that with my dad about a series in the school art show, we ended up having this big talk.

The show was the highlight of the year for the art teacher, Mrs. Butler, and for all the parents, too. The parish hall was packed with families gushing over all their kids' artwork, especially the kindergartners'. My parents were no exception. They went crazy over the fifth-graders' mosaic self-portraits, and I had to admit, Andrew's was pretty good and he was happy with himself, you could tell. I thought, *Good for him.*

Mrs. Butler had assigned the seventh grade the theme "Portland: Place or Thing," which we had to do in graphite. Some kids picked bridges or public buildings or a statues. A bunch drew their houses.

I did these three sketches—six, really—two sets each of three of some of Portland's oldest firehouses that were museums now. For each pair, the first sketch was of the station back in the old days, and the second was its partner today, restored and decorated, without the gritty spirit they used to have. Now they were fancy places people took tours of or rented for parties.

When my parents saw them, they went on and on, but it put me in a bad mood and I wanted them to stop with all their amazement. Like they didn't see my drawings all the time. Since I kept being sulky and quiet, my mom finally quit all the hoopla and patted my back. But my dad kept standing there next to me at the art show, squeezing my shoulder.

"My God, Brian," he said, "I don't even know what to say. These are really incredible. I hope you're proud of this. It's obvious you worked hard. I'll bet Mrs. Butler was impressed."

I looked at my shoes. "Yeah, she's 'tickled,'" I said. "That's what she told me." I'd been embarrassed when she'd said that, like, *Come on, you can't pick another word?* "But I think if I'd had more time, they'd be better."

My dad nodded. "Better?" he said. He looked at them some more. "You're going to get to bring these home?"

"Yeah," I said. "After the show."

"I want to frame them. What do you think?" he said. "Think of a good place where we can hang them. You ready to go? Let's get out of here."

When we got home, he sat down in the living room and asked me to sit too. I thought he was mad.

"You know I have a naturally high opinion of everything you do," he said. He smiled. "Good for balancing things out when you screw up."

"I know," I said.

"But listen, I've got to tell you something," he said. "You're going to have to get used to people being impressed with your art even though everything you do isn't going to be a masterpiece. And I get it, *you* think everything you draw is never a masterpiece."

I nodded. We were all always polite—since we were little kids our parents had made us be—but when people made a big deal with their compliments, it was uncomfortable, and it was harder to be polite, I don't know why.

"So, it's okay if you think that, and maybe that will change too," my dad said. "Not so you're an arrogant jerk or anything, but privately prouder, and confident, even if you're confident you could make it better, or the next one better."

I nodded again. I wasn't sure where all this was going. I wanted him to stop talking.

"But if you're going to show people your work," he said, "you're going to have to learn to accept their praise graciously. Do you know what I mean?"

I shrugged. "I don't know."

"Think of it this way," he said. "Someone really likes a book or a movie and maybe you didn't. You could get into a discussion about your different opinions. But you'd never tell someone what they liked was unlikable, right? Because that's an insult to their opinion, which they're entitled to. Even if you disagree."

He waited and looked at me.

"So no matter what you think of your work, you can't insult people's opinions by implying what they like is crap," he said. "Before too long you and your brothers are going to find out there are plenty of people who love to tear down—whatever it is—who someone is, who someone isn't, what they think, what they create. You've got to take the thanks when it comes, and be gracious like you've always been, even if it bothers you."

"It feels weird, though. Like 'Thanks' is all, 'Yeah, I'm really good at drawing,'" I said.

He put his hands on my leg and pressed down a little.

"But they don't hear that," he said. "Is that what you hear when someone says thanks? When Mom runs a good race and we tell her she was great and we're proud and she thanks us, do you think she's saying 'Yeah, I'm all that'?"

I shook my head.

"Right," he said. "She's happy that we recognized how hard she worked and what she accomplished. I'm telling you, take those compliments while you can."

The talk went on longer than I wanted it to, but it was cool. And after that whenever I showed him a drawing, he'd always like *something* about it, even if he wasn't crazy about the whole thing, though sometimes he was. So I'd thank him, and he'd say, "You're welcome, Brian." And I tried to get better thanking other people too. But I was still glad I could always go back and change the parts that weren't perfect, and maybe never would be, but sooner or later I could make better.

Audrey

---

n early March, Kevin Gallagher sent me an email, which he also sent to about five thousand other people. In it, he wrote that the men from Twenty-Five had gotten the owners of Kells to agree to host a fundraiser for Leo—the night of St. Patrick's Day, the culmination of their annual three-day St. Patrick's Irish Festival. For years, since the boys were babies, we'd gone to Kells at least once a month for brunch, and Leo had been a dedicated regular at the bar—he and Kevin both had. Just like the Pittock, Kells offered a generous exception, and Kevin invited the email recipients to forward the invitation to anyone else we wanted to include.

"Jesus Christ," I said. For years, the fire department brotherhood had been like another wife I'd had to share Leo with—for the camping weekends, the late nights out drinking, the marathon golf days—a presence I had to check with before I knew if he would be available to spend time with his family. That presence hadn't died with him; she was the other widow, still with her own demands.

"Garrett, will you come look at this?" I said. "This is unbelievable."

"What?" he said.

"This email—you have to come here and see it."

He looked over my shoulder at Kevin's email.

"Wow," he said. "That's quite a thing."

"I know," I said. "They're completely out of line. No one asked me. I'm not a charity."

"What? No, Audrey, listen." He put his hands on my shoulders. "Turn around. Look at me for a minute."

I closed the computer. "What?" I said. "You don't think this is completely inappropriate? I don't want this. No one cared to think about what I want."

He squatted in front of me. "They're doing this for them. They're doing what they can," he said. "That's what this is about. What else can they do? If they raise a bunch of money and want to give it to you, you'll deal with that then. There's nothing but goodwill behind what they're doing. As much as it might be nothing you want."

I started to cry. "I can't have what I want. I want him back. I want a fundraiser that's going to raise enough money to bring him back."

"I know," he said. "You don't know how many times I've wished God could be bought."

"I don't know what to do."

"Write back to Kevin," he said. "Thank him and tell him you're grateful and overwhelmed by his gesture, in the lovely way you always do. That's all you have to do today. You'll deal with St. Patrick's when it gets here. Right?"

"Okay," I said. "I guess you're right."

"Okay," he said. "I have to run to Lowe's. You want me to wait? I will if you want to go."

I didn't want to go to Lowe's, but I didn't feel like staying in the house by myself. "Sure, I'll go," I said. "Let me send this first."

"Take as much time as you need," Garrett said. "No hurry. We'll go when you're ready."

"I miss him," I said.

"So do I," said Garrett.

Garrett

After I'd laid the tarpaper, I was surprised to discover that Leo had bought three-tab roof shingles but he'd gotten no flashing, and no roofing nails that I could find anywhere. I should've checked before I got to that point, but it wasn't the end of the world. Of course he hadn't had anyone else to answer to and had planned to go back and buy what he needed when he needed it, which was a terrible thing for me to think about, given that I was the one doing the shopping.

I was surprised that Audrey agreed to come with me, but I was glad she did. I knew she was forcing herself, going through the motions, but that counted for something. I drove and she kept fiddling with the radio, keeping it on the music station if there was a song she liked, I guessed, and if one came on that she didn't, changing it to NPR, which is what we listened to for most of the drive. When we got to Lowe's, she went to the garden center and I went to the opposite end of the store for what I needed. Then I rolled my awkward dolly across the store, with the flashing and its sharp edges jutting out on both ends. I found her looking at seed packets with her arms around a potted hydrangea.

"Can you plant something now?" I said, and put the pot on the dolly. "Isn't it still too cold? Don't you have to wait until, I don't know, May?"

"It's too early for starts. It'll be a few weeks," she said, but she wasn't paying any attention to me. She was scanning the seed packets, picking them out and reading the backs, deciding. "But I can start my own seeds inside."

I stood next to her while she chose a packet, put it back, then took out another one. "That's good," she said. She had a seed-starter kit and the seed envelopes in her hand. "Are you ready?"

We walked to the cashier and while the guy starting ringing up the flashing and the nails, I put the hydrangea on the conveyor belt and pulled out my wallet. I had my card ready to swipe when Audrey closed her hand over my hand, and the card, stopping me.

"No, Garrett," she said. "You're not paying for this."

"Of course I am," I said. "Why wouldn't I?"

"Because it's my house," she said. "I've got it."

The guy had finished ringing up everything and told us the total. He was waiting.

"No, I've got it," I said. "It's what I need, so I'm buying it."

She had let go of my hand and moved it to the top of the swiper, preventing me from running the card. A line of other customers started forming behind us while she just stood there staring at me, keeping her hand where it was. Our cashier was the only one open.

"You want to split the payment?" the cashier asked.

"No," said Audrey.

"Listen," I said. "How about this? I'll buy my stuff and you buy yours." I turned to the cashier. "Can we do this stuff first? And then she'll pay for this here." I pointed to the hardware, then put the hydrangea, seeds, and starter kit back on the conveyor belt, where they'd just been before the cashier had scanned them. He picked up the phone and said a code, which came over the PA system in the store. We were making him call for assistance.

"I'm sorry," Audrey said to the cashier. "We don't mean to be causing problems, but we have a misunderstanding. I really am sorry." She still hadn't moved her hand from the swiper. I put my hand on top of hers and gently pulled it off the swiper and held it in mine.

"I'll make a deal with you," I said. "The person who buys the stuff has to be the one who uses it. So, you can pay for the flashing if you're going to put it up. If not," I said, "end of story. You buy your plant things and I won't have a thing to do with them. I won't even water them."

She took her hand out of mine. She shook her head. "That's not fair. You're ridiculous," she said. "Fine."

"I'll keep all the receipts," I said. "You can pay me back."

Another cashier had opened a register and the people behind us milled over to that one.

"So we're all set then?" the cashier asked me. I saw the new total and swiped my card, and then he rang up Audrey's share. She swiped her card and the guy gave us our receipts.

"Oh, for God's sake," said the man behind us in line, who was next, after the people in front of him had moved to the new register. He had a dolly loaded with lumber and spools of cable and materials I couldn't identify. He looked like a contractor, with the air of a pro. Who knows how long he'd been waiting while we'd had our standoff.

Audrey turned around and looked at him. "If waiting in this line is the worst thing that happens to you today, you've won the lottery. Congratulations." Then she walked around me and pushed the dolly toward the door, and I followed her out.

I caught up with her and took over the dolly, and we walked together through the lot to the car.

"I'm sorry," I said. "I guess we should have talked about that before. And I think we should talk about it later. It's not a big deal and nothing that can't wait. I just have to get what I need when I need it and we can work out the details whenever."

We loaded everything, the flashing taking up and bisecting the length of the car, resting on the dashboard, almost touching the windshield. I got in and started the car while she returned the dolly, then got in. The metal between us was like a fence we talked over.

"No, I'm sorry." She sighed. "We should have discussed it."

I reached under the flashing and touched her arm. "It's okay," I said. "We still can. We will." I put the car in gear and backed out.

"Lowe's and Home Depot always make me a little crazy," she said. "I don't know why. They always start some kind of drama."

"Drama?" I said. "What are you talking about? They're just stores."

"You know, I'd go with Leo sometimes, like today—he'd say he'd just be running in for something but then I couldn't get him out of there," she said. "At first it was fine, I'd walk around, go to the garden center, or whatever, and then it would be forty-five minutes later and I'd look for him, then I'd have to text him, and when I'd find him he'd be looking at something we weren't even there for, and didn't even need, like patio furniture. I don't know, I guess men need their own version of what women do. You know, *shop*."

"Well, it's fun," I said. "I think it's fun going to those stores. I can't blame him. I might have done that today if I'd been by myself."

"There's another thing," she said. "Why they make me crazy. When I wouldn't go with him, most of the time I didn't, he'd tell me, 'I have to run out and get a drill bit I need, I don't have the right size.' Simple enough, right?" She looked at me.

I shrugged.

"Then he'd come home with three bags of stuff and I'd say 'How many drill bits did you need?' And he'd tell me there were other things he might need *later* and he wanted to get them now instead of making another trip, but he'd say, 'If it turns out I don't need them, don't worry, I'll just return them.'" She shook her head and looked out the window. It was like she wasn't even talking to me, so I didn't say anything. "And he never did—he never did take anything back. When I'd ask him about it later, ask him when he was going to return stuff, by that time the story had changed. By then he'd tell me he might need it for another project so he may as well keep what he bought. He would have bought one of everything in that place if he could have, just to have it on hand."

We were almost back to the house.

"I guess that's what's a little funny about today," she said. "I can't believe there was anything you needed that he didn't already have."

Garrett

S t. Patrick's, the night of the fundraiser at Kells, was on a Saturday. Audrey made corned beef and cabbage, and after dinner I worked for a few hours. We hadn't talked about it since she got the email. She wrote back to Kevin Gallagher, but I don't know what she said and she hadn't told me if he responded.

Christopher was at a friend's and Audrey and the boys were watching a movie.

"Hey." I sat down on the couch next to her.

"Hey," she said.

"So I think I'm going to head down there. To that thing at Kells. Just stop in. Do you mind if I go?"

"No," she said. "Go, report back. Go. Tell everyone I said thank you again."

I looked it up on MapQuest and drove Audrey's car over the Burnside Bridge into downtown. The closest parking spot I could find was five blocks away. It wasn't a dive or a hole in the wall like I expected. There was a poster on an easel by the front door declaring half of tonight's proceeds were going to the Leo McGeary Memorial Fund. *Goddamn. Half.* At the door, a massive guy was collecting the cover.

"Ten bucks," he said. I handed him a twenty.

"No change," I said.

I didn't realize at first—because it was packed—but the place was cavernous, with bottles glittering up to the ceiling behind the bar. I joined the crush of people there and waited for a bartender.

"What're you having?" he shouted.

"Glenlivet!" I yelled back. "Your oldest!"

He came back with it. "Forty-five!"

I handed him two twenties and a ten. "No change!"

I stood and sipped before I took on the maze of overflowing tables and people, all strangers, and squeezed through the loud darkness. I went downstairs to the cigar room and found them there. The firefighters, some I recognized, dominated the room—the small tables, the booths against the walls, and the one long table in the middle of the room with leather chairs all around it. The last time I'd seen Kevin was Leo's funeral. When he saw me, he left the big middle table and came over.

"Hey, professor," he said around his cigar. "Glad you could make it tonight."

"This is quite a thing you've pulled off," I said.

He shrugged. "I just asked. Kells is the one pulling it off. The owners knew Leo. They know the whole family. They wouldn't do it for just anybody."

A waiter passed us and Kevin flagged him. "You want another drink?" he said.

"Sure," I said. "Whatever you're having."

"Let's sit." We took a four top against the wall. He pointed at his cigar. "You want? Padrón. The Cadillac of cigars."

"Why not." He went back to the big table and came back with one and lit it for me. "Audrey wanted me to say thanks again," I said.

"How's she doing?"

"One day at a time, I think," I said.

"And what about you?" he said.

"I'm okay," I said. "I'm putting in a lot of work every day. It's a good thing to have to do."

"Oh, good, good, glad to hear it," he said. "And how's shacking up? How's that coming?" He puffed the Padrón hands-free, his arms crossed over his chest.

I hadn't expected to have to throw my weight around, or be ready for a fight, not tonight. I crushed out the long cigar, barely smoked, in the ashtray. "Are you kidding me?" I said. "That's very stand up." I pushed the chair back. "You're going to be an asshole, tonight? That's gallant." I stood up.

"Come on, man," Gallagher said. "Sit down. I'm just telling you what the talk is."

"The *talk*." I pushed the chair in. "You don't know me. I don't give a shit about your talk, Kevin. I loved him and I love his family. I've known him since we were kids. Talk it up all you want."

"Will you sit down? Come on. We're his family too," he said. "That's all. Relax. People have their opinions. We all have them every day when we walk down the street. Nothing you can do about it. But if you're going to be here like you are I wanted to say something. Like I'd want to know if it was me. Sit." He flung his hands at my empty chair.

I slid the chair out and sat again, leaning back, my legs stretched out in front of me. "You drive a truck, Kevin?" I said. "A really big truck?"

He laughed. "Nah, minivan. Not my choice. My wife and I have three daughters."

I smirked and shook my head. "I understand."

He laughed again. "How about you, Garrett?" he said. "Everyone know your big truck around campus?"

"Prius."

"Prius," he snorted.

We let that sit there.

"You doing it by yourself?" He puffed. "The work? I could come by. I helped Leo quite a bit."

"I'll let you know," I said. "I work pretty well alone."

"What's your number?" He pulled out his phone and punched it in when I told him, then dialed. My phone lit up. "That's me," he said. "Call me if you want. Many hands, light work. Up to you."

"I appreciate the offer," I said.

"Sure thing," he said.

He tapped his ash. "You know what never leaves the firehouse, Garrett?" he said.

"Is this a joke?" I said.

"No," he said. "It's a question. Do you know the answer?"

"I have no idea what you're talking about," I said.

"Trucks and wives," said Kevin.

I didn't get it at first. He looked at me and waited.

"Oh, right," I said. "Like the mob? That's reassuring. For the trucks and wives, I mean."

"Jesus, don't get all assed up," Kevin said. "It's an expression. What I'm saying is that Audrey and the boys will be taken care of. We'll take care of them. It's what we do. You can't stay here forever, right? Don't you have to get back to school?"

Audrey was still awake, wrapped in a blanket watching TV, when I got home after midnight.

"Wow." She looked at her watch. "Did they hold you against your will?"

I sat down next to her. She fanned at the cigar stink that clung to me.

"No," I said. "It was a big night down there. I talked to Kevin for a while. I told him thanks for you. Despite being kind of a dick, he offered to help with the work. I may call him, I may not. I don't know."

"No, he's a good guy," she said.

"Good and macho," I said.

"Posturing. They can't help it. Don't buy into any of their bullshit."

"Like 'Wives and trucks never leave the firehouse'?" I said.

She shook her head and closed her eyes.

"You know they're donating fifty percent from tonight," I said.

Audrey pulled the blanket up to her chin. "Shit," she said. "Shit, shit."

"Just wait," I said. "Wait until they offer you something. You can always have them hang on to it and tell them you'll let them know. You don't have to do anything tonight. Or even tomorrow."

She nodded.

"It was a nice night," I said. "Leo would have been there if it had been for someone else. It was a good party. Any party with Leo was always a good one, and tonight was no exception."

"I'm glad," she said. "I'm going to bed." She stood up and made a big show of holding her breath before she hugged me. "God, you reek."

Garrett

T he next week, I was reading and having a beer in the living room while Audrey made dinner. The day's last rays sliced through the clouds that had hovered for hours, and streamed in through the windows over the fireplace. I stood up to get a better look—I was acclimating to Portland's strange weather and its unpredictable, unlikely transitions. Christopher was texting on his phone and Brian was doodling. We were the picture of domestic contentment—none of us talking, but none of us very far away from each other. Except for Andrew. He was outside in front of the house, shooting hoops alone. I watched him. He looked unhappy even though he made one basket after another. The only sounds came from the kitchen and the intermittent, then more frequent text alerts from Christopher's phone.

"Can you silence that thing?" said Brian.

"Go somewhere else," said Christopher.

"You go somewhere else," said Brian, "or turn that thing off. It's distracting."

"Who keeps texting you?" I said.

"*Meredith,* I bet," said Brian. "His girlfriend."

"No, and she's not my girlfriend, ass," Christopher hissed.

"Language!" said Audrey from the kitchen. I don't know how she heard it.

"Well, she wants to be," Brian said, and Christopher flipped him the bird.

"Boys," Audrey said. Like that, she was in the middle of the room between her sons. "If you can't keep it clean, it's going to cost you. The next time, I collect five dollars from the offending party."

"Sorry, Mom," Christopher said.

"Will you make him turn that thing off, please?" said Brian.

Audrey looked at me and rolled her eyes. "Chris, can you please mute it, or relocate? It was so peaceful there for a few minutes that I thought I was in someone else's house." She walked back to the kitchen.

"So, Chris," I said. "What's wrong with Meredith, anyway? Not saying you need a girlfriend. Brian, your love life's next."

"Gah!" said Brian.

"You keep your yap shut, Brian," Christopher said. He shrugged. "She's cool, I guess. She just bugs me. I don't want that drama. I have the rest of my life to have a girlfriend. The whole idea seems kind of lame."

"Yeah," I said. "I get that." He had no idea how much.

"Plus there's Mrs. Maguire," Brian said, under his breath.

"What did I say, loser?" Christopher gritted his teeth.

"Who's that?" I said.

Brian leaned forward in his chair. "Chris thinks his friend's mom is hot."

Christopher didn't say anything. He sat there and simmered, glaring at Brian.

I felt bad for Chris; Brian was being a shit. "So how come you know so much, FBI?" I said.

Brian shrugged and looked down at his sketchpad. "I've caught him stalking her Facebook page."

"You don't have anything better to do?" I laughed. "You're spying on him while you think he's stalking? You don't see the irony in that? You're on the hook too, bro."

Brian shrank a little. "I just want to have some time on the computer, which is impossible since he's always hogging it."

"So you can look at naked pictures," said Christopher.

"They're *nudes,*" said Brian. "They're paintings. It's fine art. God."

"Guys, as much fun as this has been, and it really has," I said, "I'm going to go out and shoot with Andrew for a few minutes."

"Whatever," they both said. I left them at an impasse, glaring at each other. I felt like I had egged each of them on, and I felt bad about it. *Are they always like this?* I wanted to ask Leo. I could ask Audrey, but boys are different in front of their mothers, I knew. Not better, but different.

"Dinner in ten!" said Audrey as I walked past her and got another beer. "What was that in there?"

"I don't know," I said. "But I stepped right in the middle of it and made it worse."

She shook her head. "They never sit with me like that anymore. They hardly ever tell me anything without me prying it from them."

"I'll get Andrew," I said.

I walked outside and set my beer on the porch. "Throw it here," I said.

Andrew scowled.

"How about a quick game of HORSE?" I said. "We're almost ready to eat."

"HORSE is retarded," said Andrew.

"Jesus, *really,* Andrew? Don't say 'retarded,'" I said. "It's unkind and you sound like you have a lousy vocabulary. Very unbecoming. And, if I tell your mom, she'll fine you. Let's play and I won't rat you out."

Andrew rolled his eyes. "Sorry," he muttered. He threw me the ball.

I started out in the middle of the street and made it.

"Great," he said. "You couldn't start closer?"

"Why should I?" I said. "As good as you are."

He made his shot from my spot. He looked a little less unhappy.

We were matched shot for shot for a while, but by the time Audrey opened the front door and called us in, I was at "R" and he only had "H." The kid was good. I wasn't letting him win.

"Hang on, Mom! Just a sec!" Andrew yelled.

"We'll be right there," I said. Both of us were sweating and committed.

Audrey stood on the porch watching us, waiting.

Andrew could lay up from either side, but I couldn't nail it from the left, so with those last two shots, I was done.

"Shit," I said. I couldn't make the shots he did, not like I used to.

"Language!" Andrew called as he ran past me to go inside. Audrey held out her hand and he high-fived her on the way. I followed him inside and she closed the door.

Brian and Christopher were already at the table. "I beat Garrett at HORSE!" Andrew gloated.

"Go wash your hands," said Audrey.

"You hate HORSE," said Brian.

Chris laughed.

"Not anymore!" Andrew called from the bathroom. "Garrett's pretty good, but I'm better!"

He came out and sat down. "Nice job, but don't be a little shit when you win," I said. "Very unbecoming."

"Language," Audrey said. "*Garrett*. Jesus."

The boys all howled.

"Sorry," I said.

"Sorry," said Andrew. "Good game."

"Yeah, good game." I winked at him, and while we ate, we were all content and everyone was friends again.

Garrett

After the sparring between Christopher and Brian, I looked up Colleen Maguire on Facebook. Once I eliminated the teenagers and the women who in my opinion *weren't* hot, I figured out who I thought she was. And she was a looker, I had to give Chris that. Poor guy. Who knows if what Brian said was true. That afternoon Chris had been so vulnerable, to Brian and to me, in his own house—it really hadn't been fair.

One night when Audrey and Andrew were at the Dougy Center, Chris, Brian, and I were home alone. Brian was watching TV in the living room, and Chris was on the computer in the kitchen. He closed it when I walked in the room.

"Hey," I said.

"Hey, Garrett, what's up?"

"You know, I want to apologize for the other night," I said.

He looked confused. "What do you mean?"

"When you and Brian and I were sitting around and he got in your business about Meredith and that shit about your friend's mom," I said. "I stirred the pot and it was none of my business. I'm sorry if I made things worse."

"That's okay," he said. "It's cool."

"Well, okay, thanks. But I've been thinking about it," I said. "You know, I never have a girlfriend for very long, even now, so you've got *my* blessing to be single. But your dad gave me a lot of grief about how I did things in that department."

"Do you think you'll ever get married?" he said.

"I don't know," I said. "Probably not. If I haven't by now, it's kind of hard to imagine. Either I haven't found the right person or I'm just not built that way."

"Huh." Christopher folded his hands and looked at his feet. "What if you found the right person but it wasn't possible? Or it was impossible for the time being? Because of certain circumstances."

I didn't know if he was talking about Colleen Maguire or not, but my heart went out to him—I knew how he felt. There was an undergraduate, or two, every term, who made me think, *If I could just get my hands on you.* Like the senior who'd blossomed into a beauty from the shy, bookish freshman I'd taught. I saw her a few times at a bar near campus, and I would catch her staring at me. I always lifted my hand and waved, friendly, to diffuse any tension and to clarify any uncertainty. She always waved back, and on those nights I never looked her way again. But one night, after she returned the acknowledgment by wiggling her fingers at me, like an invitation, I settled my tab and went home. I'd done what I could to keep the lines from blurring into something I wouldn't be able to reverse. And there was the black-haired, blue-eyed junior, three years ago, with her tiny, glittering nose ring, who was a very good writer. She's stayed with me too.

"I'm no expert," I said to Christopher. "You should know that right off. But what I think are two things: If something is impossible right now, but *could* be possible later, having to wait tests you for how much you want it."

He looked up from his feet and nodded at me. He looked hopeful.

"Or, it's impossible right now and will never be possible, but having found that person changes you—it makes you know what it is you're looking for. You know, gives you some criteria. You won't settle for anything less than as close as you can get to that."

He nodded again, more slowly. He looked less hopeful.

"You can talk to me if you want," I said. "I'm not your dad, and I'm clueless more than not about this stuff. Ask your mom."

He laughed.

"I mean it," I said. "I am. All I know is, don't toy with Meredith. Just be kind even if you don't like her 'that way.' I can't always say I've done the same."

He shrugged. "She's a pain in my ass. Girls are a pain in the ass. If I'm even a little bit nice, she's going to think it's something totally different anyway. You don't know her."

"For whatever it's worth, Chris," I said. "We're a pain in their ass too."

"Yeah," he laughed. "Probably."

I left him to go back to the computer and sat down next to Brian on the couch. He was watching PBS.

"Hey," he said.

"What's this?" I said.

"A thing on the Sistine Chapel and Michelangelo," he said.

We watched for a few minutes.

"Hey, Brian," I said. "Sorry about the other night. I didn't need to get in the middle of your business with Chris. You guys didn't need me doing that. I just couldn't help myself."

He laughed. "You've been worrying about that? It's cool, Garrett."

"Okay, well, I wanted you to know I shouldn't have gotten in the middle," I said. "You guys know how to figure that stuff out."

"Yeah," he said. "But thanks anyway."

I stood up.

"You can stay and watch this if you want," he said. "It's pretty amazing."

"Yeah, maybe," I said. I sat back down.

"Well, I'm recording it too," Brian said. "So you can always watch it later if you change your mind."

After I'd talked to them I felt like a jackass. Christopher and Brian had been working out their sibling kinks long before I'd appeared. But, in my defense to myself, I felt like I had only done what I would have if Leo and Audrey had taken a trip somewhere together and asked me to watch the boys while they were gone. Temporary, but as long I was there, I'd do what I could. I imagined Audrey prepping me with all the minute instructions for everything I'd need to know for every possible scenario, and after she'd finished, I imagined Leo adding, *And as for everything else, well, you'll figure it out.*

Christopher

My friends had all been hanging out together right after school since Thanksgiving, at one of our houses. Sometimes people were missing because of a practice or a game, but it was always the same group. Me, my best friend, Joe Assante, Mike Doyle, and Ben Maguire. And the girls, Meredith McCann, Rose Ferguson, Theresa Murphy, and M. H. Chandler. It had just kind of happened; Joe and I were friends, but I'd worked to include Ben, and he brought Mike along with him. The girls came as a unit of four, and since Rose lived on the same street as Ben, they already had years of hanging out together in the neighborhood, and now combined all their people. It was easy, since all our houses were within walking distance of the school. But since my dad died, I'd stayed away. After the accident, Joe sometimes walked home with me and did homework, and went home after.

After everyone had finally stopped being weird around me, I thought about joining them again, so one day after school, I checked in with Meredith, who I knew I could rely on.

"Hey," I said. "What're you doing this afternoon?"

"Hey yourself." She smiled. "You're not going home today?"

"Maybe. What's everybody else doing?"

"Going to Maguire's," she said.

"I'll tell Joe," I said. "We'll see you there."

In the Maguires' basement, we had chips and salsa and soda, and the iPod played on the dock. The girls clustered together, texting, Ben played his guitar, and Joe and Mike played tennis on the Wii, until Rose challenged Mike and everyone watched her kick his ass. While she was texting, I caught Meredith watching me, and when I did, I looked away. Ben's mom wasn't there like I'd hoped she would be. If it had been anyone else's house this afternoon, I might have gone home like usual.

I knew where the bathroom was, but I cruised through the basement, checking it out. Everyone was oblivious, doing what they were doing, but I was ready to say that my mom wanted to remodel our basement too if anyone asked.

Around the corner from the party room, I opened a door. Inside was the furnace, mechanical stuff. I closed the door. Down the hall I opened another. Tools, shop stuff. I closed that door. The third door was the laundry room. In front of the washer and dryer stood two drying racks. Jeans, khakis, and a fancy blouse hung on one. Perched on the end of the other was a black pair of panties and a pink bra. I shut the door behind me. I grabbed the panties, wadded them in my front pocket, walked out, and closed the door behind me. When I got back to everyone, they were doing the same things as when I'd left.

"Hey, Ben, I've got to go," I said. "I got a text from my mom and I have to go home and watch my brothers."

"Okay, later, Chris," Ben said. He lifted his head but kept his fingers on the strings of his guitar.

"Thanks," I said. "See you all tomorrow."

Meredith got off the couch and came over. "You're leaving?" she said. "You just got here."

"I know," I said. "Sorry, I have to help my mom when she needs me."

"Yeah, too bad." She touched my arm. "I'm glad you came to-day—it's nice hanging out with you again. See you later."

"Yeah," I said, "later."

I sprinted from Ben's house and back to mine. I'd never stolen anything in my life, but I had taken Colleen Maguire's underwear.

Garrett

The next time I went to meet Brian and Andrew, I got to the school early. I hadn't planned to, but when I didn't see anyone else waiting and checked my watch, I realized dismissal wasn't for another fifteen minutes. I took the ball and went to the courts and warmed up by myself. I figured I'd look for the boys when I saw cars pulling up and parents standing around, but after I'd been there a few minutes a voice yelled, "Hey."

I caught the ball when it bounced back, and turned. Frank Keegan stood on the sidewalk next to the court. He was dressed in a suit and his arms were crossed over his buttoned jacket.

"Was that for me?" I said.

He walked over. "Yeah," he said. "Gary, right?"

"No," I said. "It's Garrett. What's on your mind, Frank?"

"Garrett, sorry," he said. "I wanted a word."

"I'm listening," I said.

"I don't know what you think you're doing," he said.

"I'm shooting some hoops," I said. "Waiting on some friends."

"Gannon was one of the best players on his team this year," Frank said. "He lives for basketball."

"Okay," I said. "The season's over."

"You're here playing after school with some of his teammates, and he's not been asked to play," said Frank. "Gannon's feeling left out and it's because of you. You don't even have a kid at this school."

After all the people I'd met, places I'd been, things I'd done, I didn't think much could surprise me anymore, but Frank did. *Is this what it's like?* I thought. *Being a parent? Having kids? Dealing with adults like this?*

I dribbled the ball a few times. I threw it at the closest net and made it. I caught it after the bounce, then put it between my feet and stood in front of Frank. I put my hands in my pockets. Cars were starting to pull into the lot and groups of parents were collecting.

"Come on, Frank. I'm here to meet Andrew and Brian," I said. "If they ask friends to play and Gannon's not one of them, he shouldn't be surprised. Why don't you lose the suit, make some time, and play with Gannon yourself?" I looked at my watch. "Things seem to have settled down between the boys. If you've had a part in that, thanks. It's three o'clock," I said. "Was there anything else?" He stood there, and after I waited a few beats, I walked past him toward the school.

"So what's the deal with Gannon's mom?" I asked Audrey that night.

"Margot?" she said. "What do you mean, 'the deal'?"

"Is she ever at school?" I said. "Frank's always there. Does she exist?"

"She travels a lot for work, I think," Audrey said. "I imagine she's around when she can be. You probably wouldn't know it if you saw her."

"I see Frank there all the time," I said. "So I was wondering."

"Anything unpleasant?" she said. "Everything okay?"

"Oh, yeah," I said. "I may ask him if he wants to start a book group with me."

She laughed. "Stop it."

"So his mother travels?" I said. "That explains a lot. Have you seen that kid? When's the last time he had a haircut?"

She laughed again. "Watch it, Garrett," she said. "You're starting to sound like a parent."

She wasn't wrong. But I didn't mind.

Garrett

O n April Fool's, Gallagher and I went out for drinks after we finished working. I'd been there five weeks when he came over the week after St. Patrick's. I hadn't called him; he'd just shown up in his minivan, dressed for the job, with his own tools. Together we finished the roof, which felt like a step toward integrating the addition into the house. We listened to sports talk radio, and sometimes music that either or both of us would sing along to without self-consciousness. We were together but we each might as well have been alone. He was easy to work with, and his work was good. I liked those things about him, and when he came the first time, just three days after the balance between Audrey and me was upset, I welcomed the presence of someone else in the house, even if it wasn't every day.

That morning had started the same as any other. Audrey got the boys off to school and then had hours to herself. I had made a second, partial pot of coffee and gone into the kitchen to get a cup, and she walked in wearing her bathrobe and poured one for herself.

"Thanks for making this," she said.

"Of course," I said. "Fuel for the day."

I went back into the addition to pick up where I'd left off the previous day, and although I was sure I'd left them where I'd been working,

I couldn't find the tin shears to cut the flashing, and thought I must have left them in the basement the night before, where I'd been last thing before I quit, so I ran down the stairs without thinking.

It was an unlikely place for me to surprise Audrey in her underwear, next to the washer and dryer, pulling on a pair of jeans, wearing only a bra on top.

"Oh, Christ, sorry," I said. I turned and ran up the stairs, faster than I'd come down, and back into the addition. I had never imagined Audrey in that state of undress—or imagined that it was something I would ever see—but after I had, it wasn't an image I could let go of.

She came into the addition, fully dressed, with her bathrobe draped over her arm. She looked sheepish but at the same time like she was about to crack up.

"God, Garrett, I'm so sorry," she said. "I don't know what's wrong with me. I'm just walking around clueless like I'm the only one in the house. It was just easier to change down there. I didn't even think."

"No, no, that's fine," I said. Of the two of us, I seemed far more uncomfortable. "It's your house—you shouldn't do anything differently than you normally would just because I'm here. I've had a bunch of coffee and I'm in the zone, and I just thought you'd gone back upstairs. I'll check the next time I have to run down there. Call before I head down."

"You'll check to make sure I'm not getting dressed in the basement the next time you have to run down there?" she said. "Right, because that's totally normal."

"Well, normal or not, that's what I'll do," I said. "I'm really sorry."

"Garrett, it's okay," she said. "We're adults—it's not a big deal. Don't you think it's kind of funny?"

"No, I really don't, but it's fine if you do," I said.

"I do," she said. "I don't know why, but since hardly anything seems funny these days, I'll take it where I can get it."

"Okay," I said. "I'm going to the basement now."

"Okay," she said. "It's all clear. Go for it."

So I was glad for Kevin being around for more reasons than he knew, and that first afternoon in April, when we had sat down at the bar and ordered beers, he said, "I want to tell you something. We don't know each other very well, but I like you. I admire what you're doing. There's something I want to tell you, and no one except one other person knows this, and she's across the country."

"Don't say something you're going to regret on my account," I said.

"I wouldn't," he said. "I just want to say, based on my observations, I think it would present some temptations, being there. Doing what you're doing." He raised his hand for the bartender. "Can we get two shots of Jameson each? We're here for a while."

"Temptations," I said. "Really."

"Shut up," he said, "just listen."

The shots came and I drank one.

He drank his both, one after the other, and didn't even sip his beer afterward.

"Things seem pretty cozy there, at the house," he said. "I'm not judging."

"Cozy? This bullshit again," I said. "I thought we were past that. You need a hobby. Pick up a book. See a movie." I drank my second shot.

"You're listening, remember," he said. "Shut up."

He looked at me, waiting to see if I was going to be quiet. I looked back and stayed quiet.

"On Nine/Eleven," he said, "I was in the department back in New York then. I lost a lot of friends. I've been where you are. I lost my best friend that day. Jimmy Sullivan."

"Jesus Christ, Kevin," I said. "I'm sorry. I didn't know. Man, I'm really sorry." I wished for something far better to say, but nothing came to me.

He nodded at me, then looked down at the bar and kept talking.

"So, Jimmy, he left a wife and two boys behind," he said. "I stepped in to help. They needed a lot of help. Sully and I were each other's best man, you know? Of course I would have done anything. And part of what I ended up doing was taking care of his wife, who was my friend too, in ways that my own wife doesn't and can't ever know."

I stayed quiet.

"Anyway," Gallagher said, "Jimmy's wife, Brenda, she had nothing to do with Alyssa. As insane as it sounds, I don't consider myself unfaithful. Brenda's since remarried. She's happy. I'm just wondering what being there with Audrey poses for you. You can't blame me. Things might have been different if I hadn't been married."

We sat there next to each other with his confession between us. When I looked up at the mirror behind the bar, I saw my reflection looking back and Kevin looking down, his elbows resting on the wood. He twirled one of the empties.

"He was a good guy," said Kevin.

"Yes, he was," I said. I wanted to tell him, *And by the way, he made me sign a piece of paper that I'd marry her. And what if what I'm thinking is completely out of line and I'm falling for her? Falling for all of them?* But while that unspoken question nagged at me, I knew what Kevin would do. He'd take care of the woman his dead friend had loved, no matter what.

Christopher

There was a loose floorboard in my closet that my dad never got around to fixing, I don't even know if my mom knew about it. It was a place where I stashed certain things, and after I took Colleen Maguire's underwear—her panties—I put them under the board with the other things I had hidden there. Knowing they were in my house, my room, my closet, made me giddy and distracted. I pulled them out when I was in my room alone, when I told my mom I was studying and I didn't want to be disturbed.

When I was at school and thought about the panties, I panicked about them being found, but my mom was cool about not snooping, and I think if she had known about the loose board, she would have made my dad fix it pronto, because that's how she was. So when I was out of the house I relaxed as much as I could.

Meredith had sent me a sympathy card; that was under the floorboard. *Dearest Christopher, I am hurting for you and sending you prayers. I am always here if you need anything. Much love, Meredith.* I had taken it out and looked at it after I first got it—not as often as I did Colleen's panties—Meredith had nice handwriting and no girl had ever written *much love* to me before, although the card wasn't a regular letter, obviously. Still, the *much love* stood out. I had two bottle caps with the words *Bravely Done* printed on the bottom from one night last summer when Joe and I stole some beers from his parents' fridge and went and played basketball after we drank them. There was a box of condoms in there too, a small one that had three in it that I hadn't opened. When Joe had dared me to buy it over Christmas break, I did. I wouldn't balk at a dare. I even stood in the aisle for a while, shopping, reading all the boxes, browsing all the special features the different brands of condoms had. But after I'd bought the box and told Joe it was easy and suggested he buy a box too, he chickened out and wouldn't. I wasn't going to be an asshole and make a big deal about how I didn't hesitate but he balked and couldn't pull the trigger himself even though it had been his idea. I wouldn't embarrass him and give him shit by saying, *It's not like you're buying booze or crack,* although I could have.

I also had the St. Christopher medal my dad always wore, the one he was wearing when he died. My mom gave it to me after the accident, along with a picture of my dad holding me when I was a baby, which he'd carried in his wallet. *I want you to have these, Chris.* She was a little crazy—we all were. I wasn't going to wear the medal. *A lot of good it did him* was all I could think, but never would have said that to my mom. The picture and the medal weren't secret like the other stuff; I just didn't want to lose them.

The one thing I hadn't thought about was washing Colleen's underwear. After I pulled them out a few times, they needed it. So I told my mom I wanted to start doing my own laundry.

"What?" She was clearly shocked. If only she knew. "I have enough trouble getting you guys to fold and put away your stuff."

"I know," I said, "that's why I want to help. Would it help?"

"Yes, Chris, it really would." She looked at me like she was waiting for the punch line of a joke.

"You know how to use the washer, right?" she said. "Do normal on cold."

"Sure, Mom, thanks," I said.

"No, thank you, sweetie," she said. "God, you're really growing up. Come here." She pulled me against her and I let her. I was already taller than her, taller than Colleen. A long way from that picture of my dad holding me.

"I love you, Mom," I said.

"I love you too, Christopher," she said. "More than the world."

Audrey

Leo hadn't even been dead three months when it happened the first time, in April, and it was because of me. And because Garrett had been so great with the boys and getting Kevin to help him with the work, without letting the whole fire department take over and overwhelm me with their generosity. That was what I told myself. And because I hated the color yellow—I always had—the color our bedroom was when we bought the house, when I was pregnant with Brian, and had lived with since. It wasn't awful, but it was a color I never would have picked, and I always thought it was harsh and mocking, nothing sunny or cheerful about it, though for some reason I'd never gotten around to repainting. With Garrett here, the two of us could get it done fast with him cutting in and me rolling. I went to Miller Paint and debated the swatches against each other. I wanted something blue, a peaceful color with some depth. The color that was my favorite—and I really tried to find one I liked better, I did, because it was like a slap, or one of Leo's jokes—was called "C'est la Vie." It was a dusty indigo. A color I would have liked to wear.

That afternoon I moved furniture, took everything off the walls. Leo had hung Brian's firehouse series that he'd done for school in our room—*So we'll see it first thing every morning*—and taking it down with the other pictures, I remembered the day he'd drilled the molly anchor and hung it. I draped sheets around the room and washed the walls with TSP, and that night after homework, dinner, and dishes, Garrett and I started painting. The boys came in and watched. Christopher asked to roll so I let him, then Brian and Andrew did too.

"You want to try cutting in?" Garrett asked Christopher.

"Sure," he said, "I guess. It looks hard."

"Nah, just takes practice." Garrett got another brush for Chris and the two of them worked next to each other along the baseboard. Brian and Andrew got bored and went to their room. After twenty minutes, Christopher was bored too.

"Thanks, Garrett," he said. "It's not so hard."

"You bet," said Garrett. "You're a natural."

"Good night," Chris said.

Garrett gave him a wave and I hugged and kissed him.

"Good night, Mom," he said, and left.

"You want anything to drink?" I asked Garrett. "I'm going to have a glass of wine."

"Wine's good," he said from the floor. He was lying on his side, propped on his elbow, still at the baseboard.

I came back up with glasses and a bottle and put my iPod in the dock. We painted in silence except for the music. After my first glass I poured another and sat on the floor next to Garrett. He had worked his way to the other side of the room by then.

"Do you think it's gloomy?" I said. "The color?"

"No," said Garrett, "it's fetching. Evocative."

"Of what?" I said. "What does that even mean for paint?"

"Nothing specific," he said. "It makes you think."

"I guess," I said. "Do you know what it's called?"

"What what's called?" he said.

"The paint," I said, "the name of the paint."

"What?" he said.

" 'C'est la Vie.' "

"That's a fucking riot," he said. "Is that why you bought it?"

"No, I bought it in spite of the name. It was the one I liked best. Paint names are always awful. Who do you think names them, anyway? A bunch of executives sitting around losing sleep till they're finished?"

"Maybe," he said.

I loaded the roller again, and we kept painting. I took a break to check on the boys and get another bottle. It was after midnight when the first coat was finished and both bottles were empty.

"I'll go clean these out," said Garrett. He picked up the tray, the brushes, the roller, all of it. "It looks good, it really does. A nice color with a terrible name."

"Let me help," I said. "You're going to drop something."

"No, I won't," he said, "but okay."

We weren't drunk, but weren't sober either. In the basement he washed everything at the utility sink as I handed it to him. I was feeling loose and tired—in a good way, having accomplished something, not with the dead weight of fatigue and sadness I'd grown used to.

"We'll finish tomorrow?" Garrett said. He'd laid everything out to dry.

"Yeah, tomorrow," I said. And he hugged me, not unlike the other times he had since he'd been here, but when he pulled away from the embrace I hung on, looked at him before I closed my eyes, and kissed him on the mouth.

I could feel his body freeze and tighten, but he stayed put, my arms around his waist keeping him anchored. I imagine he felt cornered at first, until he kissed me back for only seconds before he pulled away with some authority.

"Jesus, Audrey," he said. "I'm sorry."

"No, I'm sorry."

"It's late," he said.

"I know. I'm sorry," I said again. "The painting, that was fun. It was nice to have a little fun."

"Yeah," he said. "I know. It was. I'm heading up. See you tomorrow. Good night."

From my room I could hear the sink running in the downstairs bathroom.

I'm sorry, Leo. I walked down the steps, tiptoeing around the creaky spots in the floors. The guest room was dark and the door was open a crack. I peered in and Garrett lay on his side, facing away from me. I took off my clothes in the hallway, carried them in with me, and closed the door. He rolled over, toward me. I got in bed.

Except for slivers from the streetlight leaking through either side of the roller shades, the only light came from a hole in the fabric. As a toddler, Andrew had poked it with a paper clip and over time it had grown into the size of a dime.

He touched my face. "Audrey," he said.

"Garrett," I said. "Please." I reached under the covers for his hips and pulled his waistband down. I kissed him and when he kissed me back, I slipped my other arm under him and pulled him on top of me.

Audrey

God, what have I done? I woke up the next morning and looked at that first coat of the new paint with that terrible feeling of having done something I couldn't undo. *I can't take this back.*

I didn't know what to say or how to act when I saw Garrett. I felt like I had cheated on Leo, which I had never done or been tempted to do, with the worst possible person, the one person I couldn't afford to ruin anything with, the one person who was indispensable.

I had never thought about Garrett that way. He was handsome and charming, like a handsome and charming brother, or a coworker you would never want to date because you shook your head and counted your blessings every time he shared the antics of his personal life. He was terrible with women in the long term, though the women had no idea in the short term, the ones who fell for him and ended up disappointed at best or heartbroken at worst. The painting the night before had been uncomplicated, the first, small bit of something productive and positive and *normal*. The wine—you could always blame that—and the steadiness of our friendship had loosened my inhibitions. But it hadn't just been about sex. I wanted something to make me feel like I was in possession of my body, to make me feel like the person I thought I was, or used to be, after the soldiering and flailing that had become part of every day for months.

I was steeped in regret that morning and had to rehearse before I could go downstairs. I remembered everything from the night before, but it might have been better if I hadn't. I had been married to Leo for nineteen years, we had been together for more than twenty, and our history had been built on—among other non-negotiables—our chemistry in the bedroom. Garrett was the first man I'd slept with after more than two decades of sleeping only with my husband, but it hadn't felt like a first time. What I struggled with while I stalled wasn't just that I was embarrassed and ashamed. He made me feel loved, and it had thrown me completely.

Garrett

After it was over, Audrey turned away from me, sat up on her side of the bed, and cried. I didn't know what to do or say. I went into the bathroom and cried too. When I came back to the bedroom she was gone. I got into bed and smelled the indent in the pillow where her head had just been, but sleep didn't come for several hours. I lay there waiting for it, the whole time thinking how far away I was from someone I wished I were right next to.

I was up early the next morning, reading the paper in the kitchen when Audrey came downstairs. Today I would finish the new exterior door and start on the siding.

"Hey," she said. "Thanks for making coffee."

"Hey, yeah, it was no problem," I said. "I didn't want to start working until everyone was up." I had no idea what we were going to say to each other, what I should say to her. I couldn't remember the last time I'd felt more awkward with a woman.

"Garrett," she said. I didn't want her to say anything—couldn't we both just say nothing? Ignore it like we were kids?

"Audrey, you don't have to say anything," I said. "I should say something but I don't know what. I'm sorry."

She shook her head. "You don't have anything to be sorry for," she said. "I owe you an apology. I was out of line and I'm so embarrassed. I'm obviously spiraling out of control, and you were in the way." She started to cry. "I just don't want to ruin this, to screw up anything. I'm so grateful you're here, and I treasure your friendship. Jesus, I sound like I'm nineteen years old."

I wanted to say something comforting and wise, but I couldn't imagine what would make this less uncomfortable. *Six hours ago I slept with my best friend's wife and I liked it.*

"I think you're doing the best you can," I said. "I think we're all in unchartered waters here and it's likely some unexpected things are going to happen." I got up to refill my cup and stood in front of her. I wanted to touch her, but it seemed like the last thing I should do. "Let yourself off the hook. I could have stopped you. I could have and I didn't. We're okay, Audrey. Right?"

She looked up at me and wiped her face. "I've got to make sure the boys are up," she said. "Go ahead and start working if you want."

Well, that went well, I thought. *I suppose it could have been worse.* At that moment I felt like any woman I had any involvement with was subject to some measure of ruin, and I would have given anything for Audrey not to be one of them. I wondered whether if she knew what Leo had asked me, it would have made any difference.

Christopher

In April, Ben turned seventeen. When he was a kid, his family had moved from Denver to Portland, and to help with the transition, his parents had made him repeat kindergarten. I never knew he was a year older than the rest of us until middle school. Since he had already had his driver's license for a year, for his birthday he had told his mom, told Colleen, he wanted to drive us all downtown and go to the movies, and she said he could. That night we all met at Ben's house.

All seven of us were there with presents and cards, some of those that played a song when you opened it, and we sat in the living room waiting for Ben to open them all before we left. Everybody was cracking up at the cards. Colleen lit candles on the mantel over the fireplace and sat next to Mr. Maguire on the couch, and they kept looking at each other and smiling with each present Ben opened, and smiled even more and laughed when all of us hooted at what he got. You could tell they were like, *Our baby is seventeen, all grown up, can you believe it*. I'd seen the same look on my mom's face.

I couldn't look at either of the Maguires. I was standing between M.H. and Meredith, and as we stood there watching, I could feel Meredith move closer to me. I couldn't really move away from her because M.H. was on my other side. If I had moved, I would have done the same thing to M.H. that Meredith was doing to me, and that wouldn't have been good, so I just stood there. I felt pinned between the girls. I had to do something. I wanted to sprint from being in the same room with Colleen and Mr. Maguire and Meredith.

"Mrs. Maguire," I said. "Can I go get a glass of water?"

"Sure, Chris," she said. "Help yourself. Any of you guys, help yourselves. Ben, you guys are going to have to leave soon if you're going to make the movie."

"I know, Mom," said Ben. "I just have two more." He was having a blast. He was all right, really he was, but looking at all of us there in his living room, knowing that I had brought him into the group not because of him but because of Colleen, I felt like shit.

The kitchen was through the dining room and around a corner. I was glad to get away from feeling like Meredith was trapping me between her and M.H. I half expected Meredith to follow me, and since I couldn't see the living room from the kitchen, I listened for her, for anyone, but I didn't hear anything. The Maguires had those water and ice dispensers in the door of their refrigerator, and I picked up a glass from the dish rack beside the sink and filled it. I pretty much wanted to leave and get going to the movie so I wouldn't have to worry about Meredith standing so close to me, and trying not to look at Colleen or Mr. Maguire, but it wasn't my call, so instead I stalled in the kitchen.

Like everybody, the Maguires had a gallery of stuff on the front of their fridge, stuck there with magnets. There were a few school pictures of Ben and his younger brother Will, and some of their dog at the beach and one of their whole family. There were sports schedules and school schedules, the beginning of a shopping list. Because it was so small it took me a while to see a photo of Colleen and a woman I didn't know—a friend or her sister maybe—taken in one of the photo booths with the curtain you have to cram into and never get a good picture from, but this one of Colleen was really good. She looked like a girl, not like anyone's mom or wife. I wanted that picture. After I had drunk the first glass of water, I pressed my glass against the lever and refilled it and listened again. I heard the mood in the living room shift; Ben must have opened the last present. I downed the second glass and put it on the counter next to the fridge.

I pulled the picture of Colleen and the other woman out from under the magnet and shoved it in my pocket, and picked up the glass and filled it a third time and kept staring at the fridge, now at the empty space where the picture had been.

Meredith came into the kitchen. "We're getting ready to go," she said. "This is going to be great! Come on."

"Yeah," I said. "Cool."

All of us clustered by the door. Colleen and Mr. Maguire, too. Their foyer wasn't small, but I felt like we were packed in there, all ten of us, closer than we needed to be.

"Ben," Colleen said. "Text or call us if you need to, okay? You guys have fun. Be careful, okay?"

I wanted to call or text Colleen. I had the picture in my hand in my pocket. My hand started to sweat.

"I know, Mom," said Ben. "Can we go?"

"Yes, yes, go," Colleen said. She grabbed Ben around the neck and kissed his hair. "Okay, go, have fun. Remember—"

"I know, Mom," Ben said. "Call or text, be careful. Let's go, guys."

The eight of us left the house and got into Colleen's minivan. I was in the middle of the bunch of us, so I ended up in the backseat behind Ben; Meredith, Rose, and M.H. were in the third row. "Shotgun!" said Theresa, so Joe and Mike sat with me. Ben backed out of the driveway and Theresa and Mike rolled down their windows. We all waved back to Colleen and Mr. Maguire standing in the doorway.

"Let's get this party started," Ben said.

Theresa turned on the radio and put her iPhone in the dock.

"What do we want to hear?" she yelled into the car, and everyone started shouting suggestions.

I wished I were sitting in the front seat instead of in the back like a kid. So I nabbed shotgun for the ride home, and we did have a pretty fun time, but for the whole night I hoped the picture of Colleen wouldn't slip out of my pocket.

Garrett

We couldn't go back to the way things were before—you never can—but I tried. *Fake it till you make it.* The next day I cut in the second coat by myself, and later she rolled it out, alone, and the bedroom was done. Then in the days and the weeks after, I worked more steadily than I had been, took every one of Gallagher's offers to help, and concentrated on trying to act the same with Audrey as I had for twenty years. I still had dinner with them, then went back to work afterward, and Audrey was guarded and careful. When we all ate together she seemed as if she'd spent the day thinking about what she'd say and how she'd say it. She still asked if I wanted a beer or a glass of wine, but we didn't linger over our drinks and talk, easy, like we had before. I went out for beers with Gallagher, and a few times another firefighter joined us. I wondered if any of the single ones considered courting Audrey after a respectable amount of time had passed. I thought about telling Kevin what had happened—all of it, Leo's outlandish request, and Audrey and me—especially after what he'd shared. But for what, his approval? Advice? I didn't even live in Portland. I was a grown man and I knew Audrey better than I knew Kevin, but I wondered what he would say, and if I was honest with myself, I didn't tell him anything because of what I was afraid he *would* say.

After a week of our newly navigating each other, I told Audrey I wanted to take the class at the school, so I could volunteer, and asked her what I needed to do.

"The Call to Protect class?" she said. "Garrett, you don't have to do that."

"I want to do it," I said. "If Andrew has a field trip or whatever, Brian too, I could go if they invited me."

She rolled her eyes. "It's so ridiculous. The need for such a thing makes me so angry."

"Maybe," I said, "but if it's what I've got to do, it's what I've got to do."

There was a class scheduled the following week at another parish, so I signed up, and I saw what Audrey meant. I could see it was a safeguard—after the unspeakable things priests everywhere had done—but I felt simultaneously insulted and empowered. God knew I didn't want anyone to suspect anything untoward about my behavior around kids—I was an educator myself—but I appreciated being charged with looking for signs or tendencies in others. That made it feel worth my while.

When I got back to the house, Audrey was working in the front yard.

"You survived," she said. "Awful, isn't it?"

"Yeah," I said. "That creepiness sticks with you for a while. Now I'm looking at everyone like they're a predator."

She laughed, and it was the first time we'd felt a little like our old selves.

"Hey, let's go get lunch, want to? We can go to the carts on Mississippi. It's too nice a day to not be outside," she said. "We should enjoy it while it lasts. I can work more when we come back."

"Sure," I said. "Okay." So we went. We had to eat, after all.

Audrey

I t hadn't occurred to me when I said we should go to lunch, but when we got to the food carts on Mississippi, it felt like a date. The courtyard was full of couples and friends and groups, and I saw how women looked at him as we walked through and I felt possessive—*He's with me*—which was absurd and irrational. But as we approached an empty table, he put his hand on the small of my back.

"This is okay?" he said.

"Yeah," I said.

We sat down. "What's good?" Garrett said.

"I'm having barbecue," I said. "But get what you want. All of it's good."

"No, barbecue's good," he said. "Tell me what you want. Lunch is on me."

"Garrett, I can buy my own lunch," I said.

"Stop, I'm starving." He laughed. "Come on, you're not making me pay rent."

In Portland, the question wasn't if you would run into someone you knew when you went out; it was how many of them you would run into. While we ordered, I saw Chris's classmate, Meredith

McCann, and her mother, Julie, at another table across the courtyard. I used to see them both every day for years, before the kids were in high school. The last time I'd seen them was the funeral.

We sat back down with our food. "It's nice to be out," I said. It was the first time I had been out like this, eaten out, since Leo died. We had eaten at the carts a lot.

"Yeah," Garrett said. "The weather was starting to get to me. I didn't know spring could be this nice. God, this is great."

"It can be," I said, "you never know. Tomorrow it will probably pour again. You get used to it." It was such a cliché, that we were out on what felt like a date, but wasn't, talking about the weather, Garrett joking about rent. It was a place to start.

We were quiet for a few minutes, eating. It wasn't an unpleasant silence, but I didn't love it. At that point, neither of us had more to offer about the weather, or about anything else, to keep the insignificant talk going, and there was the food to work on.

"So, you know—" Garrett said. "Man, this is good." He wiped his mouth and sat sideways on the bench. "I don't want to get in your business, but have you thought about going down there? Maybe visit the station? I get from Gallagher that they all wonder how you're doing. Maybe you and the boys go down there, just say hello. I think it would mean a lot to them to see you."

"I don't know," I said. "Maybe. I'll think about it."

I didn't feel like I was on a date anymore. I felt like I was back at the reception at the Pittock Mansion, fielding condolences in my suit from Ann Taylor.

"I just wanted you to know, he told me they were asking about you," he said. "I don't have an opinion. I'm sorry if I said the wrong thing. It's just, they've asked. You'll go, if you want, when the time's right. You know what you're doing, Audrey." It all sounded like an apology.

I had no idea what I was doing. As I sat in the sun and watched

Garrett, I wondered, could a person *rebound* after their spouse died, like after a romance ended? The idea seemed so profoundly wrong, and I was ashamed at the thought, but that was what I felt like I'd done with Garrett. I would never have gone out somewhere and picked up a stranger, but there had been an opportunity that I'd created, then taken advantage of, and I wasn't sure of my own motive. What was the motive when someone rebounded after a heartbreak? To temporarily fill the absence and postpone dealing with the loss that only time would make less acute—it was an unwise choice, emotional self-medication for which even the most unlikely but available person would do. Everyone who ever rebounded, or knew someone who did, knew that. But with Garrett, it was something different, because we had a history—we knew each other, we had both loved the same man, and I trusted him. He wasn't disposable. So what did that make it?

Out in the light, in the air, part of a crowd, I wanted to say something to him about what had happened. In a neutral, public place—that's where people went when they needed composure and structure for confronting a delicate matter—I wanted to tidy the mess of the business between us that I had started. I didn't know what to say, but I just wanted it said.

Before I could say anything, though, Julie and Meredith walked over to our table.

"Hi, Audrey," said Julie. I stood up and she hugged me.

"Hi, Mrs. McGeary," Meredith said.

"Hi, Meredith. This is Garrett," I said to them both. "I don't know if you've met."

Garrett stood and Julie and Meredith shook his hand. "I remember you from the funeral," said Julie. "It's nice to see you again."

Garrett and I sat back down.

"We're on our way out. Off to the dentist," Julie said. "I just wanted to say hello. I've been thinking about you a lot."

"Thanks, Julie," I said. "It's nice to see you both."

"Take care," said Julie. Meredith waved, and when they left I returned to the thoughts I'd been having before they came over, no clearer than I had been about them before, or what to say to Garrett.

Audrey

I wasn't ready to go to the fire station. It was too much of a step. The station had been his second home, and I had enough trouble being in my own house without him. Although, maybe Leo *would have wanted* me to go—the expression drove me crazy, but I thought it anyway; it had a life of its own, out of my control. When I planted new vegetables that spring, were they what Leo *would have wanted*? When I talked to Andrew's principal, had I done what Leo *would have wanted*? Changing the bedroom's paint color—but then I couldn't think any more about that because of what the painting had triggered between Garrett and me. Some days when I couldn't stop the loop of that question in my head and I imagined what Leo would have wanted, I came up with only one response: *I would have wanted you not to sleep with Garrett, and also I would have wanted not to be dead. Not necessarily in that order.*

The wives offered me no comfort either. Some had reached out from other parts of the state—beyond just Twenty-Five and Multnomah County—*I'm here, I'm here, I'm here,* their emails said, yet there wasn't a single thing any of them could do for me. But I was a hard sell, I knew that.

As a college freshman my entire happiness had hinged on joining a sorority—it was the only thing I'd wanted—and it hadn't happened. Subject to my own naive whims and ignorant of the political stakes, a one-night tangle with the wrong guy had sealed my exclusion. I had gotten over that particular painful rejection, but I had learned something from it: those women and the guy hadn't known me at all beyond one fact that didn't define me, but my poor judgment, insignificant on a large scale, had cost me. So since then, I'd always been suspicious of a collective mind-set of women, and had no interest in being a participant. As a result, I'd never embraced a membership in the firefighter wives' cultural sisterhood.

We *were* all in the same boat—single parents for days on end when our husbands' shifts dragged, and the worst weeks made any one of us crazy. But when the wives got together, the bitching and griping could be magnified into sport, and after Leo died, I wanted to tell every one of them, *Save your fucking breath. Wait until he's dead, then you'll really have something to complain about.* And the group offered no immunity. Turning on each other was not rare: on the one who had dared to wear *that* to an event, on the one who'd had too much to drink and flirted with the wrong husband, on the one who'd dressed her husband down in front of God and everybody.

I should have been kinder. I knew many other firefighters didn't accommodate their wives with the flexibility Leo had given me when I needed it—two days at the coast alone, or a visit with Charlotte in San Francisco by myself for a week. Even so, when tension in our house built up, I unleashed my own wrath on Leo rather than share it with other wives. We had some terrible rows the times I'd come to the end of my rope because of the job, and because of the lifestyle of the job. But women could be awful. I learned that early on. I didn't want their pity or anything else they had to offer, contrived or genuine. I didn't want to be fodder for their gossip. The food they'd sent was the extent of what I would accept. Of all of them I had been the closest to Alyssa Gallagher, but when Leo died, what had been mutual was erased. She was still a firefighter's wife and I was a firefighter's widow, and I saw no way to maintain the friendship under those new conditions. If I changed my mind later, I could only hope that she'd still be receptive.

So instead of visiting the station or connecting with the wives, I tried to take the small steps I *was* capable of to get out of myself, to get out of my own head. I talked to my parents and Leo's parents when they called. Garrett talked to his father when he called him. I talked to Garrett about my calls. I told him my mother wanted to come back out and that she'd cried when I told her she could if she wanted to but that we were managing. I told him my father and Glenn wondered when Garrett would be finished with the addition and I'd said I didn't know. Garrett told me his father had asked him the same question and that he'd told Julian the same thing. I asked him about Boston and his last girlfriend, Celia, and how he'd managed to leave so easily.

He waved away Celia. "A further waste of my time I was saved from. She wasn't a bad person, but she was a phony and I can't stand phonies." That was all he would say. About leaving his job, he said, "Audrey, what were they going to do? You know how easy I uproot."

"Like a weed," I said, and he laughed.

"Exactly."

That's what you do to engage other people, you ask them questions instead of talking about yourself, so I focused on the small goal of giving my thoughts and time to someone else, trying to catch up with Garrett like it was just a regular visit, trying to replace my mistake by efforts to resume the role I'd always had with him. I asked him endless questions about the addition—what was next, what I needed to make decisions on. Garrett had put his mark on the place after all his work, and after he and Kevin had finished the roof and moved forward on things Leo hadn't started, I could start to envision it as a part of the house we could spread out into and live in.

Since I'd slept with Garrett, I'd avoided Erin and dodged her phones calls and texts as best I could, and she'd given me space the way friends will for a time before they call you on it. We shared our secrets with each other and over time had accumulated details about each other that no one else knew. She didn't know about Garrett. She knew I was a terrible liar and I knew she knew I was. When I decided I'd start running with her again, I figured we would talk or we wouldn't. I knew that my being out running at all would be enough for her. So I took one of those small steps and texted her. She came by the next morning and let herself in.

"Hey," she said, "you ready?" She looked proud of me.

"Yeah," I said, "I just need shoes. Go check the progress."

I put on my shoes and walked back to the addition myself.

"Hi, Garrett," said Erin. "Wow. It looks great."

"Hey," Garrett said. "Thanks. It's coming along."

"I'll be back," I said.

He waved.

We left the house and started one of our regular routes.

We were three blocks in and Erin said, "Why is he single, again? It really looks terrific. *I* want an addition."

My neighbor passed us walking her dog and I lifted my hand. What a simple thing to be doing. I envied her.

"I slept with him," I said. I stopped running, then so did Erin.

"What?" she said.

"I slept with him," I said. "I slept with Garrett."

"What?" she said. "When?"

"A couple weeks ago," I said. "It was terrible."

"Oh, God," she said. "Do you want to sit down?"

"Can we just walk for a minute?" I said.

"Okay," she said. "God, it was terrible?"

"No, it wasn't terrible." I started to laugh and cry at the same time. "I did a terrible thing. It was me. I initiated it."

"Oh," she said. "What happened?"

I covered my face with my palms.

"Jesus," I said. "We were painting, we were repainting our bedroom. My bedroom. All of us, the boys too. And then the boys went to bed and we were drinking wine and then when we finished I kissed him. It was awkward, he was mortified, and we both went to bed. Then I went and got in bed with him."

"Oh," she said again.

"Aren't you going to say anything?" I said.

"What do you want me to say?" she said. "Can you give me a minute? You just told me."

"Erin, say what friends say. What is there to think about?" I said. "That it was terrible and that I'm crazy and you can't believe I did such a thing."

"Oh, sweetie." She dropped her head and looked up at me with just her eyes. "I don't think that, though."

"I feel like I cheated on him," I said. "Who does such a thing after her husband just died?"

"You didn't, Audrey," she said. "It may feel like it, but you didn't cheat on Leo."

"Well, what am I supposed to do?" I said.

"I don't know," she said. "What happened after? Did you talk about it? How has it been?"

"It was awkward the next day," I said. "And then we just kind of pretended it didn't happen and went back to the way things were. Well, not really. It's obvious how hard we're both trying. It's not easy like it was before."

"Well, no," she said. "Of course it would have to be different."

"I don't know what to do," I said again. We walked for a half a block, quiet.

"What is there to do?" she said. "Do you mean to get back to the way things were? Or do you mean something else?"

"I don't know," I said. "It *wasn't* terrible. So I feel terrible about that. Are you mad at me?"

"Audrey, of course not," she said. "Stop it. This doesn't have anything to do with me. Why would I be mad?"

"Because you don't want to have a friend who's an idiot," I raised my voice. "Isn't that what you're here for, to let me know when I'm being an idiot?"

She laughed but it wasn't a funny laugh. "You don't even need me here to have this conversation, do you? You're having it all by yourself."

I hadn't expected to almost be arguing with Erin because she wouldn't agree with me. I had just dumped it on her, so I knew it wasn't fair. But after my confession, I'd expected her to reprimand me, quickly, and forgive me just as quickly, and that would be it.

"We've known each other too long, Audrey. If I thought I needed to scold you about something, I wouldn't need you to coach me through it," she said. "I'm sorry I'm not piling on. I don't agree that you're an idiot, sorry."

"Leo hasn't even been dead for three months," I said.

"I know," said Erin. "And I'm sorry if I'm not saying the right things. I don't know what the right thing to say is. You know, it's not like you get to practice this so you know how to do it when it really happens. The very last thing I'm going to do is judge. But I'll always tell you if I think you're making a mistake, and I can't about this. Only you can, and if you think what happened was a mistake, then you know what to do, or what you have to do. Work on getting back to where you were with Garrett. If you don't think it was a mistake, that's nobody else's business."

"Let's start running again," I said. I couldn't talk any more about it.

As we put the blocks behind us, I still felt like I'd betrayed Leo with Garrett, but although sleeping with Garrett had done nothing to penetrate and diminish my grief, it had suspended it while I was in bed with him. We hit the halfway point and turned back, and I thought, *Now Garrett is the closest I'll ever be able to get to my husband.*

I knew where they were, and when I got home I found the box, packed away, that I'd never gotten rid of. I pulled out the base and receiver for the baby monitor I hadn't used in nine years. I put new batteries in both and tested them. They still worked. I put the base upstairs in the alcove bookshelf behind some books. I put the receiver in the back of the pantry, behind boxes of food, so it would be handy when I needed it.

Garrett

The second week in May, Kevin and I finished putting in the electricity and the inspection was scheduled.

One night that week, after the boys were in bed, Audrey opened a bottle of wine and poured two glasses.

"Let's go sit and look at it," she said.

We walked outside to the backyard and I headed to one of the chairs on the patio.

"No," she said. "Here." She sat on the edge of one of the planter boxes she'd been tending for weeks and patted the wood next to her.

I sat down and took a sip.

"It's great, Garrett," she said. "It's really great. I hope you think so."

"It's coming along," I said. "Thanks."

"No, thank you," she said.

I hadn't taken any time to stop and sit like we were, to have a look at the work from the outside. Kevin and I always dovetailed finishing one thing into starting the next. We hadn't taken time to reflect, so it was a new thing to take in the progress with Audrey sitting next to me. Piece by piece, day by day, I hadn't realized how far we'd come.

"Of course. You're welcome," I said.

We sipped in the dark, and I could feel her looking at me.

I turned and looked at her and looked away again. "What?" I said.

"I'm sorry," she said. "I have something to say and I need to muster some courage."

I sat there and waited, for her to say what exactly, I had no idea, but I was pretty sure I knew what it was about.

"I'm not sorry," she said. "About what happened between us. I'm not sorry it happened. For me, it wasn't a mistake."

She had put it out there. She had put herself out there. And now she was waiting. *Tell her, tell her now. Tell her about the promise, the paper, the pact, the thing, what Leo said. Tell her.*

She took a deep breath. "I'm sorry if I'm out of line. I'm sorry if I seem like I'm not in my right mind. We've known each other too long, Garrett." She paused. "I wouldn't be sorry if it happened again."

Tell her.

"Me neither," I said. "I'm not sorry either. And I wouldn't be sorry if it happened again, just so you know."

There it was. One thing was out there. Another thing wasn't.

She stood between my knees and kissed me. After the first time, I'd hoped it would happen again—dreading that it wouldn't—and now it was.

The boys were asleep, and before we went into the guest room, she went to the pantry, took out a baby monitor, and brought it in the room with us.

Brian

My mom seemed happy and I was glad. Not *happy* happy, not like normal exactly, but something closer to normal than how she had been. She worked in the garden again every day and there were flowers on the dining room table. The days she came to school she talked to other parents and she wasn't all hysterical laughing or anything like that, but she was different from the weeks before, when the days she did come to school to pick us up, she had driven and just sat in the car and waited for us when school let out. If she didn't hang out with the parents, Andrew and I couldn't hang out either. Except for the days when Garrett came and we played ball.

I thought she should think about being happy again, not like my dad didn't die or anything, but what good was it doing to go to bed right after dinner like she did right after he died? My dad shouldn't have died skiing, but he did have a dangerous job, and my mom, well, she was tough. She married someone who could die on the job, not like a miner or someone on the bomb squad, but it wasn't like my dad had sat at a desk all day.

So I felt okay doing something about my drawing. Kevin Gallagher had been helping Garrett with the house, finishing what my dad started. I guessed they were doing a good job. I guessed they were doing what they thought they should. My dad couldn't finish it and we couldn't live with the room half done at the back of the house like that. I just hoped when it was done it would be the way my dad would have wanted it, but it didn't matter if it wasn't. It wasn't like he was going to show up and complain about what other people did that he couldn't now that he was gone. He wasn't like that anyway. He didn't criticize other people, as much as he liked doing things his own way.

Since Kevin was around all the time, I could ask him. If the drawing was gone, it was gone, but at least I'd know. One day after my mom, Andrew, and I walked home from school, she drove to the store. Kevin was sitting in the kitchen with Garrett. I sat down at the table with them. A pot of coffee was brewing. Andrew got a bowl of cereal.

"How was school?" said Garrett.

"The usual," I said.

"Where's your mom?" he asked.

"She went to shop for dinner," I said.

Andrew sat down with his cereal and it was quiet except for his chewing. Now I didn't want to say anything about the drawing.

"You guys want to help us this afternoon?" Kevin said.

"Yeah," said Andrew, with a mouthful. "Can we?"

"Maybe," I said.

"Garrett's running out of steam." Kevin laughed. "He needs a rest and I can't do all the heavy lifting."

I changed my mind again.

"Hey, Kevin, I've been thinking about something I want to ask you," I said.

"Shoot." He smiled, all easy, like I was going to ask him something different from what I was.

"Well, there's something I'm looking for," I said. "And I was wondering if you could help me find it. It's going to sound stupid." I picked at a hangnail on my thumb under the table.

Garrett got up from the table to pour them coffee, and Kevin leaned forward with his elbows on the table and looked at me, all serious and helpful.

"If it's something you want help finding, I'm sure it's not stupid," he said.

"Maybe." I picked the hangnail harder. "So I drew this picture of my dad a few months ago? Like back in February, you know, before. Anyway I gave it to him and when my mom got all his stuff back, you know, from the station, she didn't get the picture. So I don't know what happened to it. I'm afraid it just got thrown away."

Garrett came back with the coffee, and Andrew, who'd finished eating, put his bowl in the sink and sat back down.

"Yeah," said Andrew. He talked too loud. "Can you find that drawing for Brian? It was a really good one. It really cracked my dad up. Maybe someone else took it because it was so good."

I wished he'd stayed quiet, and I glared at him.

Kevin sat back and crossed his arms. He was wearing a baseball cap and pulled the bill down. "Sure." Now he was quiet. "You want to go down there? Why don't we drive to the station right now?" He stood up and patted Garrett's back, then pulled at the hat's bill again and pulled up on the waistband of his pants. I waited for him to arrange something else on himself. He pushed up his sleeves. "The professor needs a break from the manual labor."

"Yeah." Garrett laughed. "I can see you're in a huge hurry to get back to work yourself."

Kevin shook his head, slow, at Garrett and when Garrett saw the serious look on Kevin's face, he stopped laughing.

We left my mom a note and the four of us got into Kevin's truck. We hadn't been to the station since December, before Christmas, when the gas grill was covered up and the basketball hoop looked cold and lonely. We used to visit my dad at the firehouse all the time when we were little, before we were in school, and my mom would take him a vase with flowers for his room, and she said the same thing every time she brought them: *Bringing you some garden.*

"I still want to help on the room," Andrew said. "Can we?"

"I'm going to hold you to it," said Kevin. "How about tomorrow?"

Andrew

"Your dad has a banner." Kevin pointed at the ceiling when we walked into the bay where the truck and engine were parked. The station hung banners from the ceiling for retired firefighters. They had their last names on them—just like the numbers of retired athletes that hung from their home stadiums—and now there was one that said *McGeary*.

All the men working approached us like a troop and shook our hands.

"It's been a while since the boys have visited," Kevin said to them. He started walking away from the other firefighters and motioned for me, Garrett, and Brian to follow him. "Let's go into the kitchen."

I was surprised the first time I'd seen the kitchen, which looked just like any plain one you'd find in any apartment building where someone's grandmother lived, except it was a lot bigger. It was one half of an open space, and the other half was like a living room, with recliners and a big-screen TV. There was nothing special about either space, just a lot of white walls, and the rooms always felt cold, even in the summer. Nothing like the illustrations I'd seen in books when I was a kid about firefighters and the stations where they worked. Kevin had told us the firehouses in New York were different, in historic buildings, and back there the beds were all in one place like a barracks, not like the bunkroom at Twenty-Five, where each guy had his own room with a door and only shared it with the other two guys who worked on the two other shifts.

I had no idea why we were going into the kitchen, and I didn't think Brian or Garrett did either, but since Kevin seemed to have something in mind, we followed him without asking. Two firefighters had gotten coffee and passed us carrying their mugs as we came in. Kevin walked over and stood by one of the long counters that divided the two spaces. He adjusted the hat on his head again. He turned and pointed toward the wall before he crossed his arms and looked down. "No one threw it away, Brian," he said.

It was hanging between the kitchen room and the living room spaces in a big green frame. The picture of my dad and the blow-dryer and our old freezer. Around it was a white mat with all kinds of writing on it. I walked closer to it so I could read the words. *I love you, Leo. Love you, my brother. See you on the Top Floor. You're with us every day. Keep us safe, Lion, just like always.*

No one was saying anything, and finally Brian walked up next to me to get a better look too. His whole body trembled, and I could tell he was crying even though he wasn't making any noise. I was afraid he was going to punch me or push me away, but I moved closer to him anyway and reached up and put my arm around his shoulder, and he let me.

Kevin walked away from the counter and stood behind us. "Brian," he said. "We should have given it back to you. I'm so sorry we didn't. It wasn't ours to keep. I'm sorry you've been worrying about it. It's my fault." His voice was husky. "It's such a great picture of your dad. We wanted it here with us so we could see it every day. But we had no right."

Brian managed to nod his head even though his body was still shaking.

Kevin walked around us and took the framed drawing off the wall. "You take it home with you today. It's yours. It doesn't belong to us."

"You keep it." Brian pushed out the words before he slipped out from under my arm and crushed himself against Kevin and sobbed.

Garrett

After Kevin and I had spent the day blowing in the insulation, we went to Kells. Kevin sat at his regular stool, and I sat on his other side, not on Leo's.

We were two beers in when I told him. I had to.

"So something's been happening with Audrey and me," I said. "Like we talked about a while back. It started and it's still going."

"I saw that coming." He wasn't surprised and I listened for judgment, but there wasn't any. He looked at me. "Didn't you?"

"No," I said. "I didn't. But now, now I can't imagine it not happening."

"You're consenting adults," he said. "Nobody else's business. Do the boys know?"

"I don't think so," I said.

"You'd know," he said.

I drained my glass and waved to the bartender. I felt compelled to explain.

"There's something else," I said. "Something nobody else knows."

"Something else?" he said. "What'd you do, propose?"

"Shut up," I said. "Listen."

He leaned back and raised his hands in surrender.

"A long time ago, it was Y2K, I was here for a visit," I said. "Leo and I got drunk and he told me he wanted me to marry her if he died. It was stupid. He made me sign this paper he wrote up. It was a joke. I still have the fucking thing."

"Man, that guy," Kevin said.

"Yeah, well, it stopped being a joke," I said. "He shouldn't be dead."

We both sat there and sipped our beers.

"So you could say he gave you a kind of a permission slip," he said. "A green light, if you will."

I shrugged.

"Does she know about the paper?" asked Kevin. "You think that's why you're in your present situation?"

I shrugged again. "I don't know. I don't think so. I think if she did, it would have come up. And I think if she found out now, she'd be pissed."

"Yeah," he said. "I could see that. No question."

We were quiet.

"You happy?" he said.

"I guess," I said. "As much as I can be given the circumstances."

"She happy?" he said.

"I don't know," I said. "Sometimes she seems happier. Sometimes just less unhappy."

"So be happy," he said. "Life's too short. Nobody's ever happy enough when they can be. You'll be unhappy again soon enough."

"Right," I said.

"Well, I appreciate you opening up to me," he said, laughing. "I think we're growing closer." His hand clutched my shoulder in mock comfort. "But I don't think you're any less burdened, my friend."

He was right.

"Don't sweat it—play the hand you've been dealt. You're being a gentleman?"

"Of course," I said.

"You can't mess around here," he said. "Audrey's not someone you can have a fling with. I know I don't have to tell you that."

"You're right, you don't have to tell me that," I said, annoyed. "It's not a fling, not for me."

"Good, good, sorry, just checking." he said. "You're all right." He squeezed my shoulder again before he took his hand away. "But, Jesus, couldn't he have picked someone who was good-looking at least?"

Audrey

S ome days were better than others. The sex with Garrett brought comfort and guilt in equal measure, the way I imagined drinking did for a drunk. The very thing that eased the shame was what caused it in the first place. It was as infinite a cycle as the snake swallowing its own tail. I felt like I had put Leo's death in a room and closed the door in order to do what I was doing with Garrett. But the room was always there to enter when I wanted to, and when I did and let myself miss him, and agonized over what I was doing, I wondered which kind of death was easier for survivors to heal from. The shocking loss of Leo in an instant, someone still so beautiful and strong and solid one minute and gone the next, dying alone, sent out of his life without anyone there to say goodbye? Or the prolonged dying some people endured, lingering and disappearing bit by bit, devastating the loved ones gathered around while they waited and hoped for the end to come as much as they wanted it not to, saying goodbye until they had no more goodbyes to say?

And what about those tragically drawn-out deaths—when someone lingered for far too long, for years—and the still-married spouse, suspended in a purgatory between the life and death of their beloved, began a companionship, a conflicted romance with someone else, and nobody blamed them? Of course, there were people who blamed them—needing something to blame—but it usually wasn't at all about the romance, but about their own reluctance to move on, their refusal to give up hope despite the undeniable evidence.

I kept it from Erin. I had never lied to her, so it was a demanding task. To make it easier on myself, I eliminated or reduced the opportunities where it could come up in conversation and I'd be forced to lie to her. I told her I'd tweaked my knee and that until it was better I'd rather go to yoga than run. During yoga, we couldn't talk, and I often met her at the studio instead of driving together. After class, if she had time, I invited her back to the house to visit. We couldn't talk about Garrett with him right there. When she got the chance, she'd give me a look or ask on the fly, "You okay? Are things okay?" I'd look her right in the eye and keep my gaze even: "I'm good. Everything's good." I remembered a time when those words were the truth, and tried to sound convincing. I was pretty sure it worked when I could see the relief on her face and she said, "Okay," and nodded, seeming satisfied. Aware of my own bald-faced dishonesty, I also considered that Erin could be letting me lie to her. I waited for her to push me beyond what I told her, and she never did.

And some nights were better than others. The nights that were bad made the following days bad, because of my dreams. There were two recurring versions, and they kept me away from Garrett until the sobering memories wore off enough that I could be with him again.

In the one dream, Leo and I are in bed, making love, and I can feel his lip between mine, and the weight of his body between my legs. In any number of ways, Garrett appears—walks through the doorway, sits in the chair in the corner, or, the worst, lies in the bed next to us—and after he sees what we're doing, leaves the room. I only get a brief look at his face, expecting but not seeing any emotion. The only thing on dream-Garrett's face is resignation and acceptance, the

way someone might look leaving a restaurant in search of another after learning their first choice has no available tables.

In the other, I'm married to Leo but Garrett and I are together,
very innocently; we never have sex. But I'm planning on it and we
both know it's going to happen. Because in this dream, although Leo
is alive and we're married, I've given myself permission to cheat on
him, but only with Garrett. That's my defense in the dream, although
it never comes up between Leo and me. I've allowed myself to sleep
with Garrett, because it's Garrett.

I still had an IUD, so when Garrett brought up that awkward
but necessary matter, I told him it was taken care of on my end, but
asked—I had to, given all his women—if I had anything to worry
about with him, risk-wise, and he'd assured me I didn't. Despite our
discussions and my wanting him to after our family was complete, Leo
had refused to get a vasectomy, to *get cut,* as he'd called it, like a bull
or a stallion. *I'm afraid,* he'd told me*, that it wouldn't be the same. That
I wouldn't be.* Nothing I could say would convince him, and while I
knew his reluctance was based on fear, it still felt selfish to me. He
hadn't been perfect.

So while I lied to Erin, and suffered the dreams and their after-
maths, I made an appointment to talk to Father John. He had said
Leo's funeral mass and called me in the weeks afterward. I thought
about going to confession, but he would know it was me anyway,
which was okay, but as much as I felt like I wanted to confess and be
absolved—before repeating the same sin and getting absolved for it
again the following week—I wanted to have a different conversation
than what the confessional offered. Although he wasn't a stranger,
talking to him seemed far easier than talking to my best friend. A little
distance for something like this wasn't a bad thing. We met in his office one morning after I'd walked the boys to school.

"I'm glad you called me," he said. "You seem well."

"Thank you, Father, I do," I said. "I know, seem well."

Father John smiled. "What you're in the middle of takes a long time," he said. "And while it will never fully end, you won't always be in the middle of it."

I nodded.

"First, let's pray," he said. We blessed ourselves and said the Hail Mary and Father said a prayer for Leo. Too late, I realized neither this meeting nor confession was going to offer the solace I'd hoped for.

"I've been keeping an eye on Brian and Andrew," he said. "How is Christopher?"

"I'm proud of all of them," I said. "They all have their moments, but I think they're doing the best they can."

He nodded. "And you? What you must do is continue to move forward every day, the best you can, especially through the days that test you the most. Putting your faith in God is what makes that possible, and over time, easier."

"I've been doing that," I said, and I had to an extent, but I had to intervene before he offered more theology than I could handle.

"Father, I thought about going to confession," I said. "My wanting to talk to you has to do with something I didn't expect. I think you'll find it unexpected as well."

Father John was a smart man, in addition to being a better priest than the ones I'd known growing up. He'd been an army chaplain and had lived around the world during his time in the service. He modeled a progressive parish; there were at least five same-sex couples I saw regularly at mass. I wanted to talk with the smart, worldly man who happened to be a priest, not the man whose job it was to spread the word of God.

"I'm here to help," he said. "Do you want to make your confession? We can do it here."

"No," I said. "I don't. I'm hoping we can just talk. There's something I'm having trouble with, something I feel guilty about."

"It's your call, Audrey," he said. "What's happening?"

"Leo and I have a very good friend, Garrett," I said. "He's been Leo's friend since they were Christopher's age. He's been here since February and he's been a great help. Maybe you remember him from the funeral. He's finishing the work on the house that Leo was doing, and he's been wonderful with the boys. He's really a very good friend. I've known him for a long time. But recently, our relationship has developed into something new, something intimate, and I'm feeling very bad about it. I know the church's position on what we're doing, so I'm sorry I'm in violation of that. But it's really about Leo that I feel the worst."

I didn't want a lecture, but if a lecture was what I was going to get, I had it coming. That certainly would have been a place for Father to start: *intimate, not married, let's talk about that.* But there was nothing in the Commandments or the Bible that I knew of that addressed my particular problem.

"Guilt is such a useless emotion," Father John said. "If you told me what you're feeling guilty about in confession and I absolved you, would it make a difference?"

"No, I don't think it would," I said.

"I'm not here to tell you what's right and wrong and what you can and can't do," he said. "I think the only time guilt serves us at all is if it helps us go to great lengths not to repeat something we truly regret."

"That's my conflict," I said. "My relationship with Garrett feels like something good, but it's too soon for it to be happening—plus I never would have expected our friendship to go in this direction. I feel guilty but I'm continuing it anyway."

"If you could name the exact reason for feeling guilty, what would it be?" he said.

"I'm betraying Leo," I said. "How can I not feel like I'm betraying Leo?"

"Did you and Leo promise each other that if either of you died, you'd never remarry or love anyone else?" he said.

"No, no we didn't," I said. "But it never came up."

"Was any of this with Garrett happening before Leo died?" Father John said.

"No, of course not, no," I said. "And Garrett's not married. He's never been married."

"That would be very different," he said.

"But it's too soon," I said again. "Garrett was his best friend. The irony, of course, is that I wish I could talk to Leo about it. And I have. I pray and apologize to him."

"*Too soon. Too long.* We all feel that way at some point, don't we? More than we'd like to admit," Father said. "You know, we're on God's time line; He's not on ours. What comes to us sometimes, maybe even the answer to our prayers, often appears in ways and at times we wouldn't consider ideal."

"I understand that," I said. "I know. But knowing that doesn't make me feel any less conflicted."

"Is your relationship with Garrett helping you live your most authentic life?" he said.

I didn't know how to answer that. I was keeping it from the boys and from Erin; that wasn't authentic. "Father, nothing feels authentic since Leo died," I said. "What I would call authentic no longer exists." Father John's question gave me pause.

"Is this relationship with Garrett making you happy, holy, and healthy?" he said. "I'm not keeping a list—these are just things for you to think about. Not even criteria, but steps toward self-examination. It's more productive than guilt."

The last thing Garrett made me feel was holy, but Leo hadn't either, and I didn't know if I'd ever felt *holy*. When the boys were born, those three times I had felt a sense of what was close to holiness, but it had existed outside of me.

"That's a tough one, Father. I'm sorry, I'm not trying to be a hard sell," I said. "I think I am closer to happy and healthy than

I would be without Garrett, but still those things feel a very long way off."

Father John nodded, like I was starting to give the right answers. "Love is a gift," he said. "The love that you're having now doesn't eradicate the years of love with Leo. All God asks is that we're good to each other, and that we love each other."

Love. I hadn't said anything about love. Of course I loved Garrett, but there was love and there was *love.*

"Audrey, in my opinion you're not betraying Leo, and you're not betraying his memory either," Father John said. "But it doesn't matter what I think or what anyone else thinks or says. God forgives us no matter what, but it's much harder for us to forgive ourselves."

I nodded.

"You know, there's a Kahlil Gibran quote that I think is very popular," he said. "It's from *The Prophet.* Do you know it, about joy and sorrow being inseparable?"

"I do, yes," I said. "It's really lovely."

"It is," he said. He got up and walked to his desk and took a frame off the wall. "But I think the piece is best in its entirety." He handed me the frame, in which the poem was preserved.

Then a woman said, "Speak to us of Joy and Sorrow."
And he answered:
"Your joy is your sorrow unmasked.
And the selfsame well from which your laughter rises was oftentimes
filled with your tears.
And how else can it be?
The deeper that sorrow carves into your being, the more joy you can
contain.
Is not the cup that holds your wine the very cup that was burned in
the potter's oven?

And is not the lute that soothes your spirit, the very wood that was
hollowed with knives?
When you are joyous, look deep into your heart and you shall find it
is only that which has given you sorrow that is giving you joy.
When you are sorrowful look again in your heart, and you shall see
that in truth you are weeping for that which has been your delight.
Some of you say, 'Joy is greater than sorrow,' and others say, 'Nay, sor-
row is the greater.'
But I say unto you, they are inseparable.
Together they come, and when one sits alone with you at your board,
remember that the other is asleep upon your bed.
Verily you are suspended like scales between your sorrow and your
joy.
Only when you are empty are you at standstill and balanced.
When the treasure-keeper lifts you to weigh his gold and his silver,
needs must your joy or your sorrow rise or fall.

I reached for the box of tissues on the table. "I've never seen the whole poem," I said. "You're right. It's far better."

"How long have you and Garrett known each other?" he asked.

"Since before Leo and I got married, more than twenty years," I said. "We met because Leo and I were together."

"Could you imagine having married anyone other than Leo?" Father said.

"No, of course not, no one," I said.

"And you wouldn't know Garrett without having married Leo?" Father John said.

"No, I don't think I would," I said.

Father John sat and waited. Maybe we would both just sit there until some shift took place inside of me.

"That's not all," I said. "I feel like I'm deceiving the boys. But they wouldn't understand."

"I think there's a difference between deception and privacy, when it comes to parents and their children," said Father John. "That's obviously something for you to think about, your honesty with the boys. But you and Garrett are consenting adults. But keep in mind, if they knew, what would you tell them?"

"I really don't know," I said. "I don't have any idea."

"You don't have to know today," he said. "But it's something to think about."

"Yes," I said. "Of course it is."

"Please, Audrey, you keep that for a while." He pointed to the frame I was still holding. "When I need it back, I'll know where to find it. And I know you know this, but you can come talk to me anytime."

I lay the frame on my lap, and we said the Our Father before I left. When I got to my car, I sat in the parking lot and read the poem over and over, so many times I lost count. After I got home, I put it in my closet next to Leo's boots. Like Father, I'd know where to find it.

Brian

When I got home from school, Garrett and Kevin were putting in the floor. I pulled back the plastic hanging in the kitchen doorway to check it out, and Kevin saw me and stood up.

"Hey, Brian," he said, "I brought you something. It's in the car. Be right back."

When he returned, he handed me a frame with my drawing of my dad. It didn't have the mat with the signatures around it.

"We made a copy and hung that up," he said. "It looks just as good. We wanted you to have yours back. It's not mounted, so you can take it out if you want."

"Thanks," I said. I didn't know why, even after finding out what had happened to the drawing and deciding it could stay at the station, it still made me so miserable. Just sad, really. It was just a drawing. You wouldn't think a drawing could mess you up like that. Especially one that you'd drawn yourself.

"Come to the station again when you can," said Kevin. "You won't even be able to tell the difference I bet. I'm glad we have it. It's what we should have done in the first place. We just weren't thinking straight."

"Sure, okay, thanks," I said.

I took the frame up to my room and took the drawing out. I rolled it up and put a rubber band around it, loose. I put it on the high shelf in my closet. I'd deal with it later. At least now I not only knew where it was, but had it back. I changed my clothes to go running.

It was my mom's idea. My terrible dreams hadn't been bad for a while, not for at least a month. My mom thought playing basketball had helped and said maybe running would too, so I started going with her. It was easy. She went slower than I wanted to but she said running slower meant you could go for longer without getting winded. So I ran slow like she did and we'd go like three miles in a half hour. Sometimes I went by myself and went faster, and she was right, I couldn't go as far. I still did it, but I didn't feel great. I felt like falling over flat and dying on the sidewalk. My mom wasn't always right, just most of the time.

She stuck her head in my room. "Are you ready to go?"

"Yeah," I said.

"You're not wiped out from school?" she said.

"Nah," I said. "I'm fine. I'll be right down. Anything in the mail today?"

"Not today," she said. "I'm looking too."

Every day I was checking the mail. I had registered for the summer pre-college program at Portland Northwest College of Art, where I'd taken some classes when I was a little kid, and I hoped I'd get accepted even though I wouldn't be in high school until next year. I wanted to learn more stuff than they taught at my school.

She was stretching on the porch. I never stretched beforehand, but she always made me afterward. "What do you say we go four today?" she said. "If you can stand to crawl along with me."

"Yeah," I said. "Four's no problem."

Garrett

I'd been sleeping with Audrey for almost a month. *We'd* been sleeping together for almost a month. The boys didn't know, I was certain. And every time seemed like the first time, in the best possible way. We were tentative at first, like there was still time to stop, then we got to a point where there was no turning back, and neither of us wanted to. Three rare nights, I stayed and slept with her until four-thirty, when the alarm on my phone went off. I listened for the all quiet before I left her bed and crept back downstairs to the guest room, where I lay still but never resumed sleeping. She spent one night with me in the guest room.

Sometimes she talked in her sleep and it was mostly gibberish, but one night she was very articulate. *Sorry, I said I'm sorry*. It was only two o'clock, but I got up and went downstairs, turned off my phone, and went back to sleep. And the nights Brian woke up screaming and Audrey ran into his room, I went downstairs for the rest of those nights too, no matter what time it was after I helped Audrey with him, if she needed it.

Each time was different, but I started the same way—it's what I couldn't help. The first thing I always kissed, after her mouth, after I traced it with my finger, was her clavicle—such a pretty word, so much more so than *collarbone*—and it was one of my favorite parts of her. Even before we went to bed the first time, I found myself again and again looking at her clavicle, bypassing her neck, whenever I got the chance to gaze without gawking. I couldn't help but think how many other men in the world noticed it and looked as long as they could too, and I wondered if it had been one of Leo's favorite parts of his wife.

We were covert, like two people having an affair, and the secrecy fueled our momentum. Playing house around everyone else, we were like coworkers or roommates, doing what life needed us to get done, side by side. There were a handful of days when the boys were at school when we were in bed more than we were out of it. Afterward, I napped, she slept curled behind me, and we showered and got back into bed. The sex was like drinking or getting high, a fleeting and artificial respite from the sadness and disorientation we were all trying to manage. But what we stole when we were alone clung to me in the best way, and made me work better, with more care and investment.

Despite all those chances I had—in bed and out of it, out to lunch and in the house, both of us working, so many opportunities—I rejected each one. I didn't know how to tell her what Leo had made me promise. If she could have read my mind, she would have known. Every day she would have seen the truth, in front of and dominating every other thought I had. It wasn't a blind decision and I felt justified: too much time had passed and too much had happened between us for me to share it now: *Oh, by the way.* Like an apology for which the time and need expire and after which expressing contrition can cause more harm than good. And although I didn't know how Audrey was doing what she was doing with me, she was doing it nonetheless, either purely of her own accord, or maybe Leo had asked her for her own agreement. Regardless, what was happening was, in the most fragile way, a kind of prelude to what he had asked of me, and I thought the less we said about it, the better. Audrey and I never talked about what we were doing—we just did it, as if we'd silently agreed to continue, without comment, what we'd started. The deeper I got, the more I resolved to keep my mouth shut.

One day when I was working alone, she came into the room and without saying a thing, stood in front of me, laced her fingers behind my neck, and pulled me toward her as she backed up against one of the addition walls. I pushed her skirt up, pulled her panties down, and dropped everything I was wearing from the waist down.

"I think it's a matter of responsibility," I whispered into her ear as we crushed against a wall that months before hadn't existed. "To see how much these walls can take."

In the middle of it all she whispered, "They can take more." And it was true; the walls took an awful lot that day.

Another: When she was at the sink one afternoon, I walked up behind her and gave her ass a light tap, then rested my palm against its curve before I slid the fabric of her sundress up then tucked my hand inside her lace waistband and against her skin. I kissed the base of her neck until she started reaching back for me, and that's how we stayed, start to finish, with her looking out the window over the sink and my face in her hair the whole time. She never even turned around until we were done, and we kissed then, until our mouths were raw, then both went back to work. The boys were home from school an hour later.

And more. I came back from Lowe's one morning and as soon as I closed the front door behind me, she texted, *Upstairs*.

I took the steps two at a time. Audrey was lying on her back on her bed, fully clothed except for panties, and her skirt was pushed up and wrinkled over her hips.

"Where have you been?" She had a wicked little look on her face. "I got started but I've been waiting for you to finish."

Only a fool would have done anything to ruin it.

It wasn't always like that. Sometimes while the boys were at school we danced in the kitchen or the living room or in the new room, to whatever I was listening to. It was very innocent—for whatever reason, dancing was never a prelude to sex for us—but still we never danced together in front of the boys. I'd wrap her up and we'd move and sway like a couple of kids. Sometimes she was happy and smiled and gazed at me like a girl, but sometimes she rested her head on my shoulder and when we separated there would be a wet spot on my shirt and she'd creep away without looking at me. I'd go back to work, but I brushed my fingers along my shoulder, fingering the spot until it dried.

We didn't—couldn't—have dates, nighttime ones, anyway, but we had a lot of nice lunches out. We never touched in public but Audrey would have two glasses of Pinot gris and I'd have a few beers, and those afternoons felt like courting—with all its chemistry and tension—that would lead a couple to do what we'd already done before we'd left the house. Occasionally we saw people we knew, or Audrey knew, when we were out for those lunches, just as we'd seen that classmate of Christopher's and her mother when we went out that first time. That was a far cry from where we were now. But neither of us ever did anything affectionate while we were out—there was nothing questionable between us for anyone to consider or interpret.

The boys had gotten cards on their own for Mother's Day, but they asked me to take them to the nursery the day before, which I did, and the neighbors let us hide her gift in their yard.

"We're buying her a eucalyptus," Andrew said. "She loves how they smell. And she loves the leaves."

I'd gotten Audrey my own card and I'd written inside, *You're the best mom I know,* and signed only my name.

The next morning I went next door and got the pot and brought it into the backyard. The boys blindfolded Audrey with one of her own bandannas. I didn't have any part in that.

"Come on, Mom," Andrew said, and took one of her arms. Brian took the other and she reached up with her hands to grasp theirs. Chris had his hands on her shoulders and, with care, they all steered her down the stairs, through the addition, and outside. I watched the four of them.

They walked her right up to the small tree and she giggled the whole time.

"Reach out," Andrew said.

Audrey pawed the air, blind.

"No, here," said Andrew. He helped her hand find a leaf.

"Rub it," Brian said. Her right index finger and thumb worked the leaf.

"Now smell!" Andrew cheered.

She lifted her hand to her face and inhaled and pushed back the bandanna and blinked at the tree.

"Oh, you guys," she said. "It's so beautiful, thank you." She caressed some of the leaves with her open palm. "This is perfect. How did you know?"

"We just did," said Andrew, the proud ambassador.

She hugged him then, and Brian and Chris too, and she patted and rubbed my forearm.

"Thanks so much," she said, "all of you. Thank you, Garrett."

We were so pleased with ourselves.

"Where should we put it?" she said.

And they chimed in with their suggestions.

On Father's Day, we all went back to the nursery and bought plants for Leo. The five of us worked together to scoop out dirt around the gravestone where Audrey told us to, and put the periwinkles and poppies in the holes we'd made. She had cut five eucalyptus branches from her tree and laid them at the base of the marker. We were all quiet while we followed her directions, but the day was sunny and the traffic of other visitors streamed in and out of the cemetery. I dug and filled my own holes, and at intervals watched other people visiting their own lost beloveds, passengers in the same boat. While Audrey collected the empty plastic pots and gardening tools and the boys gave the new plants one final check and poured water on them from the gallon bottles we'd brought, I took a rubbing of the five words beneath Leo's name. On a piece of paper I'd taken from the printer at the house, I rubbed *Friend* first—the last word on the list—with the fat pencil I'd found among Leo's things in the addition. I skimmed the graphite over the depressions of the letters shading the paper until the word surfaced on the page before I rendered the other four. I folded the rubbing and tucked it in my wallet. I made no effort to conceal doing it, but I didn't say anything and neither did anyone else. When we left, although none of us was happy, we all seemed satisfied to have done a good and simple thing.

I taught Christopher to drive and told him the story of the summer afternoon Leo and I had taken my mother's car before I'd gotten my license. My dad was at work and my mom was supposed to be at my grandmother's house for the afternoon with my aunt. Leo and I were driving down one of the main streets in Radnor, and at the exact moment I saw my mom and my aunt in my aunt's car driving in the opposite direction, my mom saw Leo and me in hers. Chris and I laughed, but I told him, "Don't ever pull that sneaky shit with your mom. Never take the car without asking. I paid for that for a long, long time." After enough time on the road with me, Christopher passed his test and got his license. That was a big day.

That's how it went as I got in deeper and deeper. When the warm of spring ripened into the hot of summer—bittersweet, the closer I got to finishing the work—and when, after all the time I'd spent, I started to think of the addition as mine.

Audrey

Leo had already decided to apply to the fire academy before he moved to Portland. I remember the conversation so clearly. We were lying in bed one morning and he was twirling my hair around his finger. I wanted to get up and make coffee, and he told me, *Wait. I want to tell you what I want to do, and if you don't want me to do it, now's the time to say so. Don't hold anything back, Audrey. This time I'm packing, then driving back out here. I'm going to apply to the fire department here, and, maybe not right away, but soon, this place will be my home as much as yours.* He had graduated with a degree in history less than a year earlier. *What the hell am I going to do with that?* he'd said. *Get a job as an historian? Right, because I hear that's where the money is.*

I didn't care. I didn't care what he did. All that mattered to me was that he was moving, and coming west to me, for me, for us. So he'd sent in his application and joined a gym, and although he'd saved money, he wanted to work until he heard back from the academy. Of course he did. He needed something to do, and he told me outright it didn't suit him for me to go to work every day and earn a paycheck while he didn't. Someone he'd met at his gym, Alan or Adam, or maybe nothing even close, told him he knew of a club that needed security and paid well. It wasn't until after he was hired that Leo told me he'd gotten a job at Doc's Bar & Grill on Powell. He'd only work three nights a week, he said, and it would be late, but the money would be good and he could take a book with him.

"What kind of place is it?" I'd asked him.

Without balking he'd said, "Dancers. It's a strip club."

I had just stared at him. Now I did care. His ambitions and my expectations of him and us didn't include this.

"Are you fucking kidding me? No," I'd told him. I didn't care if he'd been to strip clubs in the past. I did care about Leo and this particular strip club, now.

"Jesus, Audrey," he'd said. "I'm outside. I work the *door*."

"So you never see a thing?" I'd said.

"Are you serious?" he'd said. "It's a job. I'm not spending my *time* there. I'm not there because I'm looking for something to do."

It was the first thing we fought about, and we fought bitterly. It was a point of contention so early in our relationship, so soon after he'd relocated, that I'd quickly been jolted from my idea of us as an untouchable couple, because as soon as we were together, this became part of our reality. This was the employment solution he'd found, and after multiple versions of the same argument, I'd taken a leap of faith. In the end, I'd had nothing to worry about. He came home about a half hour after his shift—as long as it took to drive home—and never smelled or looked or acted like anything except a tired guy who'd been working the door at a bar.

He had worked there only six weeks when he was accepted to the academy and the Doc's stint was over. His departure from it was as unremarkable as if he'd left a summer job scooping ice cream to go to college. The focus was on what lay ahead, and I was crazy about him all over again. I'd never thought another person could make me so happy. We'd weathered a tiny, inconsequential storm.

* * *

So when the letter came in the mail one day in early June with a return address in Beaverton and handwriting I didn't recognize, I thought it was one of those solicitations made to look like genuine letters sent by real people. I just didn't even think about it. But when I opened it, I saw that it wasn't junk at all; the handwriting was real. I looked to the end for the signature, which said, *Yours truly, Wade Reynolds,* and as I read the letter, I learned Leo must not have only ever stayed outside when he worked at Doc's.

Dear Mrs. McGeary,

I saw Leo's obituary in the paper in February and thought of writing to you then, and sending a card, but I didn't and I'm so very sorry about that now, I can't tell you. But I thought you probably had enough on your plate, and we'd never met. But I can't tell you how sorry I was to hear about what happened. My son, Matthew, was devastated, and we both came to the funeral.

Years ago, it seems like forever now, I bartended at Doc's when Leo worked there. I knew he had just moved to Portland because he'd met you and that he was waiting to join the fire department. I was a single dad back then raising Matthew, who I was having a really rough go with. He was having a bad time at school, long story short, but anyway I told Leo about it and he offered to tutor Matt, which he did for six months, as I'm sure you remember, and I was very grateful for it.

I tried to mind my own business about it and just kind of held my breath. Matthew told me after we heard the news, after all that time, that your husband gave him his number back then and made him promise to stay in school and if he ever felt like he was getting off track to come and see him or call anytime, even after he left Doc's and started with his training, and Matt told me he did. So I had to let you know how good my son turned out, because of your husband, and I'm so proud of him. Matt graduated from Oregon State in 2000 and then spent two years in the Peace Corps. He's getting married next year.

I apologize again for not sending my condolences sooner, but I'm very grateful for how Leo helped Matthew, and since I couldn't thank you both, I wanted to thank you. I hope you and your family are doing as well as possible, and again I'm sorry for not writing earlier with my sincere condolences.

Yours truly,

Wade Reynolds

I read the letter a second time. *Are you kidding me? Really?* I thought. *Well, you're* still *full of surprises, aren't you?* Why Leo hadn't told me about tutoring the kid, I couldn't imagine—it wasn't something to keep secret. Unless it was because a friendship with Wade Reynolds would have revealed Leo wasn't in fact *always* outside? I had made a huge deal about it, and we were so young and new together. He'd left one side of the country for the other. But later, years after Doc's and once he was in the department, if Matt and Leo had stayed in touch, why hadn't he told me about it then? *Shared* it with me? He didn't share it with me. He didn't share.

What if Leo had asked too much of Matt Reynolds? Leo hadn't had a right to hold someone else's kid to that kind of commitment, although it had all turned out well and Matt's own father was happy. But what if Matt had wanted less, had been happy with less? To go to a vocational school and get a job after graduation? If he went to Leo with those plans, what did Leo say? Maybe Matt wanted those more modest, equally worthy goals, and because of Leo's expectations, the kid had graduated from college instead. I had no way of knowing, and it made me crazy—like I needed one more thing.

Leo had always asked too much of people. Andrew was only two when Leo had our family do fire drills; it seemed to make sense at the time, but had the boys really been old enough to understand what to do if we'd had a fire? Brian had been terrified but it had been nothing but a game to Andrew. He left Christopher, at nine, in charge of his brothers when he went out to the store for food for dinner one night when I was out—wasn't that too much to ask? He'd taught the boys to ski and bike and ride their skateboards early and well; at the time I thought it was about safety, but maybe it had been about achievement. After I had run three half marathons and was planning a fourth, Leo had said to me, "You've already nailed the halves—why don't you run a full?" And I'd laughed and said, "Because I don't *want* to run a full. If you think it's such a great idea, you do it." It wasn't the last time he brought it up.

After all the years we were married, with him gone, I was still uncovering the person Leo had been. If he were alive, would I still be discovering new things about the man I lived with every day, year after year? If we had both lived into our nineties, would he have *ever* told me about helping Matt Reynolds? Would Wade have written the same kind of letter of thanks to Leo if he hadn't died? If he had and if I'd gotten the mail and asked him about it, what would Leo have said? What if I'd answered the phone when Matt had called, before cell phones? How had I never? Leo had always held others to the same high standards that he held himself to, not higher ones, but what if what wasn't too high for Leo was too high for someone else? He wasn't critical, but he would push, sometimes more than a person wanted to be pushed. How often had the boys or I disappointed him and not known it? Had he just waited, bided his time, hoping we'd do better the next time?

Garrett

I had come up with a plan and had decided to share it with Audrey one day during the last month the boys were in school, the last month we were predictably alone. But only after we left the sheets in a twist and the pillows thrown on the floor. And after I held my hand gently over her mouth because the bedroom window was open, and when I'd closed the curtain I'd seen the neighbors across the street working in their front yard. And after we showered and I washed her hair and she shaved my face—the first time I'd ever let a woman do such a thing—concentrating to relax and not clench the whole time. I was going to tell her that after the addition was finished I was thinking about staying in Portland.

We went to lunch at the Rams Head on Northwest Twenty-Third, and since it was such a nice day we got a table outside, but it wasn't a quiet or secluded place to sit. It was a narrow sidewalk. And although it was a weekday, so many people walked by, the pedestrian traffic close enough to knock something off our table if they wanted to. Each time someone passed, it felt to me like they were about to pull up a chair and join us. And the bicyclist and skateboarder who streaked past, they shouldn't have been on the sidewalk in the first place.

I was annoyed, granted, but maybe it had more to do with my

nerves, what I was going to tell her. We ordered drinks and I pretended we were in the middle of an empty patio. It was sunny, and we both sat there drinking, wearing our sunglasses. It was far from a honeymoon, but it made me imagine a scene anyway, of a couple on an exotic, well-planned one. The honeymoons other people had.

Then at the same time:

Me: "I want to tell you something I've been thinking about."

Audrey: "Do you know someone named Wade Reynolds?"

She took a sip of wine, then, right away, another.

"Wade Reynolds?" I said. I looped back through a mental list: *Portland, neighbor, student, colleague, college, high school, childhood*. I drew a blank. I would have remembered a name like that. "No," I said. "Never heard of him. Who is it?"

"I got a letter in the mail yesterday," Audrey said. "Kevin was over and you guys were working. Just the strangest thing. From this guy named Wade Reynolds who Leo worked with when he first moved here, at this place called Doc's? Remember? It was a strip club—do you remember? Did he ever tell you about it?"

I did remember. I remembered Leo telling me what kind of deep shit he was in with her and how he thought about quitting as soon as he'd started because there was no way he was going to fuck things up. Not for such a thing, after having come so far to be with her. But the money was good and he didn't want to be a kept man. He'd get a job slinging coffee if he had to, he'd said, but it was what he had for the time being. He only ended up working there for about a month anyway, and left after he got into the academy.

"Yeah, I remember," I said. "Vaguely. He didn't work there that long, did he?"

"Did he ever tell you anything about Doc's?" she said. "He never mentioned Wade or anyone else who worked there?"

I pushed my glasses up on top of my head and took a long sip of my beer. "No," I said. "Not really. Only about the trouble it caused between the two of you. It bothered him and he was worried." I took my glasses off and put them on the table and leaned back. "That's it. Christ, that was a long time ago." I heard those last words linger in the air and how I'd said them, and felt regret and pleasure in equal measure.

On my right, Audrey's left, two women, each pushing a stroller — one headed in one direction, one in the other — converged next to our table and, each smiling with apology and understanding at the other — *We're all in this together* — negotiated the passing and continued on their way. Once they managed the pass, they each waved a hand behind them. *Carry on!*

Audrey had watched the exchange between the women too, in silence, and continued gazing over my shoulder after they were gone. Or so it seemed. The sun was behind me and she still had her sunglasses on. I waited. I finished my beer. I looked for our server to hail. I was getting more annoyed. Why hadn't we sat inside? Maybe we should finish our drink and leave and skip lunch.

I felt nasty and mean. As petulant as a child not getting his way. My temper expanded. This wasn't the lunch I wanted. I sat there, checking in with myself, aware of all of it, submerging in the simmer. I put my sunglasses back on.

"So, Audrey, and — ?" I said. "The letter. What's up?"

"Oh, sorry." Not two hours earlier, she had shuddered under me, her heels digging into my back, but now she seemed surprised not only that I was sitting across the table from her but also that I'd just spoken, and she looked back at me, away from where she'd been staring.

She took off her glasses, put them on the table, and brushed her hair away from her face. "It was a very strange letter to get. This man, Wade — it was a very nice letter too. Well, I'd never heard of him either, but he had written to tell me how sorry he was about Leo and to thank me, because back then Leo had tutored his son, Matthew. Matthew was having a hard time in school, and I guess for a long time after that he stayed in touch with the kid, told him to stay the course, you know, stay in school, and to let him know, to get in touch with him, with Leo, if he ever felt like he was getting off track."

I waited for more. She looked down at her wineglass and traced the stem, scowling.

"Okay," I said, irritated, bored. I didn't give a fuck about Wade Reynolds. "I don't get why it's strange, really. You've heard from a lot of people, haven't you? But I guess it is an awkward thing for the guy to do, to write to you now. Kind of disturbing too, I think, coming out of the woodwork all these months later."

She looked at me then with an expression that I'd never seen on her. But I recognized it. I'd seen it on plenty of other women's faces.

"Garrett, are you listening to me?" she said. As she talked, her words became quieter, not louder, and slower, not faster. "Sorry you're not interested in anything I'm saying. He wrote to me *now* because he wanted to tell me that his kid graduated from college and was in the Peace Corps and is getting married next year. He made it. He made it because of what Leo asked him to do, and the kid did it. Wade Reynolds wanted to thank *me*—he can't exactly thank Leo, now can he—because his son did what Leo had asked him to instead of turning out to be some loser, his father's worst nightmare, some criminal in jail or living on the street or dealing drugs or even pumping fucking gas, I guess. I don't know. The letter's not *disturbing*. What's strange is that I never heard of any of this happening. Leo never said anything to me about it. I find out now. I think that's fucked up. What's going to come in the mail next week? A picture of his other, secret family? You read about this kind of thing happening to wives, right? After some guy dies? The poor wife never had any idea." She finally stopped talking and exhaled. "I just assumed I could talk to you about it, you know, since." She waved her hand in the air above the table, toward me, back to her, and me again. "My mistake." She looked at her lap. "Never assume."

Jesus fucking Christ. Now, after all the times I'd grappled with it, tossed the idea back and forth, weighed the odds—*Now? No, wait. Yes? No*—I knew I could never tell her. It was too late. It had been for a long time, but what she'd just said underlined the fact. Although by comparison, what he'd asked of me would surely make her feel better about Wade and Matt Reynolds. Of that I was confident. It would help her forget all about them. And even without disclosing that, I was still fucking up, right this minute.

However familiar to me Audrey's expression was from all the times I'd seen it on the faces of other women I'd alienated and angered, their looks had never alarmed me the way hers did now. I'd never felt compelled to do whatever it would take to eradicate that look of utter disappointment and disgust overlaid with disbelief. But now I wished I had some experience with undoing the damage, had spent some time practicing such a thing. When I finally needed to do it, pull out that work ethic—now—I felt as skilled as a nine-year-old mistakenly recruited to drive the getaway car who pleaded for help at the crucial moment, *Which pedal?*

The sidewalk wasn't really wide enough, but fuck it, the fucking sidewalk, I stood up and picked up my chair and put it on the other side of the table, next to Audrey's. People could go around, walk single file, whatever they had to. The next set of opposing strollers could cross the street. And I didn't care who saw us, either. I was consoling a friend.

I didn't put my arm around her, but I set my hand on the back of her chair and leaned in, blocking out the street and whatever else was behind me. This trouble had happened to her yesterday and she'd put it aside in some holding place, a little box, and carried on, finished the day, had sex with me this morning, and now she'd brought the problem out into the light again and I'd made her regret it.

"No, Audrey, I'm sorry," I said. "You're right—it is a big deal. What a weird shock. I'm sorry I didn't know about it yesterday. You could have told me, you know. I just, you know." I knocked a knuckle against my forehead. "I didn't understand at first, I didn't get it. I wasn't really paying attention and I should have been. I was thinking about something else and I really am sorry. Maybe the guy's some kind of crackpot anyway."

She moved and turned her chair to face me better, which made me have to take my hand off its back and stretch my arm so now I could rest my hand on the metal arm.

"No, he's legit," she said. "I can tell." Her anger was cooling but she was still brooding, and my one thought about Leo was not kind. Despite what was happening between Audrey and me, I'd have had him back here alive in an instant if I could have, and I would have walked away and gone back home, but this ghost that was lingering, this ghost and the mess that he'd left, I could do without. *You're still here. Either be here or don't.*

"Okay, well, that's good," I said. "You know, whatever made Leo decide not to say anything about this to you, I know he had good intentions. He wanted to help this guy's kid, right, sure he did, and I know the trouble him having that job caused with you, even if it wasn't for very long. It was just the beginning, right? You guys were just starting out. There was no way he was going to do something to ruin it. And he couldn't decide not to help the kid if he thought he should. Right? Am I right? And, Audrey, there's no secret family, for God's sake, trust me. I know that. That's crazy talk, so stop."

She looked at me and smiled, a tiny one. "I know—what's the point of being mad now? Really, the letter was very nice. Just unexpected. I hate surprises, and it just brings up more—it brings up things for me to think about that I didn't know I'd have to." She pressed her fingers into the corners of her eyes. "And you think you know a person. You think you know the person you're married to for as long as we were."

Fuck, I should get on a plane and go home. Today. "Audrey, I loved him and I miss him and I'd do anything to have him back," I said. "So I don't want this to come out the wrong way."

Looking at me, she waited for something much more significant than what I was about to offer.

"We're idiots," I said. "Men are dumb. I don't have to tell you that."

Then she smiled more but looked down at her lap. "I know," she said. "I know you are. But I love you anyway."

I knew what she meant, but I hustled to field her slip anyway. Taken out of context, it was a string of words that she surely hadn't intended to say.

So I laughed, to divert and to relieve and to hide. "We try to make up for it by doing things that are helpful. We have to, so you'll keep us around. All the lifting, the hauling, the hammering, repairing, et cetera. We try to be funny and make you laugh." I took my arm off her chair. I thought about when I'd left the bar because of how my student had waved at me from her table. "We try to stay relevant in other ways to make up for who we are. It might not seem like it, but we're aware of our shortcomings." I looked around for our server again. I picked up my chair and put it back on the other side of the table and sat down. "Where the fuck *is* our guy, anyway?"

"Thanks," she said. "And I'm sorry I went off."

"No, I'm sorry, really," I said. "Do you want another drink? Should we order?" A new kind of lunch had appeared in our series of otherwise carefree dates—the ones when we'd been giddy and absorbed with each other, thinking no one around us could tell.

"Sure," she said. "That sounds good."

"Okay, I'm ready too."

"What were you thinking about?" she said.

"Huh?" I had turned around and was still looking for the server. Where *was* the fucking waiter? Maybe he'd show if I went behind the bar and helped myself.

"When I was talking, you said you were thinking about something else. What was it? Is the work going okay?"

"Oh, yeah, sure, and you know Kevin's been such a great help with all of it," I said.

"So, what was it then?" She was again the woman I'd been in bed with before reality had reared up, sat down between us, and given me a reminder slap on its way out—*Don't forget about me.*

"Now I'm going to seem like even more of a shithead," I said. "Really, because you were upset and I wasn't listening. I'm embarrassed to mention it."

"But I'm asking," she said. "I'm done talking about the letter. Thank you for what you said, and now I want to know what you were thinking about."

"Okay," I said. "Okay. You know, I really like it out here and I don't miss Boston. I haven't even thought about it. So I was thinking I might move out here, like in the next year or two. Or maybe check out Seattle. I've heard good things about Bellingham, too." I was rambling and I couldn't stop. I'd started and now I couldn't do anything except keep going. It was out there and I couldn't reel it back in, but what I could do was talk camouflage around it, dilute the thing. "You know, Audrey I've lived a lot of places but I've never owned my own house." I tapped my forehead. "Once again, not very smart. I know the real estate market is shit—I mean, it is everywhere—but there are a lot of neighborhoods here in town, right, that have properties I'd be smart to buy. That I could afford. In one of the neighborhoods they're bringing back, places where gentrification is happening. It's kind of a dirty word, I know, but I see the good side, improving parts of the city that need it—no one wants to dislocate people. There's no way I can buy a place in Boston. And it's not like I have a lot of overhead, so I could teach high school again and if a place needs some work, who can do the work?" I pointed my thumb at my chest. "I can do the work." I sat back in my chair, smug, and crossed my arms. "I always think about trying out a new place, the next place, after I've been in one for a while. Portland's worth thinking about. I could do a lot worse."

She was starting to say something, after I'd finally shut up, when our waiter came back.

"Sorry, disaster with someone not showing up for their shift," he said. "I know how long you've been waiting, and I'm so sorry. If you're ready to order, great, and the next drink is on the house."

He took our orders and left. "I like this place," I said. "Doing what they need to to make things right. Let's come back here."

She sat back and looked down at her lap. "Well, I can see why you weren't paying attention," she said. "That's a lot to think about, all those real estate considerations you've been mulling over. I had no idea. I'm going to use the restroom." She stood up, and as she walked past me toward the door, she stopped and put her hand on my shoulder, and I felt her thumb on my neck. "It would be nice to have you a lot closer than Boston. Even if you end up choosing Bellingham."

Christopher

I woke up at four that morning in a panic. I'd put a load of my clothes, with Colleen's underwear, in the washer the night before and fell asleep before I could switch it to the dryer. I hoped my mom hadn't moved it and found the panties in there with my jeans and socks and boxers. I ran downstairs as quietly as I could. If my mom hadn't found them, I didn't want to wake up Garrett and have him ask me what I was doing.

The door to the guest room was open and I crept to the doorway and looked in. The bed was made and empty. Shit, was he already up? But the way it was still dark and quiet in the house, I could tell I was the only one downstairs. Fuck it. I ran down to the basement and put my clothes in the dryer. I took Colleen's damp underwear out. I'd put them back under the floorboard for now. I checked the front and back doors. Both of them were locked. Had Garrett already gotten up and left the house? Both cars were in the driveway. I went back to my room and hid Colleen's underwear. My mom's bedroom door was shut and everything up here was just as quiet as downstairs. I got back into bed. I was relieved about the laundry, but now I had something else to worry about. Where was Garrett? It was ten minutes after four.

I lay there in bed, waiting and listening until the real time I could get up, at least two hours from now. I watched the minutes on my clock advance to the next number. At four-thirty I heard a phone's alarm go off and get shut off, then human movement in my mom's room. I heard weight meet the floor and the shy creak of her door opening and the stealthy sound of walking toward and down the stairs. It wasn't the sound of my mom's footsteps. I'd heard her walking my whole life, and this wasn't her. I waited ten minutes, and when there was no more activity coming from her room, I got up and went downstairs too. Garrett was sitting at the kitchen table drinking coffee and reading the paper.

He looked up when I walked in, and I could tell from the look on his face that not only was he surprised to see me, but he didn't want to.

"Hey," he said. "You're up early."

"You too," I said.

"It's nice, isn't it?" he said. "To be up and alone in the house. Well, not now. Alone, I mean. But still nice." He laughed. He was nervous. "You want any of this?" He held out the paper.

"No," I said. "I'm checking my clothes in the dryer. And I have homework to finish."

"No wonder you're up," he said. "You've got a lot to do."

He was trying to banter like usual, but it was different. I don't know how long he'd been in there, but Garrett had been sleeping in my mom's room—my parents' bedroom—with my mom, with the door closed, till four-thirty in the morning, when he'd needed an alarm to wake him up. And sitting there in the kitchen drinking his coffee, trying to act regular, talking to me—me in just my boxers and a Portland Fire & Rescue T-shirt—he knew I knew. And he didn't know what to do about it.

Christopher

I
t was Thursday, so I left for school early, like normal, for Spanish Club. I hurried past my mom after she came downstairs; I told her I was picking up Joe on the way. I skipped breakfast—I couldn't eat—and I skipped Spanish Club, too. Before I left the house, I'd put Colleen's damp underwear and her picture in a plastic baggie, wrapped it in a sweatshirt, and buried it in the bottom of my backpack under my books. Blocks away from the school, I walked around the neighborhood listening to my music, loud. I wanted to talk to someone. I wanted to talk to an adult, but not my mom or Garrett. But I didn't have anyone to talk to, and what good would talking do anyway? They were having sex. I knew it.

It wasn't like my mom was cheating on my dad or sleeping with some sketchy guy; it was Garrett. That was worse. It would have been better if she was meeting some dude we didn't know for coffee or something, some single dad. At least she would tell us then—she would have to. It would be too soon for her to be dating and she would soften it, I bet, saying, *It's just coffee,* even if she knew, and we all knew, someone was interested in her now that my dad was gone. My mom was smart. Even if she liked some new stranger, she wouldn't be having sex with him, not for a long time. I wouldn't have worried if something like that had happened, but this was way different, and now I didn't want to be around either one of them.

I felt pretty sick about what I'd been thinking about Colleen Maguire. There was a trash can at a bus stop, and I pulled out the plastic bag, took out her picture and put it in my pocket, and threw the bag with the underwear in that can. It was garbage day in the neighborhood, so every house had its own can out front. Two blocks from the bus stop, I took the picture out, ripped it into tiny pieces, and tossed it in some stranger's gray can, where it mixed with the rest of the garbage that didn't matter to anyone.

Garrett

Audrey had walked to school with Brian and Andrew and after she came back, I told her what happened, as soon as she got in the house.

I was sitting on the couch waiting. "Audrey, can you sit down for a minute?" I said. "I think Chris knows."

She sat. "Knows what?" she said.

I'd had a terrible morning and I was about to ruin hers.

"About us," I said. "I'm pretty sure he knows."

"What do you mean?" she said. "That's not possible."

"This morning," I said. "You know, I got up and I came down to the kitchen and he came down a few minutes later. And I could tell. He was different. I think he'd been up for a while. I'm sure he heard me."

"Oh, shit," she said. She rubbed her eyes.

"I'll talk to him," I said.

"No," she said. "You don't know for sure. Why was he up so early, anyway? He's almost sixteen but he acts like he thinks he's thirty. He's in his own world. It could be anything."

"Audrey, I'm pretty sure," I said.

"He's my kid," she said. "I've seen him go through all kinds of phases and moods, and this could be something else I don't know anything about. Don't you remember being his age?"

"I know, he's your kid," I said. I'd already overstepped enough, but I wanted her to hear me. "And, yes, I do remember being his age. Boys Chris's age are aware of a lot more than they let on. If I've complicated things, I'm going to take care of it. Chris and I have talked a little about this kind of thing before."

She raised her eyebrows and leaned back.

"No, not *this*," I said. "Girls, his friend Meredith, that kind of stuff. Sixteen-year-old stuff." None of this was giving her any comfort, I could tell. If anything, what I'd said made things worse. "It was just a guy conversation, no big deal. I feel like I have to make up some ground. You're his mom and he would forgive you anything. I hope you know that."

"Shit," she said again.

"Will you let me talk to him?" I said. As soon as I asked, I was worried about her response. "Chris and I are good—well, we were. I respect him enough to be honest. He's too old for me not to be."

"Fine. Talk to him. And so will I," she said. "What are you going to say?"

I had no idea what I was going to say to Chris, so I didn't have an answer for her. "For starters, I'm not going to bullshit him," I said. "But that what happens between grownups who care about each other is their own business. I'm not sure where we'll go from there."

She looked back at me with an expression I wasn't happy to see. "This changes things."

There it was. "You're right," I said. "Of course it does." No other response was an option.

Christopher

On my way to homeroom, I stopped in the Spanish Club class-room and told the teacher I'd missed the meeting because I hadn't been feeling well. Joe was walking out as I walked in. "Where were you this morning?" he said.

"I didn't feel good. I almost stayed home," I said.

He backed away, not wanting to catch what he thought I had. "See you later," he said.

I was distracted all day trying to figure out what to do. At lunch I wasn't hungry and I wasn't interested in talking, so I just let every-body else.

"Shit, McGeary," said Joe. "Why didn't you stay home? You're a pathetic fucking lump."

"I didn't feel that sick," I said.

"Could've fooled me," said Joe.

After school, I waited for Meredith. Of everyone I could think of, she seemed like the only person I could talk to. If I asked her to, I knew she would keep it a secret. She would do whatever I asked be-cause she liked me so much, and I felt shitty thinking that way, but I didn't feel shitty about counting on her because of it.

I passed all the exits looking for her and found her halfway around the school, texting.

"Hey," I said.

She looked up. "Hi, Chris." Then she went back to texting.

I stood there. "Are you walking home? Can I walk you home?"

She stopped texting and put her phone away.

"That's very old-fashioned." She smiled like it was Christmas morning. "I thought I had plans, but I just got a better offer."

"Well, maybe you didn't." I already felt mean and she wasn't helping. "I need to talk to you about something. I have a problem."

She looked all worried then. "I was just kidding, sorry," she said. "I meant it as a compliment." She hurried to say what she thought would make it right since she couldn't take it back.

"Whatever," I said. "Do you want to walk or not?"

"Yeah, sure, okay," she said, like her life depended on my offer still standing. "You weren't at Spanish Club this morning. I thought you were sick."

"I thought I was too," I said, "but I wasn't."

"Oh," she said. Now that we were walking and I hadn't split, she relaxed, but not too much, and I was glad. I liked Meredith serious better than when she was trying to be all that.

"Are you okay?" she asked. "Are you in trouble?"

"No," I said. "It's nothing like that."

"Well, that's good," she said.

"You know Garrett?" I said. "My parents' friend? He was really my dad's friend."

"Yeah," she said. "He's nice, right? My mom and I saw him with your mom at the food carts once. He's working on your house?"

I stiffened. This was a bad idea. "That's not all he's doing."

"What do you mean?" she said. "What else is he doing? I thought you liked him."

"I don't know why you thought that," I said. "But I did. I did like him, but not anymore."

She got all grave and more serious. "Why not?" she said. "Chris, is he doing something illegal?"

I laughed out loud. I wished that was the problem, that he was doing something illegal.

"Why are you laughing?" She looked crushed and confused. "What the hell is going on? What's so funny?"

I stopped laughing. "No," I said, "I'm sorry. He's not doing anything illegal. You just surprised me and I thought it was funny. That would be easier. Something's going on with him and my mom. I think they're sleeping together. Or I think they did at least once."

"Oh." She stopped to think for a minute. "Why do you think that?"

"This morning I got up early and he wasn't sleeping in the guest room. Then I heard him come out of my parents' room and go downstairs. It was *four-thirty* in the morning. Then when I saw him I could tell he knew I knew. What kind of asshole does that?"

"That would be awkward," she said. "Why were you up so early anyway? That's crazy."

"That's not the point. I just was," I said. "I had work to do."

She shrugged. "I'm sure he's got to be mortified that you know, if it's true."

"He should be mortified," I said. "He should leave, he's so mortified."

"Chris," she said. "This is obviously weird and gross, whatever." She shook her head like she was trying to avoid picturing my mom and Garrett together. "And I can't imagine how you're feeling, you know, with your dad gone." She was choosing carefully what to say, I could tell. "But what's wrong about it? Your mom's smart, you know that, right? It's their business. He's not taking advantage of her or anything, is he? She's not like that."

"Well, this is a huge help," I said. "Thanks a lot. What about my dad? Jesus Christ, doesn't anyone remember my dad died? No, they obviously don't because they're too busy jumping into bed with each other. God, Meredith, that's how you'd feel if it was your mom? I don't think so. You'd be flying off the handle all over the place, never shutting up about it. Long after we're sick of listening to you. Epic drama. Come on."

"No." She could have been really mad at what a dick I was being, but she wasn't. "You don't know what I'd do. You don't have any idea, and neither do I. I hope I never find out. People do things they never planned on doing when people die, Chris. Look at the Donner party survivors. Sorry, extreme, forget it. I just think you should cut them some slack."

"Really, Meredith?" I said. "The Donner party?"

"I said sorry."

"It just isn't okay," I said.

"Well, you're not in charge of them, are you?" she said. "Whatever made you think you were in charge of anybody besides yourself?"

I wished I hadn't started any of this with Meredith. No wonder she bugged me. She was an idiot.

She stopped walking and grabbed my hand to stop me too, and then she let it go. "No one has forgotten about your dad. Especially your mom." I felt like a child getting talked to by his babysitter. I rolled my eyes. "Neither of them have forgotten him—how could they? I'm sure they're just doing the best they can even if it's something you don't like. Even if it is gross to think about them and that kind of thing." She shook her head again.

"This isn't really what I wanted to hear," I said.

"Aren't they good friends?" she said. "Aren't you glad it isn't some skanky sketcher? She'd never do that anyway."

"She has Erin," I said. I refused to have Meredith's reason sway me, at least in front of her.

"Erin's her best friend," said Meredith. "Two different things."

"Jesus," I said. I was tired. I *had* been awake forever.

She started walking again. "I'm sorry I wasn't any help." We were half a block from her house. "Even if I didn't help, I'm glad you talked to me. And I'm really sorry about it," she said. "I won't say anything. Let me know if you want to talk again, okay?"

"Yeah," I said.

"Okay," she said. "I'll see you at school." She walked fast to her house and I stood on the sidewalk, understanding I wasn't invited to follow her.

Garrett

C hris arrived home later than usual. I'd heard a story about conflict resolution on NPR—useful between coworkers, and employees and their bosses—how walking in the same direction facilitated solutions. Something about the physical motion of sharing the same simple goal of their feet moving forward lent itself to a mental agreement of the minds, or at least contributed to compromise. I had no idea if it worked with parents and children—I was no one's parent—or adults and teenagers.

Chris was in his room, and I went up and knocked on the door. I knocked again, louder, when there was no answer, and then a third time.

Chris opened the door, one earbud in, one out. "What." His expression was flat.

"How about we take a walk," I said.

"I'm not really interested," said Chris.

"Yeah, I figured," I said. "But there's something we need to talk about."

"So talk here," Chris said. He fingered the dangling earbud. "We don't need to walk."

"I need to walk," I said. "I'd consider it a favor."

Chris rolled his eyes. "Whatever," he said. "I'll be down in a minute."

"Okay," I said. "I'll wait."

After ten minutes, Chris came down. "Let's go," he said.

I followed him out to the sidewalk and we started walking.

"I have homework," said Chris.

"I know you do," I said.

We walked a block in silence while I mentally rehearsed. I wondered how many times walking in the same direction hadn't solved the conflicts people had hoped it would. How the expectation of something so basic might instead deliver crushing disappointment.

"I need to explain something," I said. "I'm just going to say it and you tell me if I'm wrong."

Chris shrugged.

"I think," I said, "on account of a feeling I got this morning, that you know about a part of my relationship with your mom that's private, and I'm sorry you're aware of it. It's not something you should have to think or worry about. It's between us."

"You mean sex," Chris said.

I rubbed my face and crossed my arms. "If it helps, you should know this makes me very uncomfortable."

"Like I'm having the time of my life." Chris glared at me. "You're an asshole," he said. "I'm going home."

"There's more to it," I said. "Keep walking with me. There's something I need you to know, and it's even more uncomfortable, as unlikely as that seems. Chris, please."

Chris rolled his eyes. "God. What."

"You're right," I said. "You're right to feel the way you do. Your mom and I have been friends for a long time. Sometimes that changes into something else."

"My dad is dead," Chris said. "You were his best friend. *Something* shouldn't change between your best friend's wife and you because he's dead. Strictly off-limits."

"I know how you feel," I said.

"No, you fucking don't know," said Chris. "You don't know anything. You think you do, but you don't know anything about me."

With his anger tapped so deep, he resembled Leo even more. He looked just like his father had when he was angry, the same unwavering carriage and attitude and rock-hard fury. *Getting your Irish on,* we used to call it. His was a rage you were protected by if you had it on your side, and God help you if you were on the wrong side of it. The resemblance was so uncanny, I wanted to stop having this terrible talk and just grab Chris in my arms and not let go.

"You're right," I said. With each step this walk was proving to be nothing but a bad idea. "Let's sit." I stopped and perched on the curb mid-block.

"I thought you wanted to walk so bad," Chris said.

"I changed my mind," I said. "I'd really like you to sit."

"Jesus," said Chris. He sat.

We both looked across the street and watched a woman unloading groceries from her car.

"When you were a baby," I said, "Brian too, I came out here for a visit. It was New Year's, Y2K. It was a long time ago. I wanted to spend that time with your parents and you guys. We had a really nice visit. Your mom was pregnant with Andrew."

"So what. Spare me your story," Chris said. He picked at the pine needles in the gutter. "You obviously haven't been acting like a guy who remembers my dad being alive. Married to my mom. Her husband."

I was getting pissed. "Why don't you let me finish." Chris reminded me of the entitled students who were ready to argue over a grade until the end of time.

Chris looked at me, wounded and insulted. "Nice tone," he said.

"I'm not the one on the hook here. Why don't you go home. We don't need you."

I ignored him. "When I was here, during that visit, on New Year's Eve, Leo and I—your dad and I—we drank a bunch, as we sometimes did when we celebrated—and you know what? I loved your dad. He was like my brother." This was not what I was planning to say; the words just came out.

Chris abandoned the pine needles in the gutter and stared at me.

I picked up a stone from the street and rubbed it. I had to get this over with. "That night, on New Year's Eve, your dad asked me to promise to marry your mom if he died. Because he was a firefighter. He got very sentimental about our friendship, and he wrote it up and he made me sign it. It was a stupid thing. We were acting your age, younger."

"Well, whatever it was, he didn't mean it," said Chris. "It *was* stupid." For a second we were on the same side. In agreement, and we weren't even walking.

"You're telling me," I said. "Your dad was like that, though. Like with the fire drills. He didn't like the unexpected. I don't know anyone who does. Although it was childish, he did it, and I signed it. And I forgot about it. That has nothing to do with your mom and me, but it's been bothering me. It's been bothering me a lot. Because it was a dumb thing and it was a joke. But he died."

"Yeah," said Chris.

"He shouldn't have," I said. "I'd give anything to have him here."

"If he was here, he would kick your ass," said Chris. "So what. He got drunk on New Year's Eve. You think my dad just told you it was okay to help yourself to his wife? Did he say that in the note? Say you had his permission to fuck my mother?"

I thought we had been making progress, but it felt like we were starting all over again.

"Chris, that's enough," I said. *Goddamn it, I've given you unlimited rope and you just hung yourself.* "I'm not talking to you anymore about your mom and me, and I don't ever want to hear you talk about her like that again. We're done. You know what you know and I'm sorry. You're pissed. Be pissed.

"They're two different things," I said. "What your dad asked me has nothing to do with what happened between your mom and me, and I'm having a lot of trouble with all of it. I just wanted to be honest with you. I thought you deserved that much from me. As pleasant as this has been for both of us. And really, it's none of your business. Sorry, but that's the fact of the matter."

"But aren't you such a player? Garrett, the legendary ladies' man." He was holding nothing back. "What did you say to me that day, that you're not a guy who's built to settle down? So you have no business. You can't treat my mom like all the hags you've brainwashed. She's nothing like them."

"You're right," I said. "She's not. This is different."

"Like you would know," he said. "Like I'm supposed to believe anything you say after that. Yeah, you're a solid bet."

We sat quietly again and I waited. I waited for it to be over for both of us.

"Do you have it?" Chris said.

"Have what?" I said.

"Do you have the paper he made you sign, or did you throw it away?"

My eyes stung. "I have it."

"Do you have it with you?" said Chris.

My admission embarrassed me and I felt as if I were the kid here, nodding to answer Chris's hard question.

"I want it," Chris said. "I want you to give it to me."

I stood up. "No, Chris. I won't. I'm not going to do that." After Leo's funeral I had tucked the paper back into a balled pair of athletic socks that I'd buried beneath everything else in the guest room's dresser drawer.

"Can I see it, at least? Jesus," said Chris. He stood too. "I've got homework."

"If it's going to make any difference," I said, "I'll show it to you when we get home." We stood up and reversed our route. *We're walking in the same direction,* I thought, *but we should have gone around the block. We're going backwards.*

"It's not your home," said Chris.

Christopher

I wished I'd gone home with Joe. Or gone anywhere else so I didn't have to talk to Garrett, but it would only have delayed the inevitable. I wasn't surprised Garrett came to me the first chance he got after the awkwardness of this morning. I wasn't sorry I'd said something to Meredith, but I hoped she would keep her mouth shut like she said she would. I still thought the advice she had given me was a far cry from how she'd feel in my situation. But I knew she could only imagine, and I hoped her imagination was as close as she ever got to what I was going through.

After Garrett said all those things I hadn't wanted to hear, I was ashamed and disgusted again about what I'd thought about Colleen Maguire, but at least her stuff was gone. I wanted Garrett to leave. We would be fine without him.

A few minutes after we got back from that terrible walk, he knocked on my door and came in and closed it behind him. He looked mad—not furious, but like he was tired of my shit. Well, I was tired of his shit too, the shit he'd done with my mom. And I wasn't even sure I believed him about the letter.

"This is it," he said. He held it out, and when I reached to take it, his fingers didn't let go. Like I was going to steal it right out from under him.

"Well, can I see it?" I said. I wanted him to let go.

"Yeah," he said, "take it."

I looked at it and it was my dad's writing after all, its sloppiness proof that he'd been drinking. What looked like Garrett's signature was just as bad.

"Did you sign this, here?" I pointed.

"Yeah, that's mine." Now he looked tired and not mad. "It was a very dark night. I could hardly see. We had a crappy flashlight."

"I doubt that," I said. "My dad never had a crappy flashlight."

"Okay," he said. "You've seen it." He held his hand out and I gave him back the paper and he left.

After dinner my mom came into my room while I was still doing homework.

"Hey." She looked uncomfortable. I knew what was coming.

"Hey, Mom," I said.

"You and Garrett talked this afternoon?" she said.

"Yeah," I said, "and I don't want to talk about it with you. I'm sorry, but I don't."

"Oh, okay." Now she looked hurt. "I just want you to know that what Garrett and I did was a mistake and I'm sorry. This is grownup stuff. I don't want you to have to deal with this kind of stuff before it's time. Especially now."

Whether it was the truth or not, she was telling me what I wanted to hear. "Mom," I said. "I really don't want to talk, really. I'm sorry. I don't mean to hurt your feelings. You can do what you want. Your business is your business, but can we please not talk about it anymore?"

"Okay," she said. "Sorry. I'm sorry."

I felt like a cat toying with a terrified mouse, and I felt bad thinking about my mom that way, I really did, but it wasn't my fault she was in this situation.

"I don't know why we need a stupid addition anyway." I was mad at everybody. "Why didn't Dad build one a long time ago when we were little kids? He waited long enough. None of us is hardly ever home anymore. We're never going to use it."

My mom still looked caught, trying to find solid footing. "You seemed pretty psyched about it when he started. It'll be a place for you to hang out with your friends like you do at other people's houses. Dad wanted that for you. He started it when he could, Chris. If he could have done it sooner, he would have." She was trying to make it up for him since he wasn't here to explain himself, but if my dad *had* been here, I wouldn't have been bitching. I just wanted Garrett to go.

"I don't know if I'd say *psyched*," I said. "Maybe Brian and Andrew were. I've never cared either way."

"Oh," she said. She had given up any fight. "Okay."

"I want to ask you something, though," I said.

"Of course, anything." Now she looked hopeful, optimistic. I was going to disappoint her.

"Don't you miss Dad?"

Her mouth got tight and small and her chin and forehead wrinkled in an ugly way. "Oh, Chris," she said. "Every minute of every day."

I didn't want her to cry and I could tell she didn't want to either, but I wasn't sorry to see how close she was, fighting hard to keep it from happening. If I'd wanted to, I could have made her cry.

"Yeah," I said. "Me too. Sorry."

She smoothed her hands over her face to wipe away her expression, and it only worked a little.

In a rush she kissed the top of my head and plucked at the neck of the Portland Fire & Rescue shirt I was wearing. "I'm washing this tomorrow," she said, her voice thick. "It needs it, and I'll have it back to you tomorrow night."

"Yeah, okay," I said. Now I really wanted her to go.

"Okay, good night," she said. "You know I love you, more than the world."

"I know," I said.

She left and I thanked God all that was over, with both of them, and I knew Garrett thought he'd taken care of business with me, nice and neat. And I knew my mom thought telling me she made a mistake solved everything too, but I didn't care. It didn't matter what they said or what they thought they'd done. I didn't want to think about them. I just didn't want to hear Garrett leaving my parents' bedroom early in the morning ever again. None of that mattered because I'd already decided that afternoon, if Garrett wasn't going to give me that paper, I was going to find it myself and take it.

Christopher

I couldn't go through his stuff right away. I had to wait until Sunday afternoon, when my mom went running and Garrett went to Home Depot. I was screwed if he kept the paper in his wallet. There was no way I'd ever get it then, but I could always put Andrew to work if I had to. He'd been such a little shit, and he could be good and sneaky, and no one would be surprised if he took Garrett's wallet, and maybe stole some money if I told him to, to cover, but he'd be forgiven fast on account of being the baby and having such a hard time lately.

I remember when Garrett got here, he only had one suitcase, so I knew he hadn't brought much stuff with him.

I closed the door of the guest room and checked the closet first. I went through the shirts on hangers and his suit. Nothing in any of the pockets—I checked twice. I checked the two pairs of shoes he had in there. I opened his suitcase and unzipped and zipped every compartment and pocket.

I felt under the mattress, on all sides, and then lay on the floor and slid under the bed and looked beneath the slats, in case it was right in the middle. I checked the pillowcases. Nothing.

There were four drawers in the dresser. In the top were boxers and socks. In the second some T-shirts, in the third three sweaters, and in the bottom three pairs of pants. I checked the pockets of the pants, which were all empty. I checked the breast pockets of the T-shirts, which were empty too, and would have been a stupid place to hide something anyway. I looked in the top drawer. It disgusted me that my mom had probably seen Garrett wearing these boxers. I pushed stuff around till I could see the wooden bottom of the drawer. Of course there was nothing there. I mashed the boxers and socks back to the way I thought they'd been before I disturbed them, and I heard a little crunch that didn't sound like fabric. I shook all the underwear and tossed them on the floor. I picked up and squeezed each pair of socks, and in the fourth pair, I heard the crunch again. I unrolled the socks and there it was, the note my dad had written and Garrett had signed. I wouldn't need Andrew after all, but Garrett was stupid for not keeping it in his wallet. I put it in my pocket and put all the boxers back in. I didn't care how they looked.

I ran up to my room and put the paper under the loose floorboard with the bottle caps, the condoms, the picture of me and my dad, the St. Christopher medal, and the card from Meredith on top.

Audrey

W e didn't belabor it, but after Garrett and I had both talked to Chris, we agreed it had gone as well as it could have and in the end, Chris hadn't wanted to talk about it any more than we'd forced him to or wanted to ourselves. As far as we could tell, Chris believed that it was a onetime thing, and he seemed so eager to brush it under the rug and move past the discomfort of it that we felt confident he wouldn't tell his brothers. I was worried about the aftermath, but while Chris wasn't as friendly as he had been toward Garrett, he wasn't as hostile as I was afraid he'd be. And with me, Chris seemed as embarrassed as I felt with him. So we all tried to continue living as we had before the awkwardness and did the best we could.

Not long after Christopher's discovery, the boys were out of school, and both realities complicated what I'd come to take for granted. I had to exercise a restraint and watchfulness with Garrett that if I'd thought about in advance I would have prepared for, but going along one day at a time as I had been, I was caught off guard.

Although I'd scheduled activities for all three of them that summer, their schedules were staggered over those months, so the boys' presences or absences were often spontaneous and unstructured, and our house—like other families'—became a revolving door for them and their friends.

We couldn't risk being caught again, so there were no more night-time trysts. Between the boys, and Kevin and Garrett working, the times for the two of us to count on being alone were scarce. A far cry from the school year.

After a few weeks of this fresh gap between Garrett and me, Erin and Mark and their kids went on vacation for two weeks and she asked me to feed their cat and water the plants. Before the first time I went over, I told Garrett that while they were away, Erin hoped he could fix the window.

"The window?" he said. "What window?"

"Right before they left," I said, "a window broke and there wasn't time to fix it. It's an upstairs window, and I told Erin I would ask you if you could take care of it."

So the first time I went over to feed the cat, Garrett came with me, and when we were both inside, he asked about the window.

"There is no broken window," I said. I tugged on his belt and pulled him through the house. "Don't say anything about it. If Brian hears, then Michael will, then Erin."

Leo and I had never had the scheduled married sex that people said they had to once their lives and families got to a point where such a thing was necessary, but for those two weeks, Erin's house was where Garrett and I had *our* scheduled sex. In the middle of that time, it felt like the most reckless thing to be doing, although in the scheme of things it certainly wasn't. And it was childish, too, sneaking around like a teenager. I had never had sex in my child-hood bed, but when we were in high school, Gabe and I had had a party while our parents were away, and my friend Lauren and her boyfriend at the time *had* had sex in my bed—and broke it in the process. Our parents never found out about the party, but I'd had to fabricate an explanation for my broken bed, by confessing to my parents that in their absence I'd gone wild by singing and dancing and jumping on it.

Erin and Mark's house was in a neighborhood where the properties weren't on top of each other, and there was an alley behind their place where I'd drop Garrett before I drove around to the front and let myself in alone, before I let him in the back door. We never stayed long and our clothes never came off completely, but neither of us was quiet. Even days when the boys weren't home, when it was *time to feed the cat and fix the window,* we got in my car and went.

"You know what this reminds me of?" he said one day afterward, when we were driving home from Erin's. His put his hand on my knee. "There was a guy I knew in high school, this guy Scott. I didn't go to school with him, he lived down the street from us, but sometimes we'd hang out and smoke pot. We called it 'walking the dog.' He'd call me and say, 'You want to come over and walk the dog?'" Garrett laughed. "We *would* walk the dog, but it was our code for getting high. We never just walked his dog."

Erin's return from vacation brought the beginning of a drought for Garrett and me, with no likely end in sight. And it hinted at the graver expiration date that was nearing. The addition was far more complete than it wasn't; Garrett had almost finished what he'd come out to do. The reality was that the job would likely be done by the end of summer, and by September, Garrett would be back in Boston, even though he was thinking about coming back, in a year or two, and I hadn't encouraged him to stay, or return sooner. I didn't know how to. With no sex, and no mention of its absence, and little discussion of the development of the new room, we went on as we had, and all we could do in the rare moments when it was completely safe was kiss.

Garrett

A t the end of July, on the morning Kevin and I started to take down the wall between the kitchen and the addition, I was the most somber I'd been since I started. It was only a wall, but removing it erased what had been the exterior of the house Leo and Audrey had bought and raised their family in. Without that barrier, the new room would be completely integrated into the rest of the house. It was a wall Leo should have been there to raze himself.

We'd turned on the radio and heard fragments of the Mariners game through the noise of our work. The sheet of plastic that hung between the kitchen and the new room waved with the breeze that blew in from the addition's new back door, which we'd left open to get some airflow. It was a hot draft but it was better than nothing. It wasn't even ten yet, but it must have been eighty degrees in that room, and later it would be unbearable.

We pulled off the slats of the wood siding one by one, then tore off the sheathing and tar paper underneath until we'd exposed the studs.

I consolidated the old planks and piles we'd dropped on the floor and passed through the plastic for a glass of water.

"Ah, fuck," Kevin said. "Goddamn it."

I walked back into the addition with my water and a glass for him.

"Look at this shit, will you?" He squatted down and peered at the innards of the wall. He poked at the studs with his knife. The tip slipped into the wood like a toothpick penetrating the top of a cake in the oven, all the way to the knife's handle. "*Every* fucking one of these is rotten."

I squatted next to him to get a better look.

"Well, shit," I said. "Better than the thing collapsing out of nowhere I guess."

"Bright side," said Kevin.

The exterior wall couldn't come out and no new wall was going up today; nothing else could happen. There was no way to progress until we replaced the studs. I was going to have to stay awhile.

Audrey

It was almost the end of July when I decided to purge the boys'
closets. It was an early afternoon and everyone was out of the
house, even Garrett. He and Kevin had been working, then
stopped and everyone left. Something had come up. It was an under-
statement that I'd neglected the closets for months, and the start of
school would be upon us before we knew it, just like every year. In the
back of Brian and Andrew's closet, I found a pair of long outgrown
cleats, a few of the previous year's school folders and notebooks, and
crumpled wads of Christmas wrapping under all of it. As I sorted
through, I worried I would find something I didn't want to, and prepared myself not to judge if I did. I purposely didn't go through the
boys' things, but if they wanted to keep it that way, they were going to
have to keep their shit from piling up. They were too old for this.

I checked Chris's closet too. He took better care of his stuff than his
brothers did, but while I was at it, I was going to get rid of anything
he'd outgrown or worn out. I wondered how old they would have to
be for me to stop thinking this was my job; at the same time, though,
I had a feeling I was the one who'd never outgrow it. With the exception of when they came for the funeral, my mother and Leo's mother
always did the same thing during their visits to my house, with the

linen closet and the spice drawer, whatever they could get their hands on. *I think I'll just clean this out,* they would say before they'd hold up a tattered towel or empty jar and determine: *This can go, it's seen better days* or *No need to keep this, nothing in it.* They left their marks by the clutter they helped rid me of and the windows they cleaned.

In the back of Chris's closet was a small mound: strewn socks, jeans, T-shirts and shorts he'd tossed, careless. Clothes that obviously hadn't made it into the loads of his laundry he'd been so intent on doing. I gathered the pile and when I tried to scoop it all up, I felt a resistance, and when I tugged harder, it was there again, like someone was pulling back, then I heard a crack. I kneeled down and plucked one item off another until I got to a pair of shorts that were caught on one of the floorboards by the waistband. I slid the shorts away. One floorboard was coming up—the one end was still secured, loosely, but the nails on the other had slipped out—exposing the cavity underneath. I assumed I was the one to discover it, so I didn't even think about what I was doing. Inside was like a little tomb. There was a collection buried under the board. Maybe it was decades old, treasures a resident from another century had hidden away. I reached in and pulled them out. I sat back. There was a card from Meredith, a box of condoms, the baby picture of Chris and Leo, and Leo's St. Christopher medal. Two bottle caps. And a piece of paper I unfolded. I fell back against the wall of the closet and stared at what was written on it. I read it until I couldn't look at it anymore.

Christopher

It was so hot we'd all gone out to Sauvie Island to swim. I had to admit, Meredith looked better in a bathing suit than any of the other girls, and since I'd talked to her that day about Garrett, she hadn't bugged me as much. I imagined stealing her bikini and hiding that in my closet. It would be a good thing to have handy.

When I got home that afternoon, my mom was sitting on the front porch. She looked weird. She looked like she did when Gannon's father had come over. Calm but angry calm. Next to her was a glass of white wine. It was pretty full. Next to the glass was the bottle. It was half empty.

"Hi," she said. "How was your time?"

"Pretty good," I said.

"I need to talk to you, Chris," she said.

"Am I late?" I said. "What's wrong?"

"No," she said. "Sit down."

"Where's everybody else?" I said.

"I have no idea," she said. "Out. I need you to sit down."

I sat.

"I thought I'd do some cleaning today," she said. "Get ready for school. As far away as that seems."

"Sorry," I said. "We should have helped."

"No, no," she said. She reached into her front pocket and pulled something out. "Chris, what is this?" She unfolded it.

Fuck. She had the paper. The paper my dad made Garrett sign.

"I don't know," I said. "I have no idea." I squinted at it. "What even is it?"

She put it on the step where our feet were. She covered and rubbed her face with her hands. Jesus, I was glad I'd gotten rid of Ben's mom's stuff. Holy shit.

"You're not in trouble," she said. "But I need you to tell me the truth. Just like you always have. Chris, I'm not mad at you. I'm sorry, I wasn't snooping. I was cleaning out closets and some of your stuff got caught on the board. I put your other things back. I'm sorry," she said again.

She didn't say anything about the bottle caps. "It's not mine, obviously," I said.

"Obviously," she said. "Where did you get it?"

"Garrett told me about it," I said. "Back when we had our stupid talk. Before school was out."

"He told you about it?" she said.

You really couldn't fuck with my mom and I knew that. I was in over my head.

"Yeah," I said.

"So how did it get in your closet?" she said. "With things that are precious to you."

"I wanted it," I said. "I wanted him to give it to me."

"He gave this to you?" she said. She was getting calmer, which scared me. She took a sip of the wine.

"No," I said. "I wanted him to but he wouldn't. So I took it."

"You knew where it was?" she said.

"No, he hid it," I said. "I looked for it till I found it." I was dead. She laughed like it was the funniest thing she ever heard.

I was freaking out. "Mom," I said. "It's no big deal. Garrett told me. It was like a joke. You know, him and Dad." I felt sick. "Mom, he doesn't even know I have it."

"A joke. Some joke." She picked up the paper off the step and folded it and put it back in her pocket. She touched the back of my hair. "Thanks, Chris," she said. "Again, I'm really sorry. I didn't mean to snoop. I thought I was the first one to find that board loose."

"It's okay," I said. But nothing was okay.

"About the condoms," she said. "If you're having sex, if you're thinking about having sex, I'm sorry but we need to talk about it. Are things getting serious with Meredith?"

I wanted to disappear. "No, Mom, I'm not. They're not. There's no one. They're not even open."

"I know," she said. "But you have them."

"Someone dared me to buy them," I said. "A while ago. I wasn't going to not buy a stupid box of condoms because of a dare. I should have just thrown them away. I'm sorry."

"Okay, but when that time comes, because it's going to," she said, "we talk, agreed?"

I nodded.

"Let's go in," she said.

I followed her through the house. She put her glass and the bottle, with what was left of it, on the counter in the kitchen.

A half hour later Garrett, Brian, and Andrew came home.

"Hey," they all said.

"Hey," I said.

"Where've you been?" my mom said.

"At the pool," Andrew said. "It was too hot to do anything else."

"Kevin and I ran into a problem this morning," Garrett said. "Things are on hold for the time being, so we just went to the pool." He laughed. "I can't say I'm that sorry about it." He put his hand on my mom's shoulder and turned toward the addition. "Come look at this mess we found."

"Can you boys go rinse and hang your wet suits outside?" she said. "Chris, you too, please."

Andrew and Brian both had that crease between their eyebrows that we all have when we're confused.

"Hey, Audrey," Garrett said. "Come here and see this." He had walked past her and was standing on the other side of the plastic sheet, holding it open.

"No, Garrett, we're going for a ride," she said. "I'll wait in the car."

She turned around after she walked past me. "You guys stay here," she said. "I'll be back soon."

Garrett

I walked back through the plastic and past Christopher.

"You okay?" I said. "Your mom okay? What's going on?"

He shook his head. He wouldn't look at me.

Audrey was in the passenger seat. I opened the driver's side and peered into the car.

"Are you okay?" I said.

"Drive," she said. She wouldn't look at me either.

I got in and started the car. "Jesus Christ, Audrey, what the fuck is going on?" I said.

She didn't answer me. I drove for three blocks.

"Pull over," she said.

I started to laugh.

"Pull over," she said again.

I pulled over. I was really laughing now. "What is all this?" I said. "All this, 'Drive. Pull over.' All this melodrama. You don't do melodrama."

"Turn off the car," she said. She still wouldn't look at me. I stopped laughing. Something wasn't right.

I turned off the car.

"What is this, Garrett?" she said. She plucked the paper from her pocket, unfolded it, and handed it to me. The paper that was in my socks. That had been. It wasn't there anymore.

I took it and folded it back up and put it on the dashboard.

"What the *fuck* is *that,* Garrett?" she said. "Is *that* why you can't keep your hands off me?" I wanted to start laughing again. "Because of my jackass husband? It's because of him you're doing what you're doing?"

Had Christopher said something to her? Circumstances had forced my hand with Chris, and my telling him what Leo asked of me had been a risk. When I made the decision, I didn't know how making him a kind of participant would turn out, but it had seemed like the right thing to do. The very thing I'd been incapable of sharing with Audrey, I had burdened her son with, and while it certainly hadn't gone well, I didn't get the sense that he would go running to her. I knew I could have been wrong, but that was weeks ago, and my mind tried to fill in the blanks. Audrey wouldn't have had any reason to search through my drawers, and in those seconds before I responded I couldn't imagine how she'd found it. And it clearly wasn't the time to ask. But I did have the answer to one question. She hadn't known anything about the paper, and I wasn't about to tell her Leo mailed it to me. I'd take that to *my* grave.

"No," I said. "None of it's because of him."

"Spare me whatever wooing works on all your other women," she said. "You did this. You both did." She grabbed the paper and unfolded it and waved it at my face. I leaned away from it. "What do you think I am? A woman who needs a keeper? Some pathetic woman two men think they can make decisions for? I was married to him, Garrett, for nineteen years. I am raising our sons. I made sure his body got off that mountain and I buried it. Anyone could finish the house. You think I need a substitute husband *willed* to me?"

She was right on every count. What I didn't know how to convince her of was that what she held in her hand had nothing to do with it.

How I felt about her. How I felt about the boys. I hadn't seen any of it coming. It would have happened with no promise, signed paper or not. I was dying inside the car. The windows were down but it didn't matter. It was so hot. I had to get out.

"I have to get out of this car," I said. I walked to the sidewalk. She got out and followed me.

"It was twelve years ago. It didn't mean anything," I said. "You know how he was. He wouldn't leave it alone. We were drunk and he got sentimental. He wasn't going to die. I did it to get him off my back. He was being a pain in the ass and I signed it and it was over."

We were fighting on the sidewalk. A couple fighting in public. People drove by and slowed down and stared at us. Someone I didn't recognize waved. A woman came out of the house we were parked in front of and sat in a chair on her porch. Wonderful.

"But he did die, Garrett," she said. "And why didn't you throw this away if it was so 'stupid'? If it didn't mean anything?" She shrieked and waved it like a lunatic. In front of God and everybody. "*You* kept it, *you* brought it out here with you and *here* it is." She wouldn't stop waving the paper. I turned my back toward the street. I didn't look at the woman on her porch.

"And *you*." She gritted her teeth and got in my face, her face as close as she could get it to mine, and I stretched my neck back as far as it would go but I left my feet where they were. I did, as the saying goes, have this coming. "When was it?" She was whispering now, her mouth inches below my chin. "When I told you about that guy Wade Reynolds and you sat there, you sat and did your fucking *Oh, Audrey, now there, there,* and I believed you. *No, Audrey, there's no other secrets. Settle down, honey. Leo only ever had good intentions.* Right, he's perfect. Leo, always so perfect. He wasn't perfect. And you're a fucking liar. Your whole sorry life is a lie, Garrett. And all this time you've spent here, that's been a lie too.

"I hate you. I hate both of you right now," Audrey said. She stepped away from me and waved the paper one last time. A big white sweep with one hand. "There *is* no promise." Then she held it between both hands and ripped it—once, twice, three, four, five, six times until she couldn't tear anymore and it was just a small white shredded pile on the sidewalk between our feet.

She walked to the car and I followed her.

"Drive me home, then get out," she said. "I don't care where you go or how you get there, but get the fuck out of my house."

Audrey

fter Garrett left, I ordered a pizza and drove the Land
Cruiser, for the first time since losing Leo, to pick it up. Even
after everything I'd done with Garrett that was far more mo-
mentous, it still upset me to move the seat forward, changing one of
the things I'd preserved inside the car for five months, and drive it
now. I brought the pizza home, told the boys they could eat and watch
a movie, and lay on my bed and sobbed into my pillow. I wished I
could undo everything. All of it. And replace it with what hadn't happened: that we had gone skiing on Brian's birthday; that I told Garrett
to go home after the funeral; that we hadn't repainted the bedroom;
that I hadn't kissed him and followed him to bed; that I hadn't started
it again after we'd put the first time behind us. That I could rewind
time and not have spent the last two months sleeping with him and,
without meaning to, let my feelings for him run away with me and al-
low him to fill a portion of the void that Leo had left. I should have
been acting like a responsible adult and I had done everything but.

I wanted to hurt Leo. He had always joked with the two of us, *If
I die, you guys have to get married. You both know all the secrets, all the
history, and you guys love each other.* But that was all it had been. So I
thought.

But the fact that he had made Garrett sign something, that Garrett had come out and played house and bedded me, made me feel like an object or property—not a person—that they thought needed a keeper. Their friendship—I didn't care how special it was. It didn't make their assumption okay. We weren't living in another century and I didn't need to be taken care of. At the very least, I couldn't believe Leo had never told me after Garrett's visit, later laughing about it, admitting he'd done such a thing. I could picture it. *Well, babe, I've made Garrett promise to marry you if I die. I should have had you sign it too, but you were in bed already, and by the next morning I'd come to my senses, and then he took it with him. You would marry Garrett, right, if you had to? Oh, come on, darlin', don't look at me like that. It was all in good fun, and you and I both know I'm not going anywhere.*

Garrett

I was never so happy to get off a sidewalk. What else could I do? I drove her home. I hated Leo a little that day. And I hated myself, for signing the paper, for hanging on to it and bringing it with me and stowing it in a place where it could be found. For wanting Audrey so badly and getting in so deep. For that, I hated myself, but it wasn't something I regretted. I left the house and called a cab a block away and had it take me to the White Eagle on Russell Street. *Fuck, fuck, fuck,* I thought. *You bring ruin everywhere you go.*

I called Kevin and asked him to meet me. "Things have changed," I said. I told him where I was.

"On my way," he said.

I explained what happened, the only part of the story I knew. I told him I had no idea how she'd found it.

"But it was inevitable," I said. "The clock was ticking."

"It was a matter of time, I suppose," he said. "Sorry the clock didn't run out different."

He put his hand on my shoulder, heavy, and left it there for a minute before he took it back. "How'd you leave it, then?" he said.

"You're looking at it," I said. "Like this. She wanted me to leave and I did, and she'll want me to go back to Boston, I'm sure, so I will.

But I'm coming back—I just don't know when." The thing was, I did know when, but I wasn't ready to tell him.

"Sure," he said. "You can do that. There you go." I'm sure I sounded like a grown man who should have known better: full of naïveté, denial, and hubris, imagining a hopeful solution for a situation that was doomed. But Kevin wasn't going to kick me while I was down, and I appreciated that.

"I don't have any expectations," I said. "It's just that I'm done back there. There may be nothing here for me, but there's even less there."

"Right," he said. "Sure, I get that. Hey, I left too. That's the pioneer spirit."

I let his levity work on us. "Yeah, embarking in unchartered territory, trail blazing, all that. I wouldn't be the first Boston ex-pat."

"Certainly not," he said.

"What about the room?" Kevin said.

"She can figure it out," I said. "In the meantime she can live with it. Those studs aren't going to give out tomorrow."

Kevin nodded. "It's been really good working with you," he said. "It really has. I'm really sorry about this. You'll figure it out. You let me know when you're back. If I don't hear, I'll find you."

"Yeah, of course," I said. "Of course I'll do that. I'll be in touch."

I didn't feel like getting drunk. I wanted to sleep. Kevin wouldn't let me leave any money on the bar, and offered me his couch for the night.

I shook my head. "Thanks, but I'm just going to get a room here. It's easy," I said. "And I'll be asleep in ten minutes."

"Come on," he said. "Really."

When I insisted, like he had paying the tab, he left and I checked into a room. I had wanted to do right by Leo, and Audrey and the boys. Up to a point I had, until whatever good I'd done I'd also unraveled. The unfortunate combination of my relationship with Audrey and my secrecy had had a far greater impact than anything else. It had been too much to ask. Leo had asked too much of me, more than I was capable of, more than anyone would have been. He had left behind shoes too big for anyone to fill, an absence no one could replace. That was my last thought before I fell asleep.

Audrey

I hadn't thought I would, but I slept. The sound of Garrett opening the front door woke me before six. I had left it unlocked. When I got downstairs, he was unloading the dishwasher.

"I made coffee," he said.

"Stop," I said. "Stop what you're doing."

"Audrey," said Garrett. "We need to talk."

"There's nothing to talk about," I said. "It's time for you to go home. I booked you on a flight at two-thirty. I printed your boarding pass. It's next to the computer."

"I know how mad you are," he said. "And I know you're grieving. I would never have dreamed of making things worse for you."

"Don't patronize me," I said. "Don't you dare tell me you know I'm *grieving*. You don't know anything. You've never been married. And you've never been married to someone who died."

"You're right," said Garrett. "But I knew him longer than you. We knew things about each other no one else did."

"You need to start packing," I said. "And keep your voice down."

"I will start packing. It won't take me that long," Garrett said. "But I have something to say and you're going to hear it."

"You have more news?" I said. "Enlighten me, Garrett. Should I take notes?"

"Don't," he said. "Don't tell me 'I don't know.' I *do* know. I'm losing you. It's happening right now. You didn't even know about it and you *still* took me to bed. Again and again and again."

"We're done," I said. "I don't need to hear this."

"I'm not done." He didn't scare me, but I'd never heard Garrett's voice so low and contained, like he was wrestling with himself not to yell. "You don't have to hear any more after I'm done. After I'm gone. After two-thirty today. You let me finish."

I shrugged like I didn't care.

"I am so fucking sorry. On behalf of Leo and me, we are both so sorry. And, Audrey, what about you? You just helped yourself to me." He said it slow and quiet. He was so angry, his lips barely moved. "*You* made me your stand-in. How did you manage it every time, Audrey? How did you live with yourself? I want to know. Every time my dick was inside you, did you just shut your eyes and pretend you were fucking a dead man?"

I didn't want to be, but I was crying. "I'm not going to listen to this," I said. "Are you done?"

"Yes, I am," he said. "I'm done."

Garrett

Packing didn't feel anything like the last time I'd packed, when I'd come out here, when I'd been ready to leave Boston in spite of the reason. But loss was forcing me to pack again. I'd left Boston because we'd lost Leo, and now I was leaving Portland because I'd lost Audrey.

I heard the boys come downstairs and mill around the kitchen. Chris walked into the guest room.

"What are you doing?" he said. My suitcase was on the stripped bed, and he touched the edge of the zipper. He looked young and fragile. Not like the man of the house he'd been playing at.

I took my stuff out of the bottom drawer and put it in the suitcase. He didn't move his hand off the zipper. "I'm packing," I said. "It's time for me to go back to Boston."

"But you're not done," he said. "The room's not finished."

I shrugged and went back to the dresser and emptied the next drawer into the suitcase.

"She asked you to leave, didn't she?" Chris said. "She's mad. Because of the note."

"What do you know about it?" I said.

"I took it," Chris pressed his lips together flat. "I found it in your drawer and I took it and I hid it in this place in my closet and she found it." He was doing everything in his power not to cry. I wouldn't have minded if he did, but I knew he would be embarrassed, so I hoped for his sake he could hold back the tears. "It's my fault." He pawed at his face. "It's my fault she's making you leave. I'm sorry I took it. I'm sorry she found it. I shouldn't have. You told me no."

Now I had the whole picture, but the details didn't matter. It was too late. "It's okay," I said. I put my arm on his shoulder. "Look at me, Chris. It's okay. We agreed it's time."

"But it's because of this. You wouldn't be leaving if this hadn't happened," he said.

"I'll come back and visit," I said. "You guys can always come to Boston."

Then he didn't look so young anymore, and stepped away from my arm. "Do you love her?" he said. "Don't you love her? If you love her, you can't go. Doesn't she love you? I mean, you know, you two—" He stopped.

Jesus, this kid. "Chris, I don't know," I said. "I don't know if she loves me. I'm her good friend, or I was. But yes, I love your mom. She doesn't have to love me back for me to feel that way. It doesn't always work out neat and easy. It's fucked up being an adult," I said. "You think it's going to be so great, but a lot of times it's not." I laughed. "Don't be in a hurry to be anything more than seventeen. You'll be okay and I will too. And for sure your mom is. We're going to be okay."

"Maybe I'll come next summer," he said. "Maybe I'll go to college in Boston."

"Yeah, maybe," I said. "That would be great. You'll see me before you know it."

I went in the kitchen and said goodbye to Brian and Andrew, too, who were both somber and confused, without knowing what Christopher did, and I told them the same things that I'd said to him.

They were easier to convince, but when they both mentioned that the addition wasn't finished, I told them it was a natural place to stop temporarily and because of some unexpected things happening back east, it was time for me to go.

I went back into the guest room, shut the door, and sat on the bed. Just like I had in my apartment—this time sober, this time in a whisper, this time in Leo's house—I said it again, *Fuck you, Leo. Goddamn you.*

But there was more now. *I'm in love with your wife.*

And I imagined him there with me, just listening, leaning against the wall in the room where I'd first slept with her.

I did all the talking. *But she's not your wife anymore, is she?*

I imagined him standing, waiting, not judging like he had by the fire pit, more than a decade ago, when he'd admonished me for all my women. He couldn't say anything now, and I would have given anything, everything, to have him here to say something, because I needed it. I really needed the one thing I couldn't have.

Is this what you wanted? I thought to the imaginary Leo, shifting his weight from one foot to the other, crossing his arms. Crossing the room to sit on the bed next to me, resting an ankle on his opposite knee.

You've fucked me up. I sat next to no one. *Because of you, I've fucked everything up. I don't want to be you, I want to be me. I want to be me with your wife, with your sons, who I could never replace with my own children. I want to stay and I can't. She doesn't want me to.*

The Leo who existed only in my addled mind continued to sit.

You and your fucking jokes, I thought. *If we had gone to bed earlier, if we hadn't drunk so much, it never would have happened. And I would be happy now, happy with the way I was living before. Happy that that was enough. I* was *happy.*

I was arguing in my mind, in an empty room in Leo's house.

How dare you? Is this what you wanted? My thoughts wouldn't stop coming, as much as I wanted them to. I wasn't done.

What about what the rest of us wanted? Audrey would have been fine. She didn't need me. She barely needed you. I wanted to laugh in his living face. *You know that, right? She barely needed you. You needed her more than she needed you. She's a woman who doesn't need anybody. You got lucky. You're lucky she married you.*

I had to get out of this room. And yet, although I had nothing else to say, to myself only—because Leo was in a Jos. A. Bank suit under six feet of dirt and clay and perfect sod—right before I stood up and walked out, I imagined him uncrossing his leg and leaning forward on the bed, resting his forearms on his thighs, clasping his hands together, and just looking at me, nodding and smiling and not saying a word.

Garrett

After I got in the cab, I didn't look back. The driver cruised through the neighborhood, headed toward the freeway, and when we were almost there, I stopped him.

What was I doing? *I'll show you, Audrey. I'm out of here.* I didn't want this.

"Shit, I'm sorry," I said. "Can you go back? I forgot something. My phone. I'm dead without it."

"Sure, buddy." He turned around and put the freeway behind us. "It's your buck."

"No kidding," I said. "But thanks."

Why had I fought with her and been such a dick? Why had I been so defensive? To make her partly responsible. She hadn't done anything wrong. My sleeping with her wasn't why she was furious. I had lied to her; that I had kept something from her that I shouldn't have was as bad as a lie, and it was all on me. As much as I wanted to spread the blame around, implicating Leo, too, I couldn't. On the drive back to the house, I realized that implicit in the promise—which had been the far-thest thing from a joke there was—to do what Leo had asked and take care of his family, was also the expectation that I wouldn't hurt his wife.

Leo had always been serious about his request. I'd never let myself come to terms with that. It was less of a burden to write it off as a joke. But now that he'd died, there was no way to interpret what he'd asked of me as anything but sincere.

Tempting fate, I made a deal with myself, which was passive and cowardly. I'd never begged a woman to stay or to keep me; it wasn't something a person did every day, or with just anyone. You begged only when it mattered, only when you couldn't bear to lose someone. Audrey had nothing to lose now—she had already endured the worst loss. Ending our romance because she felt betrayed was nothing compared to Leo's death.

So, if when I got back to the house Audrey was there—this was the deal I made with myself, this pussy deal—I'd do anything she asked, anything except let her shut me out, and I was prepared to beg. It was the only choice I had.

Then I would work to undo the ugliness I'd said this morning—I'd be contrite and self-deprecating; I'd remind her she'd said it would be nice if I were closer than Boston. I'd say the words I'd never said and tell her that because of Leo I was conflicted and guilty, but that he'd had nothing to do with how I felt about her. That the biggest mistake of my life, even at the risk of losing or changing what had happened between us, had been not telling her about the promise. That was the least I owed her, and I had failed.

We pulled up in front of the house. It hadn't taken us that long to get back.

I stood on the porch and rang the bell. Andrew opened the door.

"You're back," he said.

"Where's your mom?" I said.

"She went running. She just left. You could still catch her."

Fuck. "She doesn't want to be caught, Andrew," I said. "I just forgot something."

I went into the guest room to recover the pretended forgotten thing. I stood in the middle of the floor.

Change the plan. Pay the cab, wait for her, and stay.

That hadn't been the deal.

Fuck the deal. This "deal" business really isn't something you excel at anyway, is it?

So instead of begging—following my gut—instead of doing the risky, uncertain work of staying—when it truly mattered—I did what I knew how to do. I did the old, easy thing. Andrew stood in the living room and waited the whole time. He was still there when I walked back in.

"I've got to go," I said. "I'll see you, buddy." I squeezed his shoulder on my way to the front door. And for the second time that day, I left the house for the airport.

Audrey

fter Garrett had said individual goodbyes to the boys, we all
gathered in the living room. It felt like another mourning
had overtaken the house. The cab pulled up.

"Safe trip," I said. "Text me when you're home."

"Sure," he said. He squeezed all the boys one last time, walked out,
and shut the door behind him.

The four of us watched the black-and-white cab pull away. Then
we stood there looking at the empty street.

"I'm going for a run," I said. "You guys have plans?"

They all moped and shrugged.

"We'll decide something when I get back, okay? Maybe we'll all go
to a movie."

I put on my shoes, and stretched and headed out. It was too hot to
run, but I went anyway.

When I came back forty-five minutes later, Christopher and Andrew were taking turns shooting baskets, each with his own ball,
and Brian was sitting on the curb drawing. They seemed no less
somber than when I'd left, but at least they were all doing something.

As I started to walk up the porch stairs, Andrew ran over to me.

"Hey, Mom. Right after you left, Garrett came back. Did you see him?"

"No," I said. "I didn't. Why did he come back?"

"He said he forgot something," said Andrew.

"Well, I hope he found it," I said.

"I guess he did," Andrew said. He turned and walked back to the street and I climbed the stairs.

For the rest of that day, and during the weeks that followed, I searched the house looking for something I imagined Garrett left for me, some kind of message or sign of what, I didn't know, but I wanted one. I found nothing in every place I looked, which brought its own kind of heartbreak. More than once Leo had left me a Post-it on the bathroom mirror or a note on my windshield or inside a book I was reading. All kinds of notes: *I'm an asshole. I'm sorry.* Another: *I love you. I feel like I haven't seen you at all lately and I miss you. We need a night out.* And the one on my pillow: *This has been such a shitty week. I know the boys have been a pain in the ass. I'll see you in the morning.* After all that time, when I finally gave up, because I knew there was nothing from Garrett for me to find, I realized I'd been thinking of Leo, because that's the sort of thing he would have done.

Garrett

I had a window seat from Portland to Chicago, and for the first time I could remember, I slept on the plane. I sprinted through O'Hare for the leg to Boston, certain I wouldn't make it to the concourse, expecting to miss my connection. Although I didn't, I had the shit luck of the middle seat, and the man who got the window boarded after me and I had to stand up to let him pass when he was done stowing his things in the overhead. After he sat he nodded at me and I nodded back. He looked like the news anchor Brian Williams, a well-groomed, impervious, dashing sort of fellow, and though I knew it wasn't Williams, I wondered why the guy wasn't flying first class. It wasn't until after all the preflight instructions, taxiing, liftoff, and a half hour in the air, rising to our cruising altitude, that I noticed both of us were just sitting there, staring at the backs of the seats in front of us. I didn't want to read, watch a movie, or even shut my eyes.

"You going to Boston for business or pleasure?" I said.

"Ah, neither." He pressed his lips together. "Bit of a family emergency."

"Sorry," I said. "Since we're just both sitting here. Plane talk." I felt like an ass.

He shook his head and waved his hand. "It's all right. We just can't get there fast enough." He didn't resemble Brian Williams very much anymore.

"I've been there," I said. "Even when flying's the only way, it's still too slow."

"You have kids?" he said.

"No, I don't."

"I'm going to the Cape to get my daughter and bring her home. Back to San Francisco," he said. "She was a freshman this year and she got a summer job with her girlfriends. But she's too far away." None of this sounded like anything terrible. "My wife, Jodi, and I, we have three other daughters, so I came. We are—we were—very close, Amelia, my daughter, and I."

"I teach—I taught—at BC," I said. "Freshman year is a huge adjustment no matter how far from home you are, but she's a long way, for sure."

He looked at me with a fresh recognition of relief, like he'd found a friend in a crowd. "That's where she was last year, at BC. Good school." Then his expression grew sad and he sighed. "But she got really sick, you know, not eating. She's five foot nine and a hundred and ten pounds. I don't know what the hell happened. She's always been a good kid, talks to her mother, you know, talks to us both." I looked at the guy again, folded in his seat. He was tall.

"Sorry." He waved his hand at the air again, like he wanted to take everything back and return to sitting privately, undisturbed, until the plane landed and he could stop waiting, passive, and finally do something. "You know," he said, "once you have kids you do whatever you can, as long as you can, for them. Then you do some more. I can't just let her slip away to nothing."

"No," I said. "No, of course you can't. Sorry that's happening. Sorry I intruded. You sound like a great father. I hope she'll be okay." I wanted to take back initiating this conversation too. I wasn't sorry we'd been talking, but I felt of no use to the guy after what he'd shared.

"No, no, don't worry about it. Thanks," he said. "Thanks for listening. I think she will. At least we're doing something. My parents, their generation, would have had no idea." He extended his hand. "I'm Brad, by the way."

I took his hand and shook it and held on maybe a little longer than I should have. "I'm Garrett," I said. "Nice talking with you, circumstances aside of course. Best of luck, really."

He didn't seem to mind the extended clasp and took his hand back when I finally let go. "So." He turned his palms up over his lap. "What about you? Coming off vacation, heading back to work?" My turn.

"Something like that," I said. "I've been in Portland and I'm just heading home to pack up and go back there. It was time for a change. There's more for me in Portland than Boston, I think. Or at least there's nothing in Boston to keep me there. I don't stay in one place very long, so it was just a matter of time."

"Wanderlust," Brad said. "What a wonderful thing. It keeps you moving till you find what you're searching for, or it just keeps you moving, if that *is* the thing you're looking for. No standstill." He smiled, kindly, like a satisfied man who had found what he'd searched for, pitying someone who hadn't. "If you don't keep looking, you'll never find it, right?"

"Right." I laughed. "Even if you don't know what it is."

"But you know it when you find it," Brad said.

"Yeah," I said. "You do. You know it when you find it."

Garrett

When I got to Boston, late, I took the T home from Logan, dropped my bags at the door, and collapsed into sleep. When I woke up at six the next morning, I felt a lot of things, but the sense of being glad to be home wasn't one of them. It was a strange phenomenon to still physically inhabit a place I'd abandoned emotionally. Being back in my apartment, surrounded by my own things, felt as unfamiliar as if I'd wandered into a stranger's by mistake, my key fitting that lock and allowing my entrance.

I didn't text Audrey like she'd asked. I wanted to hurt her in some small way, as if I hadn't enough already, and the only means I had was to deny her the only thing she'd asked of me: that I let her know I had returned safely. Not only did I want to deprive her of what she wanted, but I wanted her to wonder and worry that maybe I hadn't made it. It was childish and passive aggressive; I wasn't proud, but I was aware.

So for the second time and permanently, I was done with Boston; the rest would all be formality to put it behind me. I called my father and told him I was back and planned to take the train down to see him if it was a good time to visit, which he said it was.

The whole time I'd been in Boston, I lived in a brownstone in

Brighton, off Comm. Ave.—it was a sweet place, but about as special as any sweet place in any city. Given the time of year, I was going against the tide. Faculty and off-campus students were moving in and unpacking while I packed and moved out. Fueled with coffee and music, I loaded six boxes of what I didn't want or need anymore—like a map in relief, the things I was willing to keep and pack, move and unpack, rearrange and continue to look at, wear, read, or eat off of revealed themselves, and everything else went. After I'd dropped the boxes at Goodwill, I had less to contend with and more room to do it in. What I couldn't fit in my car and haul to Goodwill I labeled *FREE* and put on the street. Within an hour the swivel desk chair I'd always hated but suffered, a forgettable bookshelf, and two lamps were gone. I spent the whole day packing, into the night, still living on Portland time, and quit at one o'clock, ten on the West Coast. The only things left in my apartment were my bed, my clothes, a coffeemaker, and one mug.

Early the next morning I took the train and stopped in New York to see the 9/11 Memorial. I had been there the previous year not long after it was completed, on my way to my father's for Christmas. It was an uncomfortable but important place to visit, especially having been there before, when the Twin Towers still stood. I had been to the city numerous times and during one visit, the Trade Center was the meeting place for friends I'd met in Europe who'd traveled to the States. But it was a different visit this time, knowing of a victim, having a hero to look for. The first responders were honored at the South Pool and I found Jimmy Sullivan's inscription there, and then his photo in the memorial exhibition. I wondered if Kevin had come back and seen it all. It was too crude a way to document them, but it was all I had, so I took pictures of his inscription and his place in the gallery with my phone. Since I would never know Jimmy Sullivan, I endowed him with qualities I imagined he had had, qualities that reminded me of Leo, which made him feel more like a friend than a stranger.

I left New York and took the train to Philadelphia. My father met me at Thirtieth Street Station and we had dinner at Bistro Romano, in Society Hill, at a table in the basement. Underground, surrounded by exposed bricks, in the most chaste terms, I told him everything, omitting Christopher's part in what had unfolded, and that I was going back to Portland, and staying.

My father never seemed surprised by much, and even when he was—by what, I couldn't imagine—I was sure he feigned the same unchanged, practiced expression. It was as though there was nothing he hadn't already heard or seen before. He could easily convey happiness or impatience or irritability, but I had never seen him shocked, and tonight was no exception. After I finished, he only nodded and smiled. As much as I'd wanted to see him taken aback by something I'd said or done when I was younger, I was grateful tonight wasn't the night it happened for the first time.

"I see," he said. "That's quite a spot you've been in." He didn't remind me of what he'd said to me in the airport right after Leo died, which I also anticipated and didn't want to hear. But what he did say surprised me. "Son, why Audrey? What is it about her? If it's not because of Leo, then why? And you don't have to tell me, but you need to know, in your own mind, before you do this."

I did know, or felt, I thought. But him asking me about it so boldly, with only love and care and no trace of judgment, invited an unveiling, and I wasn't prepared for the exposure if I answered him.

I drummed my fingers on the white tablecloth, and he finished the last of his drink. "I'm sure you do know, Garrett," he said. "And that's enough. I'm not doubting you. You're a father long enough, giving advice becomes a reflex you can't control."

Everything I could think of was a cliché. I kept drumming my fingers and watching them.

"Because she's good for me. And because I'm afraid," I said. I could answer his question, but I couldn't look at him while I did. "I'm terrified she was it for me. Because she's not perfect, and because she's not, she is. I like what kind of mother she is. Because if I live to be an old man, the sound of her voice is the first thing I want to hear every day. I like the way she looks at me. Because she knows most of what there is to know about me, all my flaws, and for a little while, I seemed to make her happy anyway." My throat was tightening. "Because even though we shouldn't have—we never should have had the chance—we *work*. Worked. Because when we worked—even during those hard months—it had felt easy. Actually, that's the only thing I should have said. Because we worked." I squeezed my head in my left hand and pressed my eyes shut several times. I still hadn't looked at him.

"Well, son," my father said. "Then of course you have to go. It's the only thing you can do."

I felt like he had just walked in on me with my dick in my hand, but he was as unperturbed as he would have been if he was sampling produce.

"But it's over," I said. "I've ruined it. I ruined the whole thing. If she can forgive me, I don't know—maybe someday she can. But that's the least of it. She won't ever feel whatever she might have, or did for a little while, with me, again."

"I don't believe it," he said. Again, his assurance, his composure, seemed to reflect a different conversation, one that we weren't having. Like one about who was likely to prevail in the next election. "But here's the thing: for as difficult as this is on your end, uncomfortable and strange, dare I say painful, you're going to have to wait, because it's harder for her. Any and all of it. So you're going to have to wait. That's also the only thing you can do. For however long."

Later, back at his condo in Radnor, I sat up alone till late, with a bottomless glass of Scotch, and pored over the photo albums my mother had amassed during my parents' marriage. They had a different significance for me now, and as I turned the pages, I recognized that they were full of many photos I hadn't known existed or had forgotten about. There were the basketball team pictures with Leo and me looking gangly and exposed in our uniforms as freshmen, and then less so with every subsequent season's photo.

I refilled my glass when I got to Leo and Audrey's wedding photos. My parents had attended, and there were copies of the professional shots the photographer had taken, but others caught me off guard. I didn't know who had taken them—my parents? I couldn't remember, but they must have brought a camera. My mother had filled all these albums because she always had a camera with her.

We looked so young, all of us, in the wedding party photos, surrounding Leo and Audrey, who radiated at the center of their friends on both sides. Then there was the series of me giving the toast. Initially I looked like I stood in front of a judge awaiting sentencing, then simply nervous, showing too many teeth, then finally raising my glass looking at last like myself. Some looked professional and others, of the same scenes, I could tell my mother had taken.

When I came to a photo of Audrey and me, I took it out of the black picture corners that held it in the album, and stared at it. I had no memory of it being taken, and though I surely must have, I couldn't remember ever having seen it before either. Nineteen years ago. We were in our twenties, babies. We look more like kids at our prom. In the picture, Audrey's arm is around my waist and mine is around her shoulder, my fingers pressed into her arm at the edge of the cap sleeve of her dress. I could tell that my hand wasn't resting there, loose, that my grasp had a gentle clutch to it. I'm still in my tux jacket, though I've lost the tie and my collar is open. Audrey is leaning under my draped arm, her free hand on my lapel. She is looking directly at the camera, with a candid but flawless smile, but I am not. I am looking off camera and lifting the glass in my free hand in the same direction. My mouth is open, not in a gaping, regrettable way—I was clearly captured mid-speech, attentive to whatever, or whomever, stood outside the frame. Comforted by the Scotch, I tried to think of possible

captions, the audio to accompany the image: What I might have ut-
tered, and to whom? To Leo, who was momentarily away from his
bride? Or to someone else, asking about Leo's whereabouts?

Can I get a refill!

Hey, where's the good stuff!

When's the band finished their break?

But now, looking at the picture so many years later, the only quote
I could attribute to myself was *I'm following her too.* Though that
wouldn't have been remotely close to what I said that day, it was the
only thing I could think of now.

It was a good picture, and I was happy to find the captured moment of the two of us alone from that day. But it was funny, too, in
a sad way. Its composition was one that today you could just as easily
have Photoshopped from two separate photographs, as incongruous as
Audrey's and my presences are to the other's—like two witnesses' dis-
parate accounts of the same accident. She is so very present and happy
and comfortably tucked close to me—who is not the groom—and I,
though unaware of the camera, am happy too, like a man in the stands
at the Derby, offering cheers to a friend because our horse has just
won. I didn't return the photo to the album and kept turning the pages
until I was past the wedding ones and came to the next series, which
was of a trip my parents had taken to Monaco with two other couples
the same year. I stopped there, took the picture of Audrey and me into
one of my father's guest rooms, put it on the nightstand next to the
bed, and went to sleep.

The next morning I took my father's car and drove to the cemetery
where my mother was buried. When I was twelve I found out she had
been married before—*Only for about ten minutes,* she'd said, as if that
was all I or anyone needed to know in the way of the story. The parents of a classmate, not a friend, were splitting up, and although I didn't
know any details, my thoughts about it had a dark hue of stigma. She'd
told me about her first marriage, I thought, not so much to normal-

ize divorce, but to cast it within the normalcy of human experience, even among Catholics. The man's name was Daniel, and his name and the mystery of his existence in my mother's life had jarred me in the same way seeing a teacher outside the classroom did: you knew teachers didn't live and sleep at school, but seeing them on the street or in a store or at the movies disrupted your sense of them and where they belonged. You didn't want to see them in a life outside the one you knew any more than you wanted to walk in on them undressing.

So I had asked my mother why, because I'd had to get a handle on reconciling this new information with the woman I'd known my mother to be five minutes earlier.

"Why what, honey?" she'd asked. "Why did I marry him or why did I divorce him?"

"Both," I'd said.

She'd responded to me in the way that people say something they've known or at least told themselves for a long time, unspoken to all but a few people, if even that. "Well, I was twenty-one and we'd gone together a long time and thought we loved each other. Why else would we have stayed together for so long?" she'd said. "And that's what you were supposed to do, or what many of us thought we were supposed to do. It's what people did. So many of us, anyway." She stopped and I thought she was finished before she said more, as if she had to balance the failure of those expectations with a quota of redemption. "For people who are still together, it was the right person and the right time. For them."

"But what happened?" I'd asked. "Wasn't he nice to you?"

She'd smiled and run her fingers through my hair. "No, no. He was nice," she'd said. "He was a very nice man. There wasn't a thing wrong with him, except that we were both too young and we didn't really even know who the other person was. I didn't even really know who I was, and as I—and we—started to figure that out, we realized we had no business being married to each other at all."

I'd nodded like I understood, but I was baffled. I couldn't picture my mother having meals with or raking leaves with or vacationing with anyone other than my father and Kate and me. I didn't begrudge her being married before and I didn't have a judgment about it either way, but what made me feel curious and strange was that she'd been another person, with another husband, in a life other people in the world had witnessed. She'd inhabited that place, and then only later became the version of her that I knew, and part of the bedrock of the history that included me and that my own history was built on.

"So," she'd said, as if concluding the whole *ten minutes* of being married, "we got an annulment and I was a single woman for three years before I met your father. I was twenty-five, so *old*." She'd laughed. "Not old at all, not by a long shot, but for back then. But I was closer to who I really was than who I'd been at twenty-one, so the second time it was right. So much more right than the first."

In my naïveté, and considering all this, I'd said, "Does Dad know?"

And with utter equanimity, she'd looked directly into my face and said, "Yes, love, he most certainly does."

But I'd remained startled that sharing a passing detail about someone in my class, while significant for them, had resulted in uncovering one of my mother's own secrets, and I worried about what others lurked, and might be revealed another day during a conversation about something that seemingly didn't have a thing to do with us. And worse, would what had happened once happen again—would she again think she wasn't really who she was and leave all of us, ultimately for a third husband?

It might have been then, timed perfectly or imperfectly with my teetering pubescence, that I'd decided I too could be cagey and withholding, given the lesson I'd learned from my mother, my first teacher. Nobody had to know everything about me, starting with my family. What an alluring and marvelous chance it offered, to live not as an open book with the very people you existed alongside every day.

Standing next to her grave, I missed her in a new way since Leo had died. I wanted to walk with her, with her arm linked through mine, telling her what I was up against with Audrey, what had happened between us, to talk about Leo, how much I missed him, how I surely couldn't have thought his request had been serious back then, could I?

My mother had been a funny and wise woman and a good friend to me my whole life, even when I wasn't one to her. She had always taken my withholdings in stride, waited for me to come around in time, addressing my revelations only when I shared them, not prying for them prematurely. It was something I'd realized in hindsight, not at the time, and I'd never thanked her for it. For adjusting to my temperament on its own terms, never lamenting I didn't do things the way Kate did or begrudging that I didn't operate according to my sister and mother's system for the mutual exchange of information. It was a fresh sorrow to want so badly to feel the weight of her arm on mine, to feel her free hand pat mine at intervals while I spilled my confusion to her. *What would you say, Mom?* I squatted, then sat cross-legged next to her headstone and tried to imagine. *"Life is short"? "Nothing risked, nothing gained"?* My mother never spoke or advised in clichés, yet whatever she shared always seemed as universal and applicable as those overused expressions, like, why hadn't anyone else ever thought of what my mother just said? *You always knew how to get the girl, Garrett, but you've never wanted to keep one, so yes, this would be new.*

As I sat and imagined her strong, well self, the woman she'd been before she was sick and so reduced, the one I'd played golf with and swam with in the Atlantic Ocean, the one who'd let me grow from a boy into a man — perhaps differently from how she'd hoped — who'd let me traipse off to Europe and be in school and school again and more school, and with woman after woman, some of whom she'd met and most of whom she hadn't. I thought, as we would have walked, after she'd listened, she would have been funny, but not unkind. She may have said, *You and Leo, always in it together, aren't you, for better or for worse?* Then, *Are you happy?* Or she may have just looked at me and smiled and shaken her head: *I haven't seen Audrey in such a long time. Tell me all about her over lunch. Where shall we have lunch?*

When we had all been in Radnor for Christmas the year Leo and Audrey were married, they had come to my parents' on Christmas Eve. The three of us stood in the kitchen while my mother poured us drinks. She handed everyone their glasses, then put her arms around my waist and rested her head against my chest. "Well, Audrey, you got Leo off the street. What are we going to do about this one?" All of us laughed. I let myself be the butt of the joke to amplify Leo's good fortune, and, taking it as far as he could, he embraced Audrey in both arms and said, "Celeste, I've found my bride. Garrett's on his own."

Audrey had basked and blushed while Leo gloated, and my mother squeezed me and kissed my cheek before she let go. In response to them all, I'd raised my glass and said, "Well, you can't fix lucky."

Staring at her headstone, I missed her and her advice and comfort more than I'd expected I would when I pulled the car into the cemetery's lot. I felt like a child again: *I want my mother.* And yet, if I had what I wanted, if she were alive and hadn't died, I knew I wouldn't revere her like I did her memory. I might have withheld all that had happened, or revealed only small, select parts. I would have had the luxury to reject and dismiss and undermine: *Never mind, Mom, you don't understand. It's hard to explain, forget it.* What I would have given for the chance to be so careless, so off hand; for the ordinary indulgence of confiding in my mother and the gift of rejecting her response, like lobbing a ball back to her side of the court, half-assed. *Oh, now, you can do better than that,* she'd say, knowing I wasn't in the mood to play, that I'd changed my mind the instant I walked on the court—brought up the topic—but not letting me get off that easy. *Mom, can we talk about it later?* I wanted her now and I wanted her later. What an enviable thing to have possible between you and another person—a later.

The entire time I was in Radnor, I fought the urge to call and visit Leo's parents. I knew that in spite of how much I wanted to see them, and surely them me, I couldn't truthfully answer the questions they'd ask me, and I couldn't lie either.

When I returned to Boston, I finalized things with my landlord and checked in with Rob and Morgan to say goodbye for good. They had repotted my plant, which I didn't recognize until they pointed it out, and asked me if I wanted it back, which I didn't. I met their baby, Mia. I rented a U-Haul that had a hitch for the Prius, and Rob and I loaded the truck. When my apartment was empty and the truck was full, I closed the driver's-side door for the last time, tucked the picture of Audrey and me in the pocket on the sun visor, got on I-90, and drove west.

After three nights on the road, putting one state line after another behind me, drinking beers in hotel bars just off the interstates and, predictably, getting a speeding ticket in Wyoming, I drove the last sixteen-hour leg straight through and followed I-84 into Oregon. I stopped in Hood River for a break. I drank coffee and watched the windsurfers put in that August morning. It had been less than two weeks since I'd left Portland, but it felt like months since I'd been here. It was, after all, still summer. The Columbia was a shimmering wild thing—a river with waves—that people were out there riding, each in their own rodeo, so unlike the tempered, manageable Charles and its refined rowing and sailing. I sat on the beach until I finished my coffee, then I drove parallel with the Columbia as long as I could until the highway bent south and away from the water and into Portland.

Audrey

I wasn't alone, of course, but after Garrett left, an invisible, unwelcome solitude came and mocked me, took up residence in my house and stayed. *No Leo. No Garrett,* it taunted with its arms spread wide. *It's just you and me.* It was a new kind of mourning, and it made me furious. I was not a woman who had never been alone before—I knew women who had never been, and though I didn't mean to, I felt superior to them that I hadn't left my parents' house and a block away and five minutes later walked into my own marriage. I'd moved across the country alone, had landed a great job, been the creator of my own happiness. Years ago, I had a neighbor who became a dear friend, who had never been alone. Selfishly, because it's what I'd have done, I thought she should be alone for a time between her divorce from her husband, whom she'd been with since she was eighteen and married six years later, and the first guy she took up with, who she lived with first, right away, then married. How could she ever know who she was or what she was made of if she never took the time to find out by herself? I couldn't say any of that to her, of course, so all I could say was "Is your life better with him or without him?" The guy moving in seemed to answer the question. We tried to stay friends but didn't, not because of her choice; the guy drew her into his circle of friends and together they cultivated new ones, away from me, and during their first year together, they moved out of the neighborhood.

So I made room for the loneliness but refused to indulge it, refused to let it get comfortable. School was starting soon, and Chris and Brian would both be in high school—I needed to gear up for that. Andrew was better, a little more each day like the kind and generous boy he'd always been.

I was compulsive for days, checking my email and phone after Garrett left, always to find nothing from him, and I was angry that he hadn't let me know that he had made it home safely. He'd said he would. *Be careful what you ask for,* the solitude gloated, from the couch where it stretched out, from half of the bed it hoarded, from the corner of the kitchen where it lurked. *You told him to go.*

Every time I stood in the kitchen, I gazed through the plastic at the unfinished room. At least once a day I'd sweep it aside and sit on the floor in the middle of the addition, such as it was, abandoned for the second time, and look at all that had been done and at what was still unfinished. I wanted the room finished. I wanted Garrett back to finish it. I wanted Garrett back. So I called my mother and told her I needed her and asked her if she would please come, and two days later she did.

She was here for a week, and if I pretended it was a different year, it wasn't unlike the visits she alone or she and my father together typically made. Summer was when they came, and it was summer. But nothing else was the same.

My mother and I were good friends, not best friends, but close and real with each other; there was a surplus of love. Yet Leo and I had been married for so long that my role as her daughter had been replaced or at least overshadowed by the years I'd spent being a wife and the mother of her grandsons. So, even though we'd talked several times a week since Leo's death, she had no idea how much in need of her help her daughter was.

The day after she arrived, we drove over to Northwest Twenty-Third for lunch at Papa Haydn, one of her favorite places to eat when she was in town. The street was crowded as always, more so in the summer, and traffic was slow and parking was scarce. When we drove by the Rams Head—I hadn't been over here since that day Garrett and I had had lunch—I looked at the table where we'd sat. Two men sat there now, drinking beers.

The next, we drove to Manzanita for the day and walked the beach. It was very windy so there were only handfuls of other walkers, but it was a good day for the three kite boarders skimming the top of ocean, as in command of the waves beneath them as Olympic skaters were of ice.

"It shouldn't have happened this way," she said. "This terrible thing. I haven't known what to pray for except for God to take care of you. I'm so far away. Daddy and I both should have been gone, and been gone for years, before you ever lost Leo."

I came right out and told her only as much as she needed to know about what had happened between Garrett and me, and about what Leo had asked of Garrett. How furious I was about all that time that Garrett had known what I hadn't. How angry I was at Leo. How he had done something I couldn't understand. I told my mother if I'd been asked about the hypothetical possibility of him doing such a thing, I would have, with mistaken confidence, answered the question wrong one hundred times out of a hundred. Every time I would have laughed and said, *No, Leo would never do something like that.*

"Oh, my love," my mother said. "No wonder."

"No wonder what?" I said.

"Well, I could never figure out why he up and left everything in Boston," she said. "Why he just came out and stayed."

"I know," I said. "Wasn't it a reckless thing for a grown man to do? Just because someone else asked or suggested it—I don't care if it was Leo. Along with everything else, I've lost a lot of respect for him."

She stopped walking, so I stopped too. "What did you say, sweetie?" she said. She put her hands on my shoulders and peered at my face. "Is that what you think? Oh, Audrey, that's not why he did it. Garrett is in love with you."

Andrew

When my mom and I went to Target for school supplies, we weren't in the store five minutes before we saw six other kids from school. My mom had always done the shopping before without me, but I didn't always like what she bought, so this year I wanted to pick out the stuff on the list. There were certain pencils and pens I liked and she never bought those. She thought she knew what I wanted but she didn't, not all the time.

We were in the aisle, putting notebooks in the cart, crossing things off, and Gannon and his dad turned the corner, then they were in the aisle with us too.

"Hello, Audrey," Gannon's dad said.

"How are you, Frank?" said my mom.

"Hi, Gannon," I said.

"Hey, Andrew," he said.

"This list," Gannon's dad said.

"A fresh slice of hell," my mom said.

As I found things and put them in the cart, I checked them off, then pushed the cart down the aisle and went around the corner to the next one.

I heard Gannon behind me. "Dad, can I have my list?" He came into the aisle where I stood scanning the shelves. "Is there only just crap left or what?" he said.

"Nah," I said. "It's not bad."

He went back to get the cart and rolled it into the aisle where I was, and started putting stuff in his cart and checking stuff off his own list. We did that together, helping each other find stuff if the other couldn't, until I'd gotten everything I needed and was finished. By then my mom and Gannon's dad had come into the aisle where we were.

"All set, Mom," I said.

"Really?" she said. "You got everything."

"Yes," I said.

I pushed the cart and she followed me.

"Take care," she said to Gannon's dad. "See you at school. Enjoy what's left of the summer."

"You too," said Gannon's dad.

We got to the checkout line and waited. All of the lines were long. We stood behind a woman unloading a full cart. Everybody had a full cart. I felt sorry for Gannon. His dad was uptight and kind of a loser and his mom was never around. He didn't have any brothers, or even sisters—it was just him. But he was a good basketball player, when he wasn't being a pain in the ass or an asshole.

"Hey, Mom," I said. "I'll be right back."

"Where are you going?" she said.

"I forgot to tell Gannon something."

"Really?" She looked confused. "Okay—" she said.

I went back to the aisle where we'd been. Gannon and his dad were still there. His dad was looking at the list, and Gannon was peering at the shelves.

"Hey, Gannon," I said.

"Hey," he said.

"So maybe you could come over some day before school starts. If you want to," I said. "We could play a little ball if you want."

"Yeah, okay, cool," he said. "That would be cool."

"See you," I said. I went back to the checkout line where my mom was still waiting.

"What was that about?" she said. She hadn't moved from the spot where she'd been when I left. The store was packed. I saw three more people from school.

"Nothing," I said. "Gannon just might come over sometime and play basketball. I invited him."

"Okay," said my mom. "That's unexpected. What made you ask him? I'm just curious."

"I just did," I said. "I just felt like it. It's not like we're going to be best friends or anything. If he's still an asshole to me, I'll still kick his ass, but I don't think he will be."

"Andrew, language."

"Geez, Mom, really?"

"Yes, *geez*," she said, but she laughed. "Really."

Christopher

Something happened between Meredith and me after I'd told her about Garrett and my mom.

I'd known her for a really long time—since we started school together when we were five. You see a girl every day for that long, by the time you're in eighth grade, she's like your sister and she thinks of you like her brother, too. But then, after we started high school, even before we kissed that time, I could tell she started to think of me *that way,* like all our years together since naptime in kindergarten up to eighth grade graduation—nerves and mess-ups in school plays and Christmas programs, doing book report presentations and group projects on birds and bridges, Outdoor School, her bloody noses and me throwing up in third grade, goofy games in PE—boring things that made us know each other so well, hadn't happened. When she started to treat me like I was a foreign exchange student, someone mysterious and new. That's what drove me crazy. That's not who she was and that's not who I was. I was embarrassed for her.

But after I told her about Garrett and my mom, she kind of went back to the way she had been, the way I liked, the kind of girl you wanted on your dodgeball or kickball team, who didn't worry how her hair looked and didn't check out her own jeans and ass when she passed a plate-glass window. I was glad she didn't seem so into herself anymore.

We all still hung out until the school year ended, and afterward, but once it got nice and after summer started, we were outside all the time, and the girls played basketball with us when we let them, girls on boys, and they weren't bad—lethal with their elbows—but as much as they fouled, they made more free throws than we did, even though we had more chances. Meredith wanted to learn to skateboard but said her brother refused to teach her—he was only twelve but he was an ace and said he couldn't be bothered—so I did, and although it was painful to watch, she wasn't afraid to fall and she wasn't afraid to look bad trying. That's what I mean: a few months before she would have been all self-conscious and vain, and that summer she wasn't. *You're a trouper,* I'd tell her. *You're getting there.* She laughed when I said that even though she was frustrated and once she said to me, *Will you shut up with that crap. I had to ask you to teach me because a* sixth-grader *blew me off.*

By August, when we went to the movies we held hands and sometimes I'd put my arm around her, but I mostly liked putting my hand on her knee and leaving it there for the whole time. I liked how my hand looked on her knee. And at parties or at night at the park we'd leave the group and go make out and when my jeans got tight and I couldn't help pushing myself against her, I wasn't embarrassed and she wasn't either. At least I didn't think so, because she pushed back pretty good.

She babysat a lot for this one family with two little boys, and I'd go over to their house the nights she was there. We'd play backgammon and Scrabble after the kids went to bed—we didn't make out there, it just wasn't a good idea.

I thought about having sex with Meredith pretty much all the time, and in the shower, in my room, and last thing in bed at night, where I didn't have to hurry. I played it out as many times as I could in one day. But I was afraid of doing it and I hoped she was too. As great as thinking about having sex with Meredith was when I was alone, if we did do it I was afraid one of two things would happen. I was afraid it would be so terrible that I'd never want to do it again and might even stop liking her as much as I did, or I'd want to do it all the time, like every second of every day, and not play Scrabble or backgammon or go to the movies, which I liked doing with her. And I worried she'd be disgusted by my boner if she saw it, that she wouldn't want to touch it and wouldn't even want it anywhere near her. And the condoms, that would be embarrassing as hell, like dressing my boner for where it was going. And the hair, there would be everyone's hair down there to deal with, who wanted to deal with that? I didn't even want to think about orgasms. The word sounded like something you'd fall into and keep falling forever without ever landing. Besides that, if Meredith had one, I didn't think I wanted to see her face while she did, and I for sure didn't want her to see mine. And the Catholic thing—I mean, Father John knew who I was, and what was I going to do? Go to confession every week, knowing Father would know it was me every time? *Me again. Had sex* again *this week with my girlfriend, forgive me,* again. Plus, I wanted to put off that talk with my mom as long as I could. I'd given her my word and I planned to keep it, but I wasn't in any hurry to have that conversation. It was just too complicated. When I was with Meredith, my body wanted more but my mind didn't.

So she was pretty much my girlfriend by the time we started junior year, but she wasn't dopey about it. It wasn't anything she had to try hard at—she just was and everyone knew it, and that felt pretty right to me.

Audrey

After Garrett left I had told Erin everything—everything except that we'd had sex in her house. She didn't need to know that.

"I thought so," she said. "I knew you would tell me when you were ready."

She surprised me because I thought I'd done a pretty good job of hiding it. But what surprised me more was what she said about Garrett and Leo.

"You know that's not the kind of thing Leo would have asked just anyone. Or would have asked because he'd had one too many. Knowing how crazy he was about you," she said. "And what happened between you and Garrett, that isn't one of those things that could happen with just anyone either. I'm so sorry that it all came to a head the way it did. That could not have been good."

I'd come clean, but I wasn't honest with her when I said I was okay, everything was okay, I was busy, and after what had been months of blundering, I was back on track, doing what I needed to, the way I needed to do it. I was grateful she let me leave it at that.

The last week in August, Erin and I took all the kids and went camping at Trillium Lake.

Fuck you, I told the solitude inside my house before I locked the front door behind me. *You're staying.*

The last time we'd been there was the previous summer, when both our families had gone together. The last time I was there, Leo had been there with me. Mark's deciding to not come with us this time didn't make the absence of Leo any less significant. It was the closest I'd been to Mount Hood since the day Leo died, but I was in no hurry to get any closer. Seeing it from our site now, six months later, its splendor and majesty rising skyward and mirrored down onto the surface of the lake, I didn't feel the way I had when I'd seen it from the Pittock Mansion the day of his funeral. When I looked at it now I only thought, *There you are. Hello, love.* That I could see the place where Leo had spent the last day of his life, with his family, doing something he loved, sometimes every day from Portland when it was clear, neither comforted nor troubled me. It only gave me a chance to say hello.

Our first night at Trillium, after the kids were in their tents, reading by flashlight, then asleep, Erin and I sat together by the fire, adding logs to keep it going, and I brought Garrett up again.

"I *was* cheating," I said. "I was looking for a shortcut. Turns out, there's no shortcut."

Erin refilled both our cups with more wine. She went to the tents and came back with two blankets. She wrapped one around me, then sat down and draped the other one around herself.

"You know how many people go their whole lives and never know one great love?" she said. "Can you imagine how few get two?"

"I have to forgive them," I said. "Right? That's what I have to do."

"For what, sweetie?" Erin said. She pulled her blanket closer and crossed her legs.

"For being grown men but acting like children," I said.

"I wouldn't say that." She laughed. "That's nothing new. We've been forgiving them for that for years."

"What, then?" I said.

"You know." Wrapped in her blanket, she leaned toward the fire. "You know, but you don't want to say it. That's okay. You don't have to."

"No, I don't know," I said. "I don't know what you mean."

She poked a stick into the burning logs. "No one loves someone because someone else says so," she said. "It doesn't work that way."

Between us the ashes floated up from the flames. I didn't say anything.

"So I'll say it," she said. "You have to forgive them for loving you, Audrey. If they did it wrong, that's the only thing they're guilty of."

I still didn't say anything.

"You'll get to that," Erin said. "After you forgive yourself."

We had no cell reception while we were away, and I was glad. I had turned my phone off. On our trip home Erin drove, and on 26 when I turned it back on, it beeped with a text. There was only one, and it was from Garrett. *Hi Audrey, I'm in Portland, I rented a place. I have a pullout couch so the boys can visit, I hope. Sorry if this comes as a shock. I was done with Boston. I hope you're well.* Then his address.

"Garrett's back," I said. "He moved to Portland."

The boys, having ignored everything else the first time I'd said it during the drive, suddenly heard me.

"He did?" Andrew said.

"Where?" said Brian.

"Cool," Chris said.

"Imagine that," said Erin. She put her hand on my knee and kept it there until she took it off when she changed lanes.

"Mom?" said Andrew.

"I'm sorry, Andrew," I said. "That's all I know."

Audrey

It was rude and careless and unkind of me, but I didn't call or email or text Garrett back. I thought about it and wanted to, then didn't want to, so I did nothing. He had moved to Portland. I couldn't deal with anything beyond knowing that. I had enough trouble thinking about the strange triangle I'd been part of, and yet I didn't know who had been more in the middle, Garrett or me, though we both had been in our own ways. When I was capable of it, I knew it had to be him, agreeing to Leo's proposal first, then my advances, years apart. Caught between us as he had been, he must have reconciled the two things the best he could, but I couldn't imagine what he had thought every time we were together, beyond that he already had Leo's blessing but hadn't told me he did. He may have felt conflicted, but I was the one who'd been in the dark.

Besides that, I couldn't stop thinking about a curious story my mother had shared during her visit, the day before she left. I got her point, and I loved her for it, but it wasn't advice I was ready to act on.

"Do you remember my best pal, Winnie, from high school?" she said. She was slicing tomatoes in my kitchen, making a salad for dinner. "It's been years since you've seen her, I know, and I haven't in a long time either. Of course we send Christmas cards, but years ago, after her husband died, she moved to Chicago to be closer to her son and his family. She called me a few weeks ago out of the blue. I can't think of the last time we talked. And it's funny, after I got off the phone, I remembered something I hadn't thought about in such a long time. Did I ever tell you the story of the night I was afraid I was going to drown in my underwear?"

I was sitting at the table with a glass of wine, and laughed out loud, almost spilling it.

"No!" I said. "Are you kidding me? What's the story, Mom?"

She laughed too and kept slicing. "The summer after we graduated from college, I spent a week with Winnie and her family in Sag Harbor. What a time we had." She looked at me from where she worked at the counter. "I know you know this already, but I wasn't born your mother. I had my own wild youth."

"I'm sure you did," I said. "I'm guessing the underwear story is part of that youth. Come on."

"There was one night that week, six of us, or seven—who knows, it was Winnie's summer gang—we'd been at a bar, having drinks, and someone thought it would be a good idea to go out on the bay. Then we all thought it was a good idea. One fellow had a boat and he motored out—he knew what he was doing—and we were all having such a good time. We got to a place far from the dock. I don't know how far from land we were, three miles or one, but we were out there and we all decided to swim. It was a hot night, even on the water—you expected it to be cooler than it was. So we went swimming. Everyone stripped down to their underwear and jumped in. The fellow whose boat it was, he didn't swim, he stayed on the boat, with the lights on and the engine idling. There we were, a bunch of supposed adults, our clothes thrown all about the boat, swimming in boxers and bras and panties." She shook her head. "It's funny now, but we were all terrified when the engine died. It was so black and dark, we couldn't see a thing. It was like being buried or drifting in space. I could hear Winnie and our friends, but I couldn't see them, or the boat. The guy on the boat yelled to us all to stay put—if any of us had started swimming, even trying to find one other person, we could have so easily gone in the wrong direction. We were in the open, but even so, I felt exactly the opposite—closed in, claustrophobic. I was a good swimmer but that wasn't going to help, as far out as we were. I treaded water, trying not to panic more. I wondered what happened: Had we run out of gas? Had the engine broken? How would it get fixed? Who would find us? No cell phones then, of course. All I could think of was after I drowned in my underwear, how disappointed my parents were going to be after how proud I'd just made them, graduating from college. I knew I was going to die out there and I wasn't scared of dying—I was mortified at the way it was going to happen. So I did what I always did and still do: I prayed. The boy on the boat couldn't see anything either, so it took him a while, but he finally found a flashlight, of course there was a flashlight on the boat, and we all made it back to the boat and climbed in, scared and sober and sopping, all hugging each other. We got the boat started again—the engine had flooded—and that was the end of the night."

"My God, Mom," I said. "What a story. I can't believe you never told me that before."

"I guess it never came up," she said. "It certainly wasn't something I meant to keep a secret. But you know what?" She sat down at the table with me, the salad made. "I was so scared out there, that after everything turned out all right, I remembered how scared I was and I promised myself that I would live in a way, or at least try, so that if I was ever in the same kind of situation again, or when I was, if the next time I was I did die, I wouldn't have any regrets. And you know, Audrey, I've done exactly that. God knows I've made mistakes, things I'm sorry about, but that wasn't part of my promise. After surviving that night out on the water, I really don't have any regrets. About anything I've done or haven't done. I don't wish harm on anyone, but I think such a night wouldn't be a bad thing for everyone to have once in their life."

After the boys were back in school, the loneliness tightened its grip, and the only way I could go on was to surrender and accept its presence. I thought of ghastly and inappropriate visuals: a useless and withered limb, and worse, a stinking, severed one that I was unable to part with. *Come on, you bitch,* I would say to the burden I couldn't cut off. *We're doing this.* And I'd stride outside and work in the yard, clean windows, do laundry, make food, help with homework, read, sleep. When it would lead me back to gaze at the addition, frozen in time, I'd stand only as long as it took to satisfy her before I'd think, *Fuck you, we're done here,* and I'd run or go to yoga or leave the house and drive, not knowing where I was going until I was there.

With no expectations, I browsed the Death and Dying section on the second floor of Powell's one morning, tilting my head to scan the understanding, comforting, and inspiring titles on the spines, without removing a single one. Shelved as they were, with only limited covers face out, the title was the first impression to make a shopper a taker, and maybe a buyer. The section was in a big, bright corner of the store, framed by large windows overlooking the Starbucks across the street. I watched all the shiny, happy people outside and below me—professionals dressed for work, mothers with strollers or children old enough to walk and hold a hand, hip singles checking their phones. Whether coming or going from the coffee shop, or waiting at the curb to cross, where they stood, they were only feet away from a panhandler with his pit bull and cardboard sign. But as long as I stood there watching the foot traffic, none of the people acknowledged him. Maybe it was intentional to put these books here, I thought, where shoppers observed the blinders of the human condition at work outside. *La, la, la, just keep moving.* I went back to the shelves and after scanning enough to orient myself to the options, I closed my eyes and picked three separate areas of the alphabet, reached out my hand, and pulled out and bought the first three books my fingers touched.

Another day I drove to the Goodwill on Broadway and spent two hours picking over the clothes there, searching for something of Leo's I'd donated. A year ago, I had forced him to purge his closets and he had, reluctantly. And after he had, I'd gone through them and picked out what he hadn't—items he had no business hanging on to—then when he saw what I'd put in the bag to donate, we ended up arguing over a terrible Western shirt that he insisted on keeping.

He'd pulled it out, furious, like I'd sold his mother for a dollar.

"You're not giving this away," he'd said.

"Leo, it's an ugly shirt," I'd told him. "It's teal. It doesn't do you any favors. Take my word for it."

We'd engaged in a bit of a battle over it, which was unexpected. It was, after all, only an ugly Western shirt.

"I look good in it," he'd said. "I know what I look good in and I'm keeping it. I'm a grown man and I'm going to wear what I want when I want."

Of all the things he looked good in, that shirt wasn't one of them, and nothing I could say would convince him of that.

So I didn't argue, I didn't fight, and he wore the shirt proudly, as he'd said, whenever he'd wanted to. And the fucking thing still hung in his closet among the things I still hadn't touched. Every time he'd worn it after our standoff I kept a straight face as best I could and he'd said, seeing through me, *Hate the shirt, not the man.* He didn't give a shit what I thought. And God damn it, why had I even? It meant nothing. If that was what we had to argue about, a Western shirt and its fashion merit, we were in good shape.

Of course I didn't find anything at Goodwill. Surely anything I had brought here a year ago was long gone. And would I have recognized anything of his anyway? Late one weekday morning I drove downtown to the art museum. *This is what we're doing today, bitch. People go to the museum every day*. But I didn't go in right away. Instead I crossed the street and sat down in the park and pretended to look at my phone. Parked two blocks from the museum were four huge white vans with the guide dog school logo on them. The same guide dog school we always passed the sign for when we drove to Mount Hood. It was way out there. I watched what all the trainers were doing. Some of them wore bright blue jackets, also bearing the school's logo, and they each got a dog out of the van and put a harness on it, like they were saddling up. Two other people, a man and a woman, who didn't get dogs, stood waiting. Then one woman put on an enormous black eyeshade and started walking with her dog, and one of the people who had been waiting, the man, followed behind them. I wanted to follow them too. I wanted to see what happened. The woman walked so confidently, and quickly, too. The dog wasn't walking slowly either; it had a bouncy little trot, like it was being walked on a leash by someone who could see. But the dog wasn't the one being walked, the woman was. I didn't know how she could surrender and follow so easily without being able to see anything, walking around downtown in complete darkness. I tried to imagine it. I would never have been able to do such a thing. If I'd had to put on that huge thing that covered my eyes and most of my face, there's no way I could have walked a step. I think the only thing I would have been able to do was crawl. I felt like a creep but I didn't care. I left the park and followed the woman and her dog and the man behind her from the other side of the street. If the man following them was doing his job, keeping an eye on the blindfolded woman, he wouldn't even notice me.

I waited for something bad to happen, although I didn't want to see it if it did. I waited for the blindfolded woman to fall, to trip and go right down on her face. Or for the dog to screw up at the same instant the man following them made a mistake and looked away. The three of them crossed a street and turned a corner and I kept following. How did those trainers pretend all the dangers they couldn't see weren't there? They still existed. It was an odd threesome to be watching. No one looked worried or scared, not even the dog. I could tell the woman in the blindfold and the man following her were talking as they all continued down the block and crossed another street. Once or twice they both laughed. I stayed with them until Pioneer Square and turned around and went back to the museum. They didn't look like they were going to do anything except keep going.

I remembered on Mother's Day how the boys had blindfolded me before giving me the tree. How afraid I'd been to walk—my arms flailing—and stumbled forward the mere ten or so steps from my own house to the yard. If I ever went blind, I could never trust a dog the way those trainers did. But if I closed my eyes, who would I trust enough to follow and keep me safe? The boys, I guessed, but very slowly, two feet at a time maybe. I would trust Erin, no question, but I'd be bossing her the whole time, I knew. Backseat driving from my darkness. I'd have trusted Leo—even now, as mad at him as I was, I knew he never would have let anything happen to me. Which was of course why he'd trusted Garrett. And Garrett, without knowing it at the time, had kept me safe when I'd walked through the dark, at least for a while. Until we both had fallen.

Garrett

From Boston, I had rented a one-bedroom apartment in Portland that I'd found on Craigslist. It was in a converted house in the Alberta Arts District, and I'd gotten practice wearing my heart on my sleeve with the landlady, who'd owned the house for decades. I could satisfy most of the move-in requirements from across the country, but beyond that I might have seemed like a tenant no one would want to gamble on, so when I told her a brief version of why I was moving, she was sympathetic.

Three weeks after I arrived in Portland, I texted Audrey, and two weeks later I still hadn't heard from her. I tried to pretend I'd moved anywhere, like I had so many times before, but it was very different. I bought a pullout sofa for my living room for when the boys came to visit. If they came to visit. I felt like an ex-husband, or like I imagined ex-husbands felt. I was nobody's ex-husband and nobody's father.

Kevin had thrown some work my way for a family that was adding in-law quarters to their house. It was good to have a job to go to where I could exert myself to fatigue. I'd visited the websites of all the colleges and universities in town, including the community colleges, and applied for all the openings I'd found.

One night Kevin came by with housewarming cigars—his

Padróns—and a bottle of Scotch, and we drank and smoked in the big yard behind the house. My apartment was one of four in the converted foursquare—built in 1915, old for Portland—which sat on a deep lot. The landlord's or the other tenants'—I wasn't sure whose—Adirondack chairs and other lawn furniture dotted the yard. I bought two chairs of my own and added them to the rest, in my own corner of the yard. When Kevin came over, we sat in my chairs. It had been a beautiful September day, which faded into the gorgeous night. I'd had no idea such a lovely day was possible in Portland.

There was one other guy who lived in the house, young, who I never saw. I think he worked at night. Single women lived alone in each of the other two apartments. I saw them regularly, Liesl and Nancy, both probably in their late twenties, and friendly and outgoing.

While Kevin and I smoked and sipped in my chairs and admired the day, Liesl and Nancy, barefoot and wearing sunglasses, came out to the yard with a bottle of wine and two glasses. They lifted their hands and walked over.

"Hey, Garrett," said Liesl. "It's a perfect night, isn't it? I adore September."

"It sure is," I said. "This is Kevin."

Everyone made their introductions.

"We'll be at the Adirondacks." Nancy tilted her head toward them. "Bring your chairs and come join if you want."

They left.

"Attractive neighbors," said Kevin. "Young."

I nodded.

"Convenient, too," he said. "Or dangerous, potentially. If you happen to be on the market, with you all right there under the same cozy roof. You looking?"

"Not right now." I shook my head. "As much good as that decision's doing for me."

He raised his glass and without words we toasted my commitment to a futile pursuit. When we finished the cigars, we capped the Scotch, Kevin left, and I went inside. On my way in I waved across the yard to where the girls sat, and they waved back.

The house was a find, no question. My apartment and yard were places I was happy enough to call home and spend time in, but not where I wanted to stay. The location was prime. I walked on Alberta every day, discovering something new. Early on, I found a neighborhood bar, Binks, and struck up a friendship with the bartender I saw regularly, Nathalie, who was beautiful, sported impressive tattoos, and took no shit. She was great to talk to if she didn't think you were trying to bed her, which I wasn't—very funny and smart. Often I took the paper and went early to Tin Shed for breakfast, to beat the crowds and lines that formed as the morning advanced. Alberta was a foodie, arty street with a bus line, and I was glad to live so close to so much vibrant activity, as if it tried to make up for what I didn't have. *Look,* boasted the neighborhood, *at how much we have to offer.* As comfortable as I felt living there, hanging out, exploring—and it was a great place to do all those things—I felt a little old to be doing and liking what I did alone, without a partner or a family to walk down the street with, stopping in at the shops where we wanted to see more. I felt like I was in Portland for the first time, and in a way I was, as a single man on my own, and it was everything any newcomer could have asked for, except I had no one to share it with.

I went over to the Rams Head one afternoon and sat at the bar and had a beer. The place was blameless, but I ached and cursed it while I drank anyway, watching the door, and through the window, at people walking past. Sitting there, I thought it wouldn't be the craziest thing if I saw Audrey walk by, and I was disappointed and surprised when she didn't.

It was only a place, but places could absorb the experiences they fostered, and then haunt you with them. Sitting there with Audrey the day of that lunch, we'd looked like any man and woman, maybe, who

304 · Polly Dugan

had started something that, while still new, had promise. And that had been the beginning of everything changing. Because of what I'd done, and what I hadn't been able to do.

I bought a bike. Portland was a bike town, after all. Businesses delivered soup and pizzas by bike. A company called B-Line, which was in the national news, delivered all kinds of things around the city on motorized trikes. For me, biking was good for thinking, and I was never alone out there when I rode. I imagined us cyclists all thinking our millions of thoughts as we cruised around the city on our own two wheels. Although none of us would collide as we rode our routes, surely our thought balloons would have, had they been able to take on shape and mass like in comic strips. A single woman fretting about a missed period, a parent awaiting an overdue return phone call from their adult child, a husband worrying over a meager checking account holding out till payday, a man, or a woman, no longer able to deny how distant their spouse had become—a landscape of worries floating alongside my thoughts about Audrey and the boys. *Pardon me,* our thoughts would say to one another's as we cruised through town. *On your left.* Maybe another cyclist was considering moving to Boston. *Go on, just do it,* my balloon would advise back. I rode to Powell's and spent an afternoon there. I went back to the food carts on Mississippi. I checked out shops on Hawthorne where I smelled patchouli for the first time in years, and made the Esplanade loop with joggers and mothers pushing strollers. I rode past dog walkers in Forest Park.

And one Saturday, like all the other days I'd ridden, I cruised home from New Seasons with my cargo bags full.

I'd wait one more week, and then I would call Audrey and invite the boys over. It wouldn't have anything to do with her. She'd have to say yes. It was only a visit. There wouldn't be a reason for her to say no. I'd invite her, too, but I would expect the boys to come without her. I'd do burgers or we could get takeout from that Thai place they all liked behind the laundry off Mississippi. Since I was renting, I couldn't put up a permanent hoop, but I would buy one of those burly freestanding ones on wheels. My landlady liked me. If I told her the hoop was for when my friend's sons came over to visit, she'd agree, no problem. I'd mention it would be good for the kids on the street, who were welcome to use it too, if that would help me sell it. I'd ask her permission after it was already assembled and ready to use. I'd hand her a nice bottle of wine while I apologized and hoped she'd consent to what I'd already done.

I rounded the corner and pedaled up the hill toward my house. Audrey was sitting on my porch, looking at an open book in her lap, so I saw her before she saw me. I braked and got off my bike, walked it to the curb, and parked it on the sidewalk. I took off my helmet and sunglasses and put them on the ground next to the front tire. When she looked up and saw me, she closed the book, took off her glasses, set them on the porch, stood up, and waited. I didn't know what I would do when I got there, but I kept walking and climbed the stairs and stopped on the step beneath the one where she stood. When she smiled, the prettiest shy lift of her lips and eyes, in her face I saw what I wanted to: clarity, courage, forgiveness. And though her expression may have meant none of these things, I felt a measure of a comfort that was unfamiliar—maybe it was what people called faith—and I clung. When she wrapped her arms around my waist and kissed my mouth, I pulled her to me, and I held tight. There was nothing to say. Nothing that couldn't wait.

Acknowledgments

For Wendy Sherman, my agent and friend: thank you for everything. The longer we work together, the greater my gratitude for what a steadfast champion of my work you are, and committed advocate for me. You were the first one to believe in this book, and because of you, others did too.

I can't imagine a smarter, kinder, more encouraging and generous editor than Judy Clain, who helped me make this book better than I ever thought it could be. My deepest thanks to you and Reagan Arthur for your early enthusiasm and confidence, and for showing me exactly where to "dig" when I needed direction. Thank you Amanda Brower, Meghan Deans, Pamela Marshall, Alison Kerr Miller, Carrie Neill, and everyone at Little, Brown whose individual and collective talents brought this book into existence and out into the world. When I think of my team, you're it.

During the course of my research, I had the great pleasure and privilege to rely on friends' histories and to meet with generous experts who were so willing to share their knowledge and experience in order for portions of this book to be as authentic as possible. Any errors or inaccuracies are mine.

For telling me about their closest, early friendships with other men,

I'm grateful to Eric Anctil, Kyle Brakensiek, Franklin Jones, and David Morrow. Thank you for sharing what was profound and lasting about the friends and relationships you had as young men, and their impact on you. Leo and Garrett are much the better for it.

Dr. Richard Manthey was the first expert I consulted in the earliest stages of writing this book. Thank you for sharing all you knew about fatal skiing injuries and accidents on Mount Hood. Richard answered every question I had, and what he didn't know from his own wealth of experience, he found out and passed along to me.

Thanks to Kathy Hurd for her personal tour of the Pittock Mansion, for sharing the rich details of the Pittock family history and also answering every question I asked.

Thank you Donna Shuurman, chief executive officer at the Dougy Center for Grieving Children and Families, for giving me your personal tour of the magnificent rebuilt facility, and for our candid and emotional discussion about the critical work Dougy does locally and nationwide for the families it serves and strives to help heal.

I'm grateful to Father Mike Biewend for sharing what spiritual advice he might have given to Audrey, and for always asking how the book is doing.

Thanks to the Tin House Writers Workshop for providing such a tremendous community of and opportunities for writers. I continue to be grateful to Steve Almond and Elissa Schappell, who were the very best teachers and remain inspiring mentors and unflagging supporters.

For everything you have given me this past year, thank you, Shanna Mahin, for being you, and for being my dear friend. There's no one I would have rather shared this journey with.

Again, my greatest thanks is to my tribe—Carolyn and Jess, Mike and Ryan. Thank you for all your help with the research and for filling in the blanks on these pages and always for your love and belief and laughter and friendship. You remain the very best version of family.

Finn and Brady, you have made me prouder and luckier than I ever thought I could be. Thank you for being my most devoted fans and for your patience on the days when the writing has had to come first.

PJ, this one's for you.

About the Author

Polly Dugan lives in Portland, Oregon, and is a reader at *Tin House* magazine. A former employee of Powell's Books and Guide Dogs for the Blind, she is an alumna of the Tin House Writer's Workshop. Dugan is the author of the story collection *So Much a Part of You*.

The Sweetheart Deal

Questions and topics
for discussion

1. Polly Dugan uses rotating narration to take us inside the minds of her characters. Compare how each family member (including honorary family member Garrett) processes grief and loss in his or her own way. Which character did you relate to the most? Whose transformation, or growth, over the course of the novel was the most gratifying for you to witness? Why?

2. Discuss Audrey's initial reaction to learning about Garrett and Leo's secret pact. Do you think her feelings are justified? Why, or why not? How do you think you would have reacted in her position?

3. Without hesitation, Garrett left his life on the East Coast to be with Audrey and her sons in the wake of Leo's death. What do you think motivated that decision? What would you have done in a similar situation?

4. When Audrey first discovers that it was a long-ago, late-night promise to Leo that brought Garrett out west, she finds herself doubting the sincerity of Garrett's emotions for her. What, in your opinion, proves that the love Garrett expresses for Audrey is real? How do you demonstrate your love to the people who matter to you?

5. How did you feel about Garrett when you first met him in the book, and how did you feel about him by the end? If your opinion of him changed over the course of the book, why?

6. Have you ever made a promise to a friend that you never expected to have to fulfill? What was it? How would your life have been altered had you been required to make good on that promise?

7. How did the multiple perspectives on Leo's death, and on life in its aftermath, color your read? Imagine if the story had been told from Audrey's point of view only. How do you think it would have changed your experience as a reader?

8. Throughout the novel, as Audrey copes with her loss and struggles to make sense of her emotions, she finds herself recalling particular scenarios in which Leo wasn't, perhaps, the most considerate partner in their relationship. Do you think that the mixture of intense love and resentment she experiences toward Leo is natural and understandable? Why, or why not?

9. Were you surprised by the ending of the book? What were your expectations, and in what ways were your expectations gratified or upended?